A CONVENTIONAL CORPSE

A CONVENTIONAL CORPSE

A
Claire Malloy
Mystery

JOAN HESS

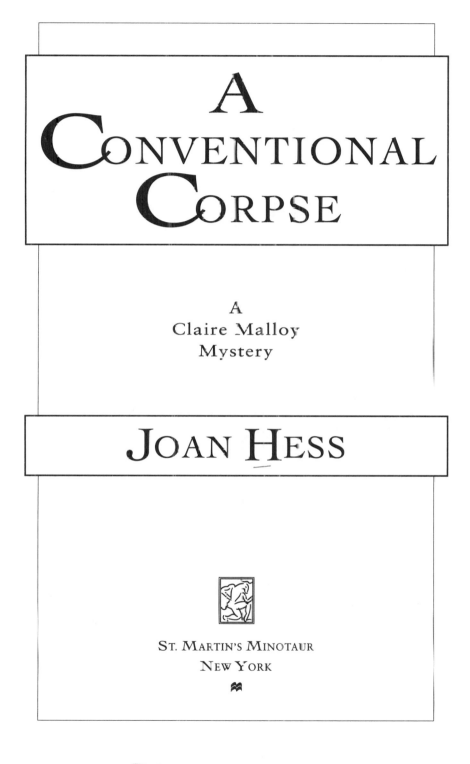

ST. MARTIN'S MINOTAUR
NEW YORK

Library of Congress Cataloging-in-Publication Data

Hess, Joan.
    A conventional corpse : a Claire Malloy mystery / Joan Hess—1st ed.
      p.   cm.
    ISBN 0-312-24662-5
    1. Malloy, Claire (Fictitious character)—Fiction. 2. Detective and mystery stories—Authorship—Fiction. 3. Booksellers and bookselling—Fiction. 4. Women detectives—Fiction. 5. Arkansas—Fiction. I. Title

PS3558.E79785 C66 2000
813'.54—dc21   00-029686

ISBN 0-312-24662-5

First Edition: June 2000

10 9 8 7 6 5 4 3 2 1

To Terry Kirkpatrick,
whose advice has been essential.
Finally, a book of your own.

A CONVENTIONAL CORPSE

CHAPTER 1

It had thus far been a reasonably agreeable day, so the last thing I wanted to see was Sally Fromberger marching down the sidewalk, clutching a clipboard to her busom as though it specified disembarkation protocol for the *Titanic*. She was smiling and nodding at her fellow pedestrians; most of them managed to return the courtesy with only a faint glint of apprehension. There is nothing about Sally that suggests she might be a serial killer in disguise, despite the fact her vanity license plate reads VEGNRULES. She has a significant girth, buttery yellow hair, ruddy cheeks, and a perpetual glow of pleasure. The tip-off was the clipboard, I concluded as I continued to arrange gardening books, flowerpots, and assorted tools in what I hoped would be an eye-catching display in the bookstore window.

Not that I wanted to catch eyes, mind you. I was much more interested in platinum credit cards. The Book Depot, situated in an old train station down the hill from the Farber College campus, certainly could use an influx. I suspect bookstores in small college towns like Farberville experience the same swings—a lull in January and February, followed by a flurry of activity before midterm exams, and then a sustained funeral interlude when students pull out blankets and coolers to bask in the sunny spring weather. At such times, a young man's fancy may turn to love (well, lust), but rarely to literature. Not even Elizabeth Barrett Browning can compete with Budweiser when the tanning season arrives.

"Good afternoon," Sally chirped as she came into the bookstore and beamed at me. "It looks as though we'll have perfect weather for the convention, doesn't it? This very morning I had quite a few cardinals and blue jays in my backyard, and there were darling little finches at the feeder. I assumed they were purple finches, but my husband was adamant that they were house finches."

I was tempted to put a flowerpot over my head and hope my red hair resembled roots, but instead descended from the footstool. "Would you like to buy a field guide to North American birds?"

Ignoring my admittedly silly question, Sally began to flip through the thick clutch of pages on her clipboard. "The steering committee met last night at my house to make sure nothing has been overlooked. Everyone attended except you and Dr. Shackley. He was presenting a paper at a seminar on the East

Coast, so we could hardly expect him to be there." She glanced up at me with the sly look of a robin assessing the caloric content of a worm. "Your role is vital, you know. The Thurber Farber Foundation for the Humanities has invested a great deal of money in our very first mystery convention. I'm hoping the board members will be adequately impressed with the outcome to continue to fund us in the future."

"So am I," I said, wondering if I could persuade the foundation to fund me in the future, too. As much as I love my musty, dusty, cobweb-riddled bookstore, I barely make enough money to keep my peevish accountant at bay and my sixteen-year-old daughter in designer jeans. When pressed into duty, the boiler at the back of the store hisses with the virulence of a deeply-offended Victorian dowager; it's only a matter of time before it shudders to a timely death—or explodes. One would think owning a bookstore is a suitable job for a widow, but there are moments when it seems perilous.

Sally paused in case I chose to offer an explanation for my unexcused absence, then sighed with enough vigor to produce small-craft warnings on area lakes, and said, "Here are your copies of all the committee reports." She began thrusting pages at me. "Registration is approaching one hundred, and we anticipate a few more. Press releases have gone out to all regional media. The schedule of activities is finalized. Your table will be in the back of the room in which the signings will be held, and you can start setting up Friday at four o'clock. Caron and Inez will be needed to fetch our authors from the airport beginning at noon. They are still willing to do this, aren't they?"

"For seven dollars an hour, they'd carry the authors on their backs." I set the papers down on the counter and attempted to look like someone with a very important chore awaiting her. "If that covers everything . . . ?"

"These are photocopies of the page proofs for the program book. They'll give you an overview of Farber College's first 'Murder Comes to the Campus.' I can't begin to tell you how excited I am, Claire. Just think of the luminaries who have agreed to be our speakers! I never expected such a response."

She didn't have to tell me how excited she was. Her face was flushed and her eyes were glittering; if the boiler didn't explode in the immediate future, she might, splattering the paperback racks with robust red corpuscles. She clearly wanted to continue, but I clasped her shoulder and steered her toward the door.

"Why don't you hurry home?" I said in a concerned voice. "It's likely people are trying to get in touch with you. Your answering machine must be jammed with messages. All of us are so grateful for your attention to details, Sally. Don't let us down now."

"It is a complex project," she said modestly, then sailed out the door to badger some other innocent soul.

I waited until it seemed safe, then went outside to admire my window display. It would not incite rabid gardeners to storm the store, but it might lure in a few green-thumbers. I most certainly was not one; the only things I grew with noticeable success were dustballs, mildew, and gray hairs. Okay, perhaps a few wrinkles, too. Gravity asserts itself at forty—with a vengeance.

Satisfied with my efforts, I went into my cramped office in back, gathered up the checkbook and a stack of invoices, and sat down behind the counter to determine if there was any way to appease some, if not all, of my creditors. Will Rogers never met publishers.

It was not an amusing way to spend a balmy afternoon, and I was gnawing on a pencil and mumbling to myself when the bell above the door jangled. I put down the pencil as Caron and Inez came across the room. "How was school?" I asked in a tritely maternal fashion.

Caron, who had mastered the art of speaking in capital letters at age fourteen, dropped her backpack on the floor and made a face reminiscent of a gargoyle gazing down from the heights of Notre Dame. "School is Such A Bore. Everybody else on the entire planet is outside, soaking up sunshine, while we're incarcerated in that dreary prison. I'm surprised the cafeteria isn't serving bread and water. What's more, the teachers seem to think their job is to torture us. All I was doing was looking out the window, for pity's sake. From the way Mrs. McLair jumped on me, you'd have thought I was skinning an armadillo."

Inez Thornton, a perfectly muted counterfoil to my melodramatic daughter, stared at her. "That's nauseating. Why would anyone skin an armadillo?"

"Who cares?" Caron picked up the pages Sally had left. "I can't believe you're involved in this dorky thing, Mother. Who would actually pay to listen to a bunch of authors talk about where they get their ideas? Mrs. McLair had this writer in to prattle to our class about poetry. My brain positively atrophied. Carrie and Emily were obliged to help me out of my desk and guide me to my next class. I had to chomp down on no less than three peppermint candies to come to my senses."

I resisted an urge to snatch the papers out of her hand. "Authors can be interesting, dear."

"Yeah, and Louis Wilderberry's going to ask me to the prom." Caron went into the office and began to open desk drawers in search of my cache of chocolate.

Inez eyed me warily. "What time are we supposed to pick them up at the airport? I have an algebra test sixth period, and I sort of said I'd help decorate the cafeteria after school for the Latin Club banquet."

"*Humanum est errare,*" I said. "You and Caron promised Sally Fromberger a month ago that you would work Friday afternoon, all day Saturday, and Sunday until whenever."

"Yeah, a month ago," Caron said as she emerged empty-handed and picked the pages up once again. After flinging the irrelevant ones over her shoulder, she paused for a moment. "There's no reason why both of us have to make every run to the airport, Inez. We'll divvy them up so you can practice draping yourself in a bedsheet. Who's this Laureen Parks, Mother? Is she an utter bore?"

"Laureen Parks," I said with admirable restraint, "has made a significant contribution to the mystery genre. She's written over sixty novels of romantic suspense."

Inez peered at me. "Like when the heroine hears a chainsaw in the attic and goes to investigate? I never could figure out why she doesn't just call the police on her cell phone."

"She can't afford one," I muttered.

"Give Me a Break," said Caron. "This author's got to be really old to have written all those books. Inez, you get her. You can tell her how you used to obsess on Azalea Twilight's gushy books."

"That was a long time ago," Inez retorted hotly. "At least two years—and you read her books, too."

Caron did not deign to respond. "Then, at one-fifteen, somebody named Sherry Lynne Blackstone. You'll have to get her, Inez. I absolutely cannot make polite conversation with somebody named Sherry Lynne. I'd feel obliged to drop her off at a bowling alley. Big hair makes me nervous."

I glared at my darling daughter. "Sherry Lynne Blackstone is responsible for a goodly portion of your wardrobe. Her books have sold steadily for fifteen years. They're a bit too cozy for my taste, but she has a loyal following of cat fanciers."

Caron raised her eyebrows. "Do her cats type clues?"

"Sometimes," I conceded, "but I've been told there are a dozen web sites devoted to Wimple, Dimple, and Doolittle. Their pedigrees, what they prefer to eat, that sort of thing."

"Wimple, Dimple, and Doolittle? That sounds like a sleazy law firm. Maybe I can persuade them to sue Mrs. McLair for vernal abuse."

I resumed my glare. "Sherry Lynne Blackstone is considered to be an outstanding practitioner of the American cozy genre. She's rumored to be gracious, which is more than I can say for certain people."

Caron looked down at the schedule. "And we have Dilys Knoxwood at two o'clock. What kind of name is *Dilys*? It sounds so scatty. If I were named Dilys, I'd find myself twirling like a bowlegged ballerina at every opportunity. Inez, you—"

"No," Inez said with surprising firmness, considering whom she was up against. "I can't leave in the middle of sixth period. All you have is study hall."

"Dilys Knoxwood," I intervened, "writes a very popular

series in the classic British tradition. Her books are considered to be the epitome of the genre introduced by Dame Agatha Christie in the nineteen-twenties."

"There's nobody with that name on the list," Inez said, reading over Caron's shoulder. "I guess she'd be pretty old, like my grandmother. Maybe older. At least we're not collecting urns at the airport."

"Okay," Caron said, "I can deal with this ditzy Dilys creature just so you can take your stupid algebra test. You have to get the next one, though. I'm not about to deal with some guy named Walter Dahl. Who *are* these people, Mother?"

"His books don't sell well for me," I said, "but he receives rave reviews in the literary journals. In my opinion, his characters are so overwhelmed with neuroses that they spend most of their time arguing about the Freudian implications of their motives. I prefer a butler with a well-deserved grudge or a pregnant parlor maid."

Caron gazed coolly at me, then looked at Inez. "If this guy doesn't mind hanging around the airport, I could grab him, Dilys, and . . ."—her composure evaporated—"Allegra Cruzetti! Oh my gawd, Inez—Allegra Cruzetti! Can you believe it? Why would she come to Farberville? She's famous! Did you read her book?"

Inez was blinking at me as though I'd added Moses to the list as an afterthought. "I thought *Courting Disaster* was the most thrilling book I've ever read in my entire life! I had this history paper due the next day, but I started reading and just couldn't make myself stop. There's this gorgeous African-American prosecuting attorney, and she's going after this incredibly handsome guy who may or may not have hacked up his mother, but he convinces her that he has an evil twin brother, and—"

"I read a review," I said to quell the impending hysteria. "The reviewer found it competent, but that's about all. Cruzetti hopped on the bandwagon at the precise moment to garner maximum attention and a Hollywood deal. A year from now, the hot topic will be sociopathic angels."

"Allegra Cruzetti," Caron trilled with the ardor of a diva, clutching Inez's arms in what must have been a painful vise. "Just think what Rhonda Maguire will say when she finds out I picked up Allegra Cruzetti at the airport! She thinks she's so hot because her father met Carl Sagan at some dumb conference. He never made the best-seller list, did he? Allegra Cruzetti's been on *Oprah*. She was on the covers of *People* and *Newsweek*. She's a real author, not some dorky mystery writer. Rhonda will Absolutely Die. Do you think Ms. Cruzetti would mind if we stopped by the high school for a minute? Mrs. McLair's teeth will fly across the room."

I held up my hands. "Under no circumstances will you use Allegra Cruzetti to undo whatever damage occurred today in your English class. Your mission on Friday is to collect the authors from the airport and deliver them to the Azalea Inn. On Saturday, you and Inez will be available to drive them back and forth from the campus as they desire. On Sunday, you will take them to the airport, and then help me pack up whatever books are unsold. This is going to be an uneventful convention to celebrate the current popularity of mystery fiction. The atmosphere will be calm and dignified, as befitting the occasion. Nothing will go wrong."

Caron and Inez wandered away to conceive of ways to utilize Allegra Cruzetti for their own dark purposes. I returned my attention to outstanding bills, sold a few books over the course of the afternoon, and locked the bookstore at a civilized hour.

I was driving home to the duplex across from the campus lawn when it occurred to me to swing by the venerable building known as Old Main, the site of the convention. I'd stockpiled two dozen boxes of books written by the attending authors; locating a convenient place from which to unload them was vital. Visitors' parking places on the Farber College campus could be as elusive as checks in the mail.

In that classes were done for the day, I had no problem finding a metered space in front of the building. Old Main was the original landmark on campus, a two-towered brick structure that had initially housed all the classes in the early 1900s. As buildings went up, departments were dispersed, but the English department clung to the bitter end. My deceased husband had held his seminars on the first floor, and his dalliances in his office on the third floor. A lack of elevators and a preponderance of asbestos had led to Old Main's condemnation, but generous alumni and a hefty contribution from the Thurber Farber Renovation Fund had restored the building and refitted the classrooms.

According to Sally's notes (which I would never, ever question), signings were to be in a room numbered 130. I walked up the brick stairs and paused to reconnoiter. I flipped a mental coin and went right. The room in question was most definitely locked.

I headed up the high staircase to the second floor and what had once been the English department office. The stale smell of yellowing, ungraded term papers and half-eaten apples in wastebaskets indicated nothing had changed, despite the years' hiatus to a hygenic space in a building on the far side of the campus. The department was continuing its struggle to convince its majors that Beowulf, Tom Wolfe, and Virginia Woolf could lead to academic, if not financial, security.

The office was much as I remembered it, with a view across the campus lawn and a redolence of pipe tobacco, despite the campuswide ban on smoking in public buildings. The aroma was pungent, sending me into an unwanted flashback of Carlton when we'd met at a party, found some inexplicable reason to pursue the relationship, drifted into marriage and parenthood—yet never achieved that most significant emotional cohesion that transcends mundane temptations. Carlton hadn't, in any case; a snow-covered mountain road, a skidding chicken truck, and the presence of a distaff student had resulted in a scandal that the college had glossed over more deftly than a losing football season.

I realized that I was standing in the doorway with a vacant expression. The young Hispanic woman seated at a desk in the center of the room gave me what might charitably be described as an inquiring look. Had her lip not been curled and her eyes narrowed, she would have been attractive. Maybe.

"What do you want?" she said. "It's after five. The office is closed, and I'm not here—okay? You wanna drop or add, call in the morning. Doctor Shackley is out of town, so don't think you're going to see him anytime soon. Not even the Dean's gonna see him. Got that?"

"I'm supplying books for the mystery convention," I said mildly. "Will it be possible to arrange for help to transport the boxes from my car to the signing room?"

"Do I look like someone who cares about this ridiculous thing? My job is to handle the department paperwork, keep Dr. Shackley's wife out of the building, listen to the grad students gripe, and—"

"A custodian, perhaps."

"Call maintenance," she said with a shrug. "When, where, whatever. Don't get your hopes up, though. I've been waiting for eleven months to get the photocopy machine fixed."

I shifted tactics. "Sounds like you're having a bad week."

"No kidding. These professors, these students—all of them seem to think a degree in English literature should qualify them to realign the planets in the solar system, probably in alphabetical order. Go to the local bookstore and ask for a copy of a book by Herman Hesse or James Joyce. If Disney hasn't come out with the cartoon version, the best you'll get is a blank stare. Why would anyone assume there's the least bit of distinction in having read a bunch of dead authors? You know where it's at?"

I'd retreated to the point that my back bumped the door. "I suppose not."

"Stephen King, Danielle Steele, Michael Crichton, John Grisham. Those are living authors, and they write real books. I am so tired of all those calcified fossils." She shoved a lock of black hair off her forehead. "Do you know that Azalea Twilight once lived in Farberville? Right here, not more than three blocks off campus."

"Yes," I murmured, "I knew her."

"You knew Azalea Twilight? Do you know Jackie Collins?"

I shook my head. "Sorry. Is there any chance you can arrange for some assistance from maintenance on Friday? I've been told I can start moving books in at four, but I'm going to need help."

"Call 'em yourself, because like I said, I'm not here." She pulled a gray plastic cover over her computer keyboard, punched several buttons on the telephone on a corner of the desk, and took a purse out of a drawer. "Now, if you'll excuse yourself from my presence, I have better things to do than—"

"I'm Claire Malloy," I said with enough warmth to heat Belaruse for the winter.

"Look, I'm just the department secretary. I can't fix the photocopy machine, dreg up some associate professors's email, or deal with the plumbing in the faculty john. Right now, being pregnant and all, I'm thinking about puking in the nearest wastebasket. You want somebody to carry in boxes, that's fine with me. This mystery convention is nothing more than one big pain in *la cula*. I've already got hemorrhoids. Carry in your boxes? I don't think so."

This was not going well. "Do you have the extension number?" I asked desperately.

"Yeah, but don't get your hopes up that it'll do any good." She pointed at the ceiling. "See that sprinkler? Every day for two months it leaked. I thought about moving my plants under it. The ceiling grew mold and the floorboards began to buckle, but nobody did one thing about it until it dripped on Dr. Shackley's wife's silk blouse. You can imagine how that went over." She stood up. "You're welcome to call maintenance. Tell 'em to fix the photocopy machine while they're here, and take a look at the toilet in the faculty lounge. It runs, which is what I've gotta do."

She nudged me out into the hall, locked the door, and scurried down the stairs. I waited, feeling as if something catastrophic ought to occur; when nothing did, I wandered to the end of the hall and looked out the window at the crisscrossing sidewalks and newly-leafing trees. A few students were meandering homeward or toward the bars on Thurber Street, but without urgency.

Resisting the temptation to visit Carlton's former office, I went back out to my car. A call to Sally, however repugnantly cheerful she might be, would resolve the problem. If not, Caron and Inez would have to find a few minutes to help me with the boxes. The problem was far from overwhelming, and I could anticipate exceedingly healthy sales from the hundred-odd registrants. Sally had not overestimated the significance of the authors who were arriving at the end of the week. Allegra Cruzetti was the current golden child, and Laureen Parks showed up on the best-seller list on occasion; the others, with the exception of Walter Dahl, were midlist but steady sellers. And I, a die-hard fan of the genre since the age of eleven, when Carolyn Keene and I first crossed paths, would meet them. In person. Caron wasn't interested in where they got their ideas, but I was. Perhaps not on Olympus—but I wouldn't rule it out.

I may have been a bit giddy as I went back to my car and drove home. I went upstairs, imagining myself in a piercingly significant conversation with Dilys Knoxwood regarding the poisoned knitting needle in Sir Attenbury's parlor, paused in the kitchen to stick a frozen dinner in the microwave, and headed for the bathroom.

And saw the flowers on the coffee table.

Flowers, in general, are good. These, in particular, were glorious: exotic orange lilies, birds-of-paradise, magenta-streaked orchids, feathery green fronds. These, in particular, were also very bad, since I could think of only one person who might have sent them.

"Caron!" I called.

She came out of her room. "They came earlier today. The guy in the downstairs apartment accepted them from the florist, then brought them up here when I came home. I didn't know what else to do but tell him thanks."

"That's all you could do," I said as I sat down on the sofa and regarded the card held aloft in a plastic fork. "Did you read it?"

She nodded. "They're from Peter."

"And?"

"All the card says is 'Love, Peter.'" Caron sat down on an armchair across from me and shifted uncomfortably for a moment. "I wish you'd tell me what's going on, Mother. It does concern me, you know."

"I know it does, dear," I said, sifting through my thoughts as if I might find a nugget of coherence. "Peter seemed to think he had the solution—mine and yours and his. We were very close to establishing a household to determine if he was right."

"A household?" Caron said carefully. "As in . . . ?"

"Well, marriage, although I would have discussed it with you before I agreed to anything. You're old enough to put forth your thoughts. I would have listened. You and I would have made the decision."

Caron swallowed. "When Dad died, you weren't looking for my thoughts. You did all the prescribed hugging, but you might as well have been wrapped like a mummy. I know Dad was with a girl when he was killed in the accident. You've never told me how to deal with that."

"As if I knew," I said as I went across the room and dragged her up for a bone-crunching embrace. She remained limp for a moment, then reciprocated with both vigor and tears. "I haven't dealt with it, either," I added. "I do know your father adored you."

"And maybe you, but not us."

Her perspicacity went well beyond her sixteen years. Unable to respond, I squeezed her until she whimpered in protest, then retreated to the sofa. "As for Peter," I said, "when last heard from, he was in the company of his ex-wife, the lovely Leslie. Leslie has Russian wolfhounds. She is a loyal attendee of the opera season in St. Petersburg. She does something on Wall Street that makes her rich and successful. Peter's mother adores her."

"You know who you sound like?" Caron asked as she flopped back across the armchair.

"Who?"

"Me, when I talk about Rhonda Maguire. Remember what you always say?"

"This is entirely different," I said. "It is not about infatuation and petty jealousy. What's more, those flowers are the wrong color."

And they were, considering.

CHAPTER

2

It may have been obvious that I wasn't dealing especially well with any of my potential problems. Peter hadn't
bothered to call, however, and no plagues had rained on my
apartment or bookstore (or on my parade, for that matter) by
the next morning. Or so I thought, until noon, when the telephone rang and I discovered that I needed an industrial-strength
umbrella.

Sally wasted no time on idle remarks. "Oh, Claire! The
most terrible thing has happened! I would rather die than tell
you this!"

It would not have been charitable of me to select the alter-
nate option. "What's wrong?"

"Well, when I was walking home yesterday, I noticed a definite discomfort in my left leg. I finally took a look at it, and it was so swollen and pasty that I called the doctor. I'm in the hospital, Claire. It's what they call a deep venal thrombosis—treatable, but I have to stay hooked up to an IV for the next few days. It could be as long as a week."

"You'll be okay?" I asked.

"I will, but what about the convention? Dr. Shackley is the sponsor, but he has no idea what's happening. His secretary snarled an obscenity at me when I called her and asked that she update the registration list. Most of the files are at my office at home, but I'm restricted by an intravenous tube. Claire. . . ."

"What, Sally? I'm the bookseller, not the co-organizer. You promised me that all I'd be needed to do is sell books. I haven't even read the schedule."

"Claire. . . ." A haggard coyote could not have howled more despondently.

I sucked in a breath. "Sally, there are plenty of other people on the committee who attended all the meetings and are more than capable of overseeing things. I'm really sorry that you can't be there, but—"

"There aren't, though. I've been wracking my brain all night, but there's not one person on the committee who's familiar with the genre and these authors. Geraldine can lick stamps. Earlene is keeping the books. Jordan suggested which wines to order for the opening night reception. Kimmie is stuffing packets. Not one of them appreciates the significance of the attending authors. I might as well rip the needle out of my hand and let an embolism do its dirty deed."

"Sally," I began soothingly, "you're—"

"No, I'm not! If you can't be bothered to do a few little things to see that everything runs smoothly, then surely you can take off an hour to attend my funeral. My condition is serious, you know; I could have a heart attack or stroke at any moment. Stress only serves to worsen my condition. My blood pressure has achieved a new personal best."

She sounded as though she'd already selected hymns and written an obituary for the local newspaper. To my dismay, I felt myself crumpling. "Look, Sally, you've done a super job organizing the conference. It ought to run as blandly as the cable weather channel. Authors have their schedules, as do registrants. No one needs to do anything else."

"I knew you'd come through for me," Sally said with a snuffle of gratitude. "All you need to do tomorrow is make sure the authors are pleased with their accommodations at the Azalea Inn. On Saturday morning, you'll introduce the panelists, pose a few questions to kick off the discussion, and keep things moving along. These authors are professionals, and may very well take over. At the picnic, you'll introduce Dr. Shackley and let him thank everyone for attending."

"That's all?" I murmured.

"Oh, Claire, if I hadn't known in my heart that I could count on you, I would have told the nurse to wheel me straight to the morgue! The very day I'm released, I'll come by the store and treat you to lunch. I know where to find the most fantastic soyburgers in all of Farberville." She re-snuffled. "I'm so totally devastated to miss the convention, but you can tell me every last thing these fabulous authors said and did."

She hung up before I could reply, although I had little to say. Sally was sincerely enthusiastic; the birth of a grandchild would have run a lukewarm second. I was looking at what might well be two thousand dollars of profit over the weekend. Welcome attendees and introduce panelists? It hardly compared to cutting off a pertinent digit on a hand, foot, or deposit slip.

It did occur to me to find the pages Sally had left behind the day before and read them with a bit more attention. The authors were slated to arrive in Farberville at various times on Friday afternoon, as well as the groupies and aspiring authors who'd paid for the privilege of goggling at them. Caron and Inez would be busy, but once I'd transported books to Old Main, my first official obligation was not until five, when the Azalea Inn would host a wine-and-cheese affair to kick off the weekend.

The Azalea Inn was a good choice for both hospitality and convenience to the campus. The original structure was pre–Civil War and rumored to have been a stop on the Underground Railroad that assisted runaway slaves moving northward. The existence of tunnels was a myth indigenous to Farber College, mostly utilized to coerce vacuous coeds into strolling along the railroad tracks late at night.

As for the house itself, various generations had maintained, remodeled, and most recently seen commercial possibilities. It now had half a dozen bedrooms with private bathrooms. If the authors found it not to their liking, it was not my problem.

No, my problem wandered into the store shortly thereafter. The curly brown hair was charmingly ruffled, the generous but not thick lips drawn in a grin, the glistening white teeth vulpine, the molasses-colored eyes as warm and enticing as pools of silken water. They'd lured me into delicious (and lascivious) adult behavior in the past, but today I wasn't tempted. Not in the least. Cocker spaniels, perhaps—but Russian wolfhounds?

"Hey," Peter said. "How are you?"

I forced a smile. "I'm fine, thank you."

He disappeared behind the paperback fiction rack. "And Caron?"

"Fine." I took a breath. "And your mother?"

"Fine."

I waited to see if his face might surface above the lurid science fiction covers, then resolutely picked up the pencil and stared at the schedule. "It sounds as though everyone's fine. I presume this means Leslie's fine, too. I'd inquire about her dogs, but I can't remember their names."

"Boris Goodenov and Prince Igor," Peter said from the direction of the self-help books. "They're fine, too."

"Be still my heart," I muttered under my breath.

"Excuse me?"

I slammed down the pencil. "I don't know what you think you're doing at the moment, but I am not amused! Thanks for the flowers. A good time was had by all. No harm, no foul. Just leave—okay?"

Peter stepped out from behind the rack. I would have preferred him to do so with a stricken expression, his eyes filled with tears, his mouth quivering with tongue-tied angst, but he was displaying none of the above. "I've tried to call you fifteen times in the last three months," he said ever so coolly. "I wanted to explain things."

"And I didn't want to hear it. You are free to do whatever you choose. In this case, you seem to have chosen to do it with your ex-wife. I'm not interested in explanations."

Despite a visible effort on his part to play the unfairly maligned hero, his eyes shifted away from me. Perry Mason would have zoomed in with an accusatory finger, nailed him, and left him whimpering in front of a jury of twelve angry men, one of whom would be toying with a neatly-tied noose.

"It's pretty complicated," he said. "Any chance you can close and go to lunch? I'd like to tell you what's going on."

"So I can agree to babysit the dogs while you're on your second honeymoon in Jamaica? You made your decision three months ago, and so did I. Let's just allow the relationship to die a dignified death. I'll scatter the cremains along the railroad tracks when I have some spare time."

"You won't give me a chance to explain?"

"I can see no reason to give you a chance to explain anything, from the global warming crisis to your rekindled relationship with Leslie, Boris, and Igor. May you all bump into the specter of Stalin during your next jaunt to St. Petersburg."

"I have not rekindled my relationship with Leslie," Peter said, although not as firmly as I would have liked. "There is a complication, but it involves all of us. I'd like to take you out for dinner and talk about it. May I come by at seven?"

"No."

"Seven-thirty?"

I picked up the pencil and made several scratches of no significance. "I have other plans. I seem to have been forced into coordinating a mystery fiction convention on the campus this weekend. I need to study my notes and prepare remarks. If

22

you're still around next week, you can call me. If not, don't worry about it."

"Why wouldn't I be around next week?" he said.

"I have no idea. Now, if you don't mind, I have some phone calls to make."

I glowered at his back until he was gone, then snatched up the telephone and called my best friend, Luanne Bradshaw, who owns and runs Secondhand Rose, a used clothing shop a few blocks up the street. "What have I done?" I wailed as soon as she answered.

"I have no idea," she said with the briskness I'd expected—and needed. "What's more, tell the detectives I take no responsibility, will not offer you an alibi, and am unable to raise bail."

"You're a lot of help."

"Doctor Ruth, I'm not. Shall I assume this has to do with Peter?"

"Maybe," I said grumpily.

"And what is it you think I should do?"

"If I knew, Luanne, I wouldn't have called you."

"Is that supposed to make sense?"

I stared at the door through which Peter had exited. "No, it's not. He asked me to go out to dinner so he can tell me all about Leslie's dogs. I said no. Now it's possible I'm overreacting, but—"

"Did he tell you that he wanted to discuss Leslie and her canine companions?"

"Luanne," I said, "stop being reasonable. If I'd wanted to know the time and the temperature, I could have called the five-five-five number. All I want is sympathy. You're my friend, not my attorney."

"Pizza later?"

"Yeah," I said and hung up.

There was most decidedly a conspiracy, although it was challenging to see Peter, Sally, and Luanne with their collective heads bent over the blueprints.

By Friday I was what might politely be called a disintegrating basket case. Peter had neither called nor dropped by, which was for the best. Sally was continuing to hyperventilate from her hospital bed, calling several times a day with increasingly convoluted details. Caron and Inez had expropriated my car; I hoped none of the luminaries expected a limousine. My aged hatchback most definitely did not fall into that category.

I was glumly watching my science fiction hippie attempt to shoplift a paperback when the telephone rang.

"Don't think about leaving with that book in your coat pocket," I called, then picked up the receiver. "Book Depot."

"Ms. Malloy?" said an unfamiliar voice.

In that the voice held undertones of an arctic breeze, I considered the possibility of resorting to a gelatinous accent and an assumed identity. However, I took the high road. "Yes, this is Claire Malloy."

"This is Laureen Parks."

"Oh," I said, gulping.

"I understand that you're now the coordinator for the conference. I am not unfamiliar with the necessity of staying in rather quaint accommodations, but this inn will not do. I specifically made it known to that other woman that I require a suite in which I may smoke. This ridiculous woman at the desk continues to avow that smoking is not allowed anywhere inside the building. I do not stand on sidewalks late at night and puff away like an unmarketable prostitute."

"Laureen Parks," I mumbled.

"You're familiar with my work?"

"Of course I am, Ms. Parks. I've read everything you've ever written."

"Admiration is always appreciated, dear, but let's save it for later. Either you reason with this woman or I take the next flight out of here."

"Please don't do that," I said. "You're the cornerstone of the convention. Over a hundred fans have registered to meet you."

"They will not meet me if I'm expected to spend two nights in a prisoner-of-war camp. I realize that smoking is a vile ploy to maim or kill everyone on the planet who has risen above the filthy habit, but I will not be sent to the woodshed to have a cigarette. This young woman at the desk has refused to back down. Am I on my way to the airport, Ms. Malloy?"

I was sorry I didn't have a spare moment to swing by the hospital and rip the IV needle from Sally's hand in hopes a bloodclot would rush to her brain. "Please, Ms. Parks," I said in what might have sounded like a pathetic whine to those tapping the phone line, "I'll be there in ten minutes. Find a bench in the garden and have a cigarette. Enjoy the azaleas."

"I have become increasingly less amenable to being treated as a pariah, Ms. Malloy. However, you sound like a reasonable person, so I'll give you ten minutes, and even a few more, to convince me not to demand to be taken back to the airport. I've always been fond of azaleas."

My hand was trembling so violently that I could hardly replace the receiver. I'd known for months that I would encounter authors whom I'd equated with gods and goddesses—now it was not just sinking in, but slamming in like a bumptious thunderstorm. Laureen Parks, on the telephone, tossing out my name as if I were a regular person. I wasn't; I was a dyed-in-wool fan who'd practically teethed on her books.

It was not the best time to close the Book Depot, but I stuck the sign in the door and turned the deadbolt. I would have hurried to my car to drive to the Azalea Inn, had not said vehicle been taken by Inez and Caron for the afternoon. I let myself out the back door and headed down the railroad tracks for the historic house that had once been owned by Farberville's most famous (or infamous) author, Azalea Twilight, prosaically known as Mildred Twiller. She'd been murdered, as had her husband, and the house had been vacant for most of a year until an obscure cousin had appeared to revitalize the property.

At the pertinent bridge, I scrambled up the embankment, paused to pull twigs and leaves out of my hair and wipe the perspiration off my face, and then took several deep breaths before I went into the Azalea Inn.

Inez was cowering just inside the doorway. "Oh, Ms. Malloy," she said, dangerously near tears, "I don't know what I'm supposed to do. That woman told me not to set one foot outside until this is resolved, but Sherry Lynne Blackstone's plane is scheduled to arrive in ten minutes. I've got to pick her up and be back at school before sixth period. My parents will kill me if I get a bad grade in algebra. They're still upset about my C-minus in biology last year because of the thing about stealing the frozen frogs. What's more, Jason—he's the president of the

Latin club—told me after first period that he's really, really counting on me to help with the banquet decorations." She blinked behind thick lenses, reminding me of a guppy in an aquarium filled with piranhas. "He acted like he might ask me to sit with him tonight at the head table."

"Can you make it back to school on foot if you leave now?" I asked her.

"If I leave right now."

I patted her on the head. "*Fortuna favet fortibus,* dear. Go for it."

She gave me a bewildered look, then wiped her nose on her shirt cuff, tossed me the car key, and dashed out the door. "Thanks, Ms. Malloy," she called as she reached the sidewalk and turned in the direction of Farber Street.

"Fortune favors the bold," I muttered through clenched teeth, then went to the sun room at the end of the hall. There was no hint of cigarette smoke in the air, but the thirtyish woman behind the desk, obviously smoldering, was close to spontaneous combustion.

"I'm Claire Malloy," I said cautiously.

"That's nice."

"I understand you're having a problem with Laureen Parks . . . ?"

"The lady in question is the one with the problem. This is a smoke-free establishment. She's not even supposed to smoke in the garden. It's bad for the botanica."

"I didn't hear any delicate coughs when I came up the walk."

"Maybe not." The woman stood up and proffered her hand, which was as dry as her expression, and, quite possibly, her life to date; she had the aura of someone whose most dramatic outbursts thus far had taken place in a junior high civics class. "I'm Lily Twiller, owner of the Azalea Inn. I had several conversations with Sally Fromberger about the conference. I guess it never occurred to either of us to bring up my nonsmoking policy."

"It's on the platter now," I said, squeezing her hand with what I hoped she interpreted as sympathy rather than annoyance. "You've booked five rooms for two nights, as well as the reception tonight and the picnic supper tomorrow night. I can't swear the other authors aren't smokers. It might be best if I call the Holiday Inn to see if they can accommodate us."

"I'll have to send the drapes and bedspreads to a dry cleaner's. I might even have to arrange for the carpets to be shampooed."

"The Thurber Farber Odor Foundation will cover any additional expenses."

"Well," Lily said rather ungraciously, "I suppose I can make an exception this time, but if I find one single cigarette butt in the rose bushes—I don't know what I'll do!"

"Go buy ashtrays." I continued down the hall and out the back door into a garden enclosed by a high, red-bricked wall. My first sight of Laureen Parks was less than impressive. She was seated on a concrete bench, slouched over as if observing ants trekking through the grass, a cigarette dangling from the corner of her mouth. One of her feet was twitching impatiently, although I'd arrived well within my promised ETA. I'd seen more dignified—or at least more optimistic—drunks in doorways.

"Ms. Parks?" I called.

She immediately straightened up, yanked the cigarette from between her lips with a shaky hand, and turned to me with a warm, if suspect, smile. "Ms. Malloy? You really ought to consider joining the cavalry. You came galloping to my rescue in record time. So which is it—the inn or the airport?"

"The inn," I said, gaping at her. She'd obviously been beautiful in her earlier days, with elegant cheekbones and a fine, smooth forehead. Now, in her seventies, age had softened her features and etched lines on her luminous complexion. Despite her gray hair, I could easily visualize her as any of the giddy heroines in her novels. "Lily has agreed to temporarily rescind the smoking ban. I'd love to talk, but I have to pick up Sherry Lynne Blackstone at the airport. Please make yourself comfortable and I'll be back."

"You're a good egg, Ms. Malloy."

"Thank you." I wiggled a hand and went back down the hallway and out the front door. My car was parked at the curb. I had five minutes to make it to the airport, so I could hope to be no more than ten minutes late. Sherry Lynne would not be met with a brass band and children holding fistfuls of daisies, but I could get there only a few minutes after the baggage had been unloaded and set on the conveyor belt.

As I drove down the highway at a speed prudently within range of the legal limit, I tried to remember Caron's casual recitation of the proposed pickup schedule. The next three authors were arriving in a fairly close clump. I could deliver Sherry Lynne Blackstone to the inn and go to the high school, but I wasn't confident Caron could be plucked out of study hall with time to drop me off and make it to the airport before the authors panicked.

Sally Fromberger was the organizer and overseer of introductions and remarks; Caron and Inez were the official gofers; I was the person meant to rack up sales in the back of the room. Quite clearly, the situation had gone haywire, but there was little time to deal with it. I pulled into the airport and parked in front of a sign that warned me that I had three minutes to conduct my business or have my car towed (at my expense) to an unknown destination. At that moment, I almost hoped it would be, thus absolving me from further responsibilities.

I'd seen Sherry Lynne's photographs on the cover flaps of her books, but I was aware that they might not be timely. I roamed through the crowd gathered by the baggage carousel. I was beginning to despair when I spotted a possibility—frizzy hair, florid complexion, paranoid eyes.

"Ms. Blackstone?" I said.

"Where is my cat?" she snapped in response.

"I'm afraid I don't know."

"Wimple is delicate. I simply cannot allow him to be left on the runway in this temperature. If he is not produced in the next sixty seconds, I shall—I don't know—scream, possibly. I cannot—"

She broke off as a pet carrier appeared on the conveyor belt. "Oh, my darling, were they unkind? Did they handle you too roughly?"

I grabbed the carrier. "We're all thrilled that you've agreed to participate in Murder Comes to the Campus, Ms. Blackstone. Why don't you let me take you and your cat to the Azalea Inn? The two of you can relax for a few hours before the reception."

Sherry Lynne Blackstone in no way resembled Laureen Parks, but when she smiled, her charisma was equally dazzling.

"You are such a dear," she said, clutching my arm and literally glowing at me as if she were a supernova and I an orbiting (but promising) chunk of rock. "So many people don't understand the enigmatic personalities of cats."

We both winced at the high-pitched yowls emanating from the carrier. "So many people," I said, thinking of Lily Twiller. Smokers had won the opening skirmish, but I wasn't sure if cats could win the second round. Perhaps if the cats smoked, I heard myself thinking irrationally.

I hustled Sherry Lynne out to my car, did the politically correct thing of setting the carrier in the backseat rather than the trunk, and politely looked away as Sherry Lynne dosed herself with nasal spray.

"Laureen Parks is already here," I said as I pulled onto the highway.

"How delightful," Sherry Lynne said. "Did she arrive on a broomstick?"

"You know each other?"

"We all attend the obligatory fan conventions every year. I've met Allegra, of course. She's entirely too famous to hobnob with the rest of us, and she's only written the one book. My first book was published about the time she was in diapers. I would never elaborate on what she was doing in them, but certain bodily functions come to mind. Some of the by-products of these functions should have been mentioned in reviews of her book."

Unable to respond, I drove back into town and sent Sherry Lynne and Wimple up the sidewalk to the Azalea Inn, then headed back to the airport, feeling like an amateur—and majorly disjointed—shuttle service.

According to Caron's cold-blooded assessment, the next

three authors could be gleaned in one fell swoop, as long as no individual minded spending quality time at the Farberville airport. I parked in the shadow of the ominous sign and went back into the airport to gather the next batch of authors—Dilys Knoxwood, Walter Dahl, and Allegra Cruzetti. I was well beyond being thrilled to meet any of them. Had I been slated to face Jane Austen or Charles Dickens, I suppose I might have shaken off my exasperation and knelt with proper reverence, but I was much too stressed to do much more than stalk over to the baggage area.

There were no suitcases rumbling by on the belt, and the only person in sight was a slight woman with curly blond hair, sprawled on the floor with a cellular phone in her hand, a flowery print skirt enveloping her like a garden on the scuffed linoleum. "Oh, dearie," she said in a lilting English accent, "do you have the slightest idea how these things work? I've punched all the buttons to no avail. That's not completely true; I just had a conversation with a very rude gentleman named Smitty. I don't believe I should care for him to fetch me."

"Dilys Knoxwood?"

"Why, yes," she said as she stood up, her eyes round with amazement and her cheeks as pink as the carnations (or whatever they were meant to be) on her skirt. "However did you guess? Are you one of my readers? I do love to meet my readers, and I shall gladly sign a book for you, but I wish you could tell me how to operate this device. My husband gave it to me just before I left, and the brochure is ever so technical. I'm not very good at these sorts of things."

"Whom are you trying to call?"

She cocked her head. "Now that you ask, I'm not sure. Do

you think I should call my husband? He becomes very annoyed, almost irate, when I interrupt him while he's in his workshop. The last time I knocked on the door, he claims he almost sliced off his thumb. However, if you think I must, then I'll risk it. He's not all thumbs, after all."

It was clear she was as dithery as her elderly village sleuth. I would have been charmed had it not occurred to me that I needed to move two dozen boxes of books before the bloody reception.

"Claire Malloy," I said briskly. "I'm here to take you and your colleagues to the inn. I hope you won't mind waiting for a few minutes. Would you like a cup of coffee?"

"I don't suppose I could have a cup of tea," she said as she dropped the cellular phone in her enormous cloth handbag. "Tea is so much more comforting when one's tummy has been tested by a bumpy flight."

I picked up the only suitcase in sight. "Let's see what the café has," I said.

Dilys obediently trailed after me. I settled her at a table, coaxed a cup of hot water and a tea bag from the waitress behind the counter, and returned with a tray. "I wasn't sure if you preferred lemon or milk and sugar," I said with an apologetic smile.

"This will do nicely." She plunked the tea bag in the water and looked up at me. "Where is it that you said we are? I thought my husband said something about Florida, but the woman sitting next to me on the airplane kept insisting it was a place called Farberville." She began to rummage through her purse. "I really do think I should call him, no matter how upset he becomes."

"You're one of the featured speakers at the Farber College mystery convention," I said. "You're in the right place. On Sunday we'll make sure you get on the flight back home."

"Are you quite sure?"

"Absolutely." I waited until she'd stirred her tea and taken a sip. "I adored your last book, Ms. Knoxwood. Until the last scene, I was so sure that the vicar had dumped the ground-up foxglove in the port that I would have bet money on it. I never for a moment expected the nanny to have done such a thing."

"Nannies are so unreliable, aren't they?"

For a fleeting second, something flashed across her face that made me wonder if she was highly amused with me. Before I could properly assimilate it, however, she gave me an engaging smile.

"Is there any hope I might have a bit of milk," she asked, "and a lump or two of sugar?"

"I'll see what I can do."

I returned with the desired items, but Dilys did little more than rattle a teaspoon in her cup and show me photographs of her grandchildren and her dogs.

After ten minutes of cooing in admiration, I glanced up at the clock. "If you don't mind waiting here, I'll meet Walter Dahl at the gate."

Her amiable expression vanished. "Walter Dahl is part of this? Why wasn't I warned? He was very rude to me at the fan convention in Portland."

"Didn't you receive a copy of the program?"

"I may have," she said, staring at the sodden teabag on her saucer. "I do not examine everything that's sent to me. The IRS in particular is always making demands, but my husband deals with them. I most definitely was not warned that Walter Dahl would be here. It might be best for me to take the next flight home." She tilted her head and gave me a sharp look. "Have we met before, Ms. Malloy? There's something very familiar about your name."

I was at a loss to respond. After a moment of deep-seated bewilderment, I said, "What happened at the convention?"

Her eyes filled with tears. "He was rude, and he embarrassed me. I am sorry that he finds my books vapid and without literary merit. I've put three children through college thus far, courtesy of my 'fluffy little works,' and started a trust fund for my grandchildren's education. As far as I'm concerned, Mr. Dahl can stick a dahlia up his arse!"

CHAPTER
3

Three down, two to go, I told myself as I handed Dilys a napkin and headed for the gate as the screechy P.A. system announced the disembarkation of passengers from the next flight. For the record, the Farberville municipal airport has precisely two gates, and all passengers enter the terminal through one doorway.

I was wondering if I'd recognize Walter Dahl among the incoming drove when I heard a man in a black turtleneck shirt, khaki shorts, distressingly translucent calves, and politically correct sandals say, "You must blame your ignorance on your parents, my dear young thing. No one should be allowed to achieve puberty without a thorough grounding in the deconstruction of Henry James."

With a curt nod, the speaker dismissed a woman who seemed less than grounded and clearly more eager than he to end the conversation. He was well over six feet tall, distinctly cadaverous, with what hair he still had pulled back in a dull brown ponytail, a wisp of a goatee that clung irresolutely to his chin, and a gold stud in his left earlobe. For a brief moment, I wondered if the last was his link to the mother ship.

"Mr. Dahl?" I said as he went past me.

To my regret, he stopped and looked back at me. "And you are . . . ?"

"Claire Malloy. I own the bookstore that's supplying books for the conference. Circumstances have obliged me to meet the authors at the airport. I hope you had a pleasant flight."

"There is nothing pleasant to be experienced on a vehicle that might best be described as a lemonade can with wings." His eyes flitted down my admittedly lithesome figure, then met mine. "A bookseller, you say? Have you read my books?"

"I'm familiar with them, Mr. Dahl. Did you check any baggage?"

"Luggage, Ms. Malloy, but not baggage. I make it a point to shed excess baggage before it burdens me. As a child, I was physically abused by my stepfather, who saw me as a threat to his tenuous grasp of masculinity. As an adolescent, I was tormented by bullies whose primary interests were drugs, alcohol, and glassy-eyed whores. My first wife came home one day with a depiction of Satan tattooed on her breast. Within a week, she left me for a biker. My second wife was a painter known locally, if not as a hot commodity on international circuits, for her depictions of wolves, one of which bore a remarkably similar likeness of me, if you observe the facial structure from a distance. My third wife—"

I held up my hands. "I was just thinking we might want to collect your—ah, luggage. If you don't mind waiting for a few minutes, I have one more author to collect. After that, I'll take the three of you to the inn so you'll have some time to unwind before the reception."

He arched his eyebrows. "So I am nothing but a fare in this mass transmit scheme?"

He was lucky he wasn't a target in a mass slaughter scheme. "This is the first year of the Murder Comes to the Campus conference, Mr. Dahl," I said. "You must excuse us if everything is chaotic. The organizer, Sally Fromberger, is in the hospital. The rest of us are doing our best to keep things moving smoothly."

I led the way to the carousel and left him staring at it, his arms crossed and his scowl more than adequate to provide him with ample breathing room. The protagonist in his books was a psychology professor, which is what I seemed to think he had been at some point. He most certainly looked like the sort to mercilessly harass students and staff alike; it was not difficult to imagine him flustering Dilys—or convincing his first three wives to live in trees and survive on shredded monkey meat.

I peered out the main entrance to make sure no tow truck was coupling itself to my car, then returned to the gate as passengers began to disembark from a plane only slightly larger than a lemonade can. I wasn't worried about recognizing Allegra Cruzetti. Her emerald eyes and cascading black hair had graced the covers of several entertainment magazines. I'd caught the tail end of an interview on a morning talk show in which she'd sounded bemused by her sudden plunge into the limelight. Bemused, but not displeased.

I eventually spotted her in the doorway of the plane, signing an autograph for a cabin steward. She was wearing her trademark scarfs and a billowy silk dress that had expended the energies of many an Asian worm. Her unrestrained hair hung to her waist, and even from fifty feet, I could see her swirly eyeshadow and scarlet lipstick.

Wondering if she considered herself a celebrity, and therefore entitled to behavior worse than Walter Dahl had exhibited thus far, I waited uneasily as she came into the terminal.

"Ms. Cruzetti?" I said. "I'm Claire Malloy."

She clasped my hand. "It's kind of you to invite me to the conference, Claire. From what I could see from the airplane, this looks like a lovely little town. I'm looking forward to spending a few days here."

Relieved, I said, "You'll have to remember that this is our first year, so there may be problems. Sally Fromberger had a medical emergency and can't be with us. She's the type who likes to do everything herself. At the moment, the other members of the committee are deciphering her cryptic notes and dividing duties."

"I'm so sorry to hear about poor Sally," Allegra said as we headed toward the carousel. "I never spoke to her in person, but my publicist at Paradigm House found her to be very enthusiastic."

"I'll bet she did," I said under my breath.

As we went past the café, I saw Dilys morosely toying with her teabag. Walter was not in view. I assumed he was either in the men's room or out by the curb, haranguing fellow travelers.

Moderating the panels might be more difficult than I'd anticipated, I thought as Allegra and I waited for the carousel to
shudder to life. Sherry Lynne, Dilys, and Allegra might allow
themselves to be bullied, but Laureen Parks had not hesitated to
insist on getting her way at the Azalea Inn. It might be prudent
to put Walter at one end and Laureen at the other, although verbal pugnacity did not require proximity.

"Do you know the other authors?" I asked Allegra.

"Laureen and I sat at the Paradigm table at the American
Crime Writers Alliance banquet just last week. She made a point
of congratulating me after the ceremony, despite never having
been so much as nominated herself. Sherry Lynne and Dilys
were at a conference in Phoenix; we had lunch with our editor,
and later, drinks and gossip in my suite. I'll have to admit I
hadn't heard of Walter Dahl until I read about him in the program book. I haven't had time to read for pleasure since I
started college. After law school, I joined a firm where associ-
ates were expected to put in seventy hours a week."

"When did you find time to write your book?"

She lapsed into what sounded like an oft-repeated response.
"Two years ago my parents died in an accident on the freeway.
I took a leave of absence to deal with their affairs. I started the
book as a way to maintain my sanity—and sobriety, for that
matter. Before I realized what was happening, the characters
took over and insisted I tell their story. It sounds rather psy-
chotic, doesn't it?"

A woman standing near us gasped. "Are you"—she held up
a hardback book—"Allegra Cruzetti? I couldn't help noticing
your resemblance to the photograph on the cover. You are,
aren't you?"

Several other people swung around to stare at her. I wasn't sure if I should lower my shoulder and prepare to tackle encroaching fans, but Allegra beamed at the woman.

"Would you like me to sign your book?" she asked. "It's always such a thrill for me to see my book in someone's hands."

I decided she had the situation under control and went to look for Walter. I checked the hallways, listened outside the men's room for his voice, and made sure he wasn't stalking around the parking lot. I gave up and went back to the café, where I found Dilys scattering shredded tea leaves on the tabletop and utilizing her fingertip to draw what looked unnervingly like hex signs to me.

I sat down across from her. "Have you seen Walter Dahl?"

"No," she said. "Are we ready to go?"

"Almost. Please wait here for just a minute or two." I returned to the carousel, expecting to find Allegra surrounded by autograph hounds. The only person there was a thickset man cursing into a pay telephone.

Little Bo Peep seemed to be losing her sheep at an alarming rate.

However, Allegra had not disappeared into the ether on an outbound flight, but was instead washing her hands in the ladies' room. "I always feel grimy when I get off an airplane," she said as she noticed me. "You'd think I'd be used to it by now, after a thirty-five city tour. What was worse were all the people who insisted on hugging me, kissing me, and coughing in my face. My editor ordered me to get a flu shot before I started the tour, and I have a prescription for antibiotics in my purse. A twentieth-century amulet, I suppose."

"You didn't seem to mind the fans by the carousel."

"I force myself to do it. I've never been an outgoing person, which is why I specialized in appellate briefs at Harvard Law School." She folded a paper towel and tossed it into a trash can. "Shall we go?"

I led her to the café and settled her down with Dilys, who seemed reasonably agreeable. While they exchanged pleasantries, I took a final, futile look for Walter, then picked up their suitcases and herded them out to my car.

"Are you no longer a Paradigm author?" Allegra asked Dilys as I drove out of the airport.

Dilys sighed. "Paradigm published my last six books, but a the moment I'm between houses. I really would like to settle down and go to work on my next Miss Palmer. I have an idea, but without a contract and a deadline, I am sadly lacking in motivation."

Allegra, who'd insisted on sitting in the backseat, leaned forward. "I hope you won't be offended if I ask why you left Paradigm."

"It was for the best," said Dilys, her voice melodious but tinged with irritation. "You, on the other hand, must be rather fond of them. Very few Paradigm authors merit a full-page ad in the New York Times and an extensive tour. The only place they ever sent me was to a mall bookstore in a town twenty miles from where I live. They paid mileage. I believe it came to three dollars and change." Her head fell against the back of the seat. "If you don't mind, I'll close my eyes for a few minutes."

I glanced at Allegra's face in the rearview mirror. She was gazing out the window as if enchanted by the gas stations and used car lots, but her expression was that of a cat with a bloodied baby rabbit between its paws.

When we arrived at the Azalea Inn, Dilys and Allegra detoured into the sitting room to examine an elegantly carved credenza. I continued to the sun porch.

Lily Twiller's expression was more like that of a cat treed by a pack of feral dogs. "Is Attila another of your authors?" she demanded. "Should I prepare for an onslaught of Huns?"

"Is Mr. Dahl here?"

"Oh, yes," she said, rolling her eyes toward the ceiling. "He came in a taxi fifteen minutes ago. He didn't like the wallpaper in the Rose Room, or the color scheme in the Lilac Room. I was about to suggest that the basement might be suitable when he decided to take the Petunia Room. I did the interior decorating myself, and all of my guests have found their rooms charming. No one has ever described the unique window treatments as 'grotesque and garish.' If Mr. Dahl prefers a prison ambiance, I'm sure some cheap motel out by the airport can provide it for him!"

"I'm sorry, Lily," I said. "We'll try to keep him occupied until he leaves Sunday afternoon. I don't think you'll have any problems with the other four."

"Then you are wrong. I do not allow pets. Your Ms. Blackstone arrived with a cat. Cat hairs are impossible to vacuum up. The Azalea Inn prides itself on offering a hypoallergenic environment." Her hands trembling, she picked up a brochure and opened it. "It's guaranteed in writing. We use biodegradable cleaning supplies. The bars of soap and bottles of shampoo come from a specialty shop in California. These mystery authors of yours are pollutants, Ms. Malloy. This is my inn—not some tawdry rooming house for transients and thieves. My integrity is at stake!"

"Where is the animal under discussion?"

"I asked Ms. Blackstone to wait in the garden until you returned. Ms. Parks is keeping her company—and no doubt smoking despite my request."

I told her that Dilys and Allegra would appear momentarily, then went out the back door. Laureen was seated on the bench where I'd left her an hour ago. Sherry Lynne sat on a nearby bench, an enormous Siamese cat draped across her lap like a moth-eaten fur stole.

Laureen gave me a little wave as I approached. "There you are, Claire. I was just telling Sherry Lynne how one of my cats came home with a broken tail last week. I was so distraught that I couldn't write a word until my secretary brought the poor thing back from the vet's office."

I sat down next to Laureen. "We have a problem."

"No, my dear," she said, "*you* have a problem. I have time for a nap before the reception." She bent down to stroke Wimple's head, then went up the path.

Sherry Lynne looked at me. "I assume you've spoken to that arrogant woman. How anyone could object to a noble creature like Wimple is beyond me. I have learned, however, that those with an aversion to cats have a streak of cruelty in them. A poll of convicted criminals would most likely prove me right."

Steeling myself, I ran my hand along Wimple's back and snatched it away before any feline fangs could find my flesh. "He's certainly a healthy specimen, isn't he? How old is he?"

"He turned nine just last month. We had a little party to celebrate, with hats and balloons and a cake made of liver paté and decorated with catnip. Would you like to see pictures?"

"Maybe later," I said as I sat down and tried to think what

to do. Locking Lily in a broom closet for the weekend would solve the immediate problem, but in that she was catering the opening reception at five o'clock and a picnic for all the attendees the next day, a new set of problems would surface. There were no motels or hotels convenient to the campus. The nearest that came to mind was a twenty-minute drive away, which meant Caron or Inez might spend most of the day carting Sherry Lynne back and forth to check on Wimple.

An iffy notion came to mind, although it might require the guile of P.T. Barnum to sell it. Pasting a bright, confident smile on my face, I said, "I have a wonderful idea, Sherry Lynne. Wimple can stay with me. My apartment's only two blocks away, so you can visit him between panels. I can assure you he'll receive royal treatment from my daughter and me. We love cats."

"How many do you have?"

A tricky question. "At the moment, none. We're planning to go by the animal shelter after the conference is over. Wimple will have his own little room with a cushion, fresh water and kibble, and whatever else his heart desires. It's only for two days, Sherry Lynne."

She lowered her head and in a gooey, high-pitched voice, said, "What does Wimple say? Would you like to stay with Claire?" We waited while Wimple considered this proposition, although he seemed more interested in a squirrel scampering across the grass. I was on the verge of mentioning that he could have his own portable TV set, remote control, and basic cable channels, when Sherry Lynne shrugged. "I didn't hear any grumbling, so I guess it's all right. Warn your daughter to be careful around him. Whenever he feels anxious, he bites. Just before

Christmas, I had to have four stitches in my arm. Dimple and Doolittle are generally imperturbable, but even they have been known to go on the defensive if startled."

"Why do you travel with your cats?"

"My fans expect it of me," she said as she poured Wimple back into the carrier and latched the door, "and since my ex-husband left me for his twenty-year-old secretary, I find it comforting to have a loyal friend with me. I'm worn out from the trip. If you don't mind taking Wimple with you, I'd like to lie down and rest."

I hadn't intended to take custody until after the reception, but I nodded. "Does he have any special dietary requirements or preferences?"

She told me the brand name of a catfood that cost as much as ground sirloin, adding that he could eat as many as six cans a day. She did not offer to pay for them. After making a few kissy noises through the mesh screen of the carrier, she handed it to me and started for the patio.

Feeling like a native in a safari movie, I trailed after her. "I'm taking the cat," I called to Lily as I went past her desk, told Sherry Lynne I would be ever vigilant in matters concerning Wimple's physical and emotional well-being, and was placing the carrier in the backseat of my car when Caron came huffing and puffing up the sidewalk.

"What's going on?" she demanded, red-faced from a combination of exertion and indignation, with an emphasis on the latter. "Inez was supposed to leave the car in the student parking lot at school. In that Everyone Else at Farber High except me has a car, it took me a long time to make sure it wasn't in some obscure corner behind a pickup truck. Sixth period had already started, so I couldn't burst into her algebra class and ask her where the car was. I called the bookstore but nobody answered. I finally decided to walk over here and find out if Inez had totally screwed up." She sank down on the low rock wall. "I'm all sweaty, and my mascara is literally dribbling down my face. Any minute now Louis Wilderberry will drive by and see me glistening like a professional wrestler. With my luck, Rhonda will be with him. I can just hear her telling everybody how hideous I looked. I might as well kill myself socially, if not literally. Remind Inez to weep at my gravesight once a week."

"Leap into the car," I said. "It's your only hope."

"What about the authors milling around at the airport?"

"They've already checked in. We encountered a problem with Laureen Parks. By the time I got it straightened out, Inez had to race back to school. I picked up the others."

"Do I still get paid?" Caron asked with a calculating look. "I should get a bonus, you know. It may not feel all that hot to you, but you didn't have to walk up a three-block hill that's steeper than Mount Everest. I thought I was going to faint before I got to the top. My head was spinning and my tongue was swollen—"

A yowl from the backseat interrupted the description of her close brush with death. "We have a houseguest," I said quickly, "but just until Sunday afternoon."

"A banshee? Good work, Mother."

"The Azalea Inn guarantees a hypoallergenic environment, as in no cat hairs in the carpet. As soon as we get the boxes of books loaded in the back, I'll drop you and said guest at home. Put him in the porch off the kitchen and make sure the screen-door is latched. Give him some water and a can of tuna fish. I'll have to go to the grocery store after the reception to buy his preferred brand of exceedingly expensive gourmet catfood. I'm afraid you won't be able to go to college after all, dear, but perhaps you can become a veterinarian's assistant or a dog groomer."

"You are not funny," she muttered. "You know cats make me nervous, and the last thing I want to do is break out. I'm not about to so much as let it out of that cage."

I parked behind the Book Depot. "Technically, you'll be doing it for the conference, so I'll see that you get paid. Let's get moving—I'm scheduled to meet a maintenance person at four o'clock."

Caron continued to mutter during the fifteen minutes it took to load the boxes, but the specter of cash precluded an outright rebellion. When I pulled up to the curb in front of the duplex, she gingerly took the carrier and trudged up the sidewalk to the front porch.

"Make sure the door's latched," I called, then drove to the campus. The bells of Old Main were tolling as I stopped at the loading entrance. A man in a khaki jumpsuit was sitting on the far side of the concrete dock, smoking a misshapen yellow cigarette. As I opened the car door, he stood up and turned around.

His eyes widened and a broad, gap-toothed grin spread across his face. "Yo, Senator! How's tricks these days?"

"Arnie," I said with a great deal less enthusiasm.

Some days it doesn't pay to get up. Period.

CHAPTER
4

A rnie was among the more ignominious of the great unwashed, in matters of both personal hygiene and ethics. His black hair, partially hidden by a greasy blue baseball cap, did not look as though it had been washed since our last skirmish, when he'd been caught peeping through windows at the Kappa Theta Eta sorority house next door to my duplex. I'd first encountered him when he'd been hired to drive a beauty pageant queen and a state senator in a Thurberfest parade. He'd shown up drunk, forcing me to take over, and he'd never quite sobered up enough to figure out my role in the fiasco. I'd long since quit trying to explain the political realities to him. His alcoholic haze was as impenetrable as his pungency.

"You know, Senator," he continued with a hiccup, "I was thinking about you the other night when I was watching C-Span and they were talking about the Asian economic crisis. Do you realize how much it's gonna take to bail out the Japanese?"

I opened the hatchback. "Do you have a dolly?"

He sucked on his lip for a moment. "Come to think of it, I brought one with me like I was supposed to, but not ten minutes ago some frat boys offered me a tidy sum for it. Something about moving kegs of beer. Maintenance has lots of them, so I figured nobody'd notice. Dollies, that is—not kegs or frat boys. Pardon my imprecision."

"Okay, Arnie," I said, sighing, "I'll set the boxes on the platform and you can carry them inside. Do you have a key to Room 130?"

He jangled a heavily-laden key ring at me. "I have keys to everything on the whole darn campus, including the college president's skybox at the football stadium. I've been living there since the season ended. It's got all the amenities, including a TV set, a bathroom, and a little refrigerator. I nailed a blanket over the window so no one will notice a light at night. The carpet's an ugly shade of mauve, but I've learned to put up with it. I'm hoping it'll be remodeled next season. I'm partial to earth tones, like chestnut and Saharan sand."

I stared at him. "You're kidding?"

"Senator, have I ever been anything but honest with you? Just don't go spreading it around."

Arnie had been anything *but* honest with me, but I let it go. "I don't have time to unpack the boxes—and I'd better not find any of them opened when I get here in the morning. You wouldn't want to find a horde of campus cops pounding on the door of your cozy little aerie, would you? There should be a table in the back of the room. Stack the boxes on it, and make sure you lock the door when you're finished." As I set the first box on the dock, I gave him a hard look. "And if some frat boys wander by and discover a sudden yearning for popular fiction, give them directions to the Book Depot as opposed to free samples. Got it?"

"I am wounded that you could say such things, Senator," Arnie said, wiping his eyes with a grubby handkerchief, "considering all we've been through together. Someday in the future you'll look back on this moment and remember what you said to Arnie Riggles, a constituent and loyal supporter, and be overwhelmed with remorse."

"Trust me, Arnie," I said as I unloaded another box, "should I ever look back on this moment—and that won't happen until well into this new millennium—I won't even be whelmed."

I left Arnie scowling at the boxes and drove to the Azalea Inn. Had I dared think things would go smoothly? Hubris, thy middle name is Malloy. Thus far, everything that could go wrong had gone wrong. The last thing left was the weather, and damned if raindrops weren't splattering my windshield as I parked.

April showers bring many things—flowers, income tax forms, Easter, and daylight savings, for example—but they do keep people inside. I eased my way through bodies clotting the hallway, doing my best not to make parallels with Sally Fromberger's veins and clumps of flaxen-hued cholesterol. Lily looked a bit tense when I found her behind a serving table with trays that had been ravaged, leaving only limp sprigs of parsley and crumbles of cheese. Wine bottles littered the tables like a defoliated glass forest.

I spotted a bottle with a few inches of its contents intact. As I looked around for a cup, I said, "Are any of the people on the organizing committee here? I should recognize them, but I missed a lot of meetings."

Like all of them.

"No," Lily said shrilly, "and Dr. Shackley called to say he and his wife were detained at a cocktail party. Sally assured me that she would handle registration at the door, but not one persona affiliated with the organization of this conference has so much as said hello. I did not agree to be in charge of this behemoth!"

I poured myself a glass of what proved to be rosé. I dislike rosé. "And our authors?"

"They're out there," she said, swiping her hand at the bodies mingling in the same fashion as salmon spawning in the immediate upstream. "People were supposed to present reception tickets at five o'clock. At four-thirty, they stormed the door. I asked to see badges or proof of registration, but they would not be held back. We could be feeding the homeless."

"The Thurber Farber Food Foundation can afford it," I said, then assessed the sunroom. Laureen Parks had appropriated an antique wicker chair that resembled a throne, and was surrounded by admirers, some of whom were literally sitting at her feet. Dilys Knoxwood was deep in conversation with a man in a clerical collar, undoubtedly debating the scruples (or lack thereof) of the bishop in her last book. Walter Dahl was slumped in a less-imposing chair in a corner, slurping red wine and gazing morosely at what I presumed he saw as the moral decay of the tatters of societal integrity. Sherry Lynne Blackstone appeared to be having a lovely time with her fans, although I noted that she was drinking club soda and taking surreptitious peeks at her wristwatch.

This left only one author unaccounted for. I stuck my head out the back door, but the garden was uninhabited. Not remarkable, since the rain had proceeded from spitty to steady. I made my way down the hall to the sitting room, where I spotted Allegra Cruzetti perched on a sofa, hemmed in on three sides by aspiring authors eager to know how to get an agent. Her face seemed pale in comparison with what I'd seen at the airport, and her eyelashes were flickering faster than bat wings.

I forced my way into the room. "Okay," I said loudly, "let's save these questions for tomorrow, please. Ms. Cruzetti has been traveling all day. She deserves a chance to relax and get her bearings before she's peppered with questions."

They quieted down, and after exchanging contrite looks, left the room. Allegra looked up with a grateful smile.

"It was getting tight in here," she said. "I'm used to having people from the publicity department nearby to keep the crowds at a civilized distance. I wouldn't have agreed to do this conference if I'd been warned that I was on my own and at the mercy of . . . well, fans . . ."

"Why did you agree to do it?" I asked bluntly.

"My editor was enthusiastic at the prospect. I'm not sure why, though. I certainly can't expect to draw the crowds I did in Atlanta and New York. I'd hoped to spend the next few weeks at my condo in Jackson Hole, doing nothing more strenuous than gazing at the mountains from my hot tub, but Roxanne was insistent that I come." She began to twist a corner of one of her scarfs around her finger. "I'm hardly in a position to argue with her. If she hadn't gone to bat for my book, it would have drifted in and out like a wave on a deserted beach. She worked hard with me, demanding revisions and helping me add secondary plot lines that initially seemed only tangential, but the bottom line is that she was right. I owe my success to her."

"You most certainly do," said a honied voice from the hallway. "Allegra, darling, how are you holding up?"

Allegra gasped, as though she were one of the salmon that had inadvertently flopped onto the shore. "Roxanne?"

"*C'est moi,*" said a fragile ash-blond woman as she swept into the room in a glitter of swirls and expensive jewelry. "I wanted to surprise you!" She bent over to kiss Allegra's cheek. "How was the tour? Are you exhausted? I'd planned to meet you in Philadelphia, but my husband insisted that we go to Bermuda that very same weekend. Men are so—oh, I don't know—immutable. Are you well?"

"I suppose," she responded without conviction.

The woman turned to me. "I'm Roxanne Small, Allegra's editor. I thought it would be fun to surprise her, as well as my other authors. Lily, and such a dear she is, has agreed to accommodate me for the weekend. It's a veritable homecoming for me, as well as an opportunity to see my authors in action. You must be Sally. When I learned you were having this conference, I was thrilled. I did my master's degree at this very college."

"Oh?" I said, obscurely wishing I were Sally, who was grazing on over-cooked green beans and Jello on a plastic tray and wondering when the IV bag might next be replaced.

Roxanne gave me a look that indicated she was cutting me

some slack for the moment. "My great-aunt had a farm a few miles out of town. I visited every summer, and for reasons I can never explain, I developed a fondness for the quaint, rustic ambiance of Farberville. My bachelor's degree is from Radcliffe, but I have a master's degree in literature from Farber College, if you can imagine the incongruity. And you, dear? Did you go to college?"

She sounded as though she expected me to confess to a high school diploma in agronomy. "English lit," I said, "mostly medieval."

"I never found Chaucer all that interesting," Roxanne said dismissively. "Allegra, you look positively worn. Should you be in bed for the night?"

"It's five-thirty," Allegra said with a trace of sullenness. "I can usually make it until seven, sometimes, eight."

Roxanne patted Allegra's cheek with a bit more intensity than might be called for. "I can tell that you're exhausted, you worn thing. I'm so excited that we're here together in Farberville. I do hope you'll have an hour of free time tomorrow so that I can show you Uncle Bediah's farm. There was a tire swing on an old oak tree that has left an indelible mark on my memories of a carefree childhood."

She was dressed in a pastel blue suit that surely cost more than the antique credenza behind her. She wasn't exactly gaunt, but it was hard to imagine she'd ever consumed more than a dozen calories at any one meal. Her shoulder-length hair brushed her shoulders, her complexion was dewy, her makeup applied by an expert hand. Small pockets of quilted softness were evident, however, and I put her age at thirty-five or more, despite the Alice-in-Wonderland packaging.

"And," she said breathlessly, "I understand that dear, dear Laureen Parks is here, as well as Sherry Lynne Blackstone and Dilys Knoxwood. Tomorrow night we must all put on our pajamas and have a party. I'm sure Sally here can arrange for chips and dip, sodas, cookies, and fingernail polish. It's so wonderful to escape the suffocating sophistication of New York! There's something so refreshing about the hinterlands!"

I wondered if I could find a way to lure her to a particular skybox for a truly heady dose of the hinterlands. "I'm not Sally," I said. "She's in the hospital. I'm Claire Malloy, the bookseller for the conference. I wish we'd known you were coming, Ms. Small. Many of our registrants hope to be published some day. They'd have been thrilled if we could have scheduled you for a session."

She clutched my hands. "That's why I didn't tell a soul. Fortunately, my husband is at a plastic surgeons' symposium in Palm Springs, so he doesn't even know I'm not spending the weekend reading dreary manuscripts in our apartment on Park Avenue. The idea of sneaking down here was too delightful to resist. The entire time the limo was taking me to the airport, I felt like a fifteen-year-old at summer camp, stealthily paddling across the moonlit lake to spy on the boys. I'm sure you must have similar memories, even though yours may involve more of a pond."

I opted to disengage my hands and change the topic. "So you have a master's degree from Farber College, Ms. Small? Is this the first time you've been back since then?"

Allegra stood up before an answer was forthcoming. "This most definitely calls for another glass of wine. Shall I bring you one, Roxanne? Red or white?"

She frowned. "A glass of Chardonnay might be nice, but I'll fetch it myself. You wait here, and when I get back, we'll have a long, lazy chat about your tour." She looked at me. "Tours can be gruelling, and Allegra was such a trooper. Media from dawn to midnight, bookstores, squealing fans, canceled flights, botched hotel reservations. I worried myself sick the entire time she was on the road. I was popping Prozac tablets as if they were candy."

"Allegra was telling me that you helped her with her manuscript," I said to Roxanne as I led her toward the sunroom.

"I've always been that kind of editor. Some of my colleagues simply buy the manuscripts and cross their fingers, but I work with my authors every step of the way. Rewrites, revisions, copyedit, and then final production. I talk with the art department, publicity, marketing, and sales to make sure Paradigm is doing everything appropriate for the end product, from print media to personal appearances. I've had eleven books on the *New York Times* best-seller list in the last five years. Quite a record, if I say so myself."

I opted not to point out that she herself had not actually written the books so warmly received by the book-buying public. "I can't promise there's any Chardonnay."

"I can tolerate Chablis, as long as it isn't that California soda pop," she said, then darted away to kiss Laureen Parks. "Darling, isn't this a wonderful surprise?"

Laureen recoiled, splashing wine on her skirt. "Roxanne?"

"Yes, dear, I decided at the very last minute to fly down and surprise all of you. We have so much to talk about!"

"We most certainly do. Jennifer called earlier in the week."

Roxanne flinched as though Laureen had leaned forward

and pinched her—and not playfully. "I was thinking we might have a long discussion about all this while I'm here. Not everything at Paradigm House is under my control. I'm responsible to my boss, and he to his. Ultimately, the bottom line goes to a faceless executive at the conglomerate in God knows what country. I can assure you that he or she is not interested in contributions to contemporary literature."

"I've heard it before, Roxanne." Laureen turned toward a plump young woman hovering nearby. "As I was saying, credibility can only be established through the character's motivation. Does that answer your question?"

The woman ignored her. "Roxanne Pickett? Do you remember me? I was in your freshman comp class."

Roxanne stared at her. "Tweetie?"

"Ammie Threety, actually," she said. "You used to get irritated with me when I wouldn't participate in the discussions."

Roxanne was still staring, but she finally managed a shaky laugh. "Of course I remember you, Ammie. I always thought of you as a sugar-dusted doughnut, and you haven't changed all that much. How are you doing? Did you ever graduate?"

Ammie shook her head. "I had to drop out and work full time after my father got sick. I always meant to go back and finish up, but I never did. One of these days. . . ."

"That's what we tell ourselves," Roxanne murmured. "Laureen, let's sit down tomorrow and talk things over. If you'll excuse me, I must say hello to Sherry Lynne and Dilys." She slipped into the crowd.

I smiled at Ammie, who seemed paralyzed. "Are you working on a manuscript?"

She finally realized I'd spoken to her. "I try, but I guess I'm just not smart enough to ever write anything worth reading. I come up with ideas without too much trouble; I've been making up stories since I was a little kid. Putting them on paper's the hard part. My manuscript started way back in college as a short story, but I kept thinking of complications and ways it might go. Now it's over six hundred pages."

Laureen patted her on the arm. "The important thing is to keep right on trying. A college degree doesn't get you published. Perseverance does. Why don't you tell me about your manuscript and its evolution?"

I left them chatting and followed Roxanne, whom I suspected was not quite the beloved editor of all concerned. She'd zeroed in on Dilys by the time I caught up with her.

"Dilys," she was trilling, "Paradigm will always remain supportive of your backlist, despite this current unpleasantness."

Dilys smiled tightly. "I've been told that my first is 'unavailable,' and my others are in the warehouse in limited quantities. Has Paradigm considered reverting the rights to me?"

"We still adore your books," Roxanne said as she sat down beside her. "And we adore you, too. Is there any chance I can take you to lunch tomorrow?"

I intervened. "I'm sorry, Roxanne, but all the authors have agreed to attend a luncheon at the college. Since it's basically a one-day conference, we're working them really hard. Morning panels, lunch, afternoon panels, and then the picnic here at seven o'clock."

"Slave labor," said Roxanne.

"It seems as such," I said, trying not to wither under her piercing gaze. "Sally prepared the program, and asked the attending authors to agree to it. The honorariums are not shoddy for what amounts to a day and a half of availability. Had we known you were coming, I'm sure we could have provided the same offer to you."

Roxanne produced an abashed smile. "Yes, of course. I should have let you know that I was thinking about coming, but I did so want to swoop in like a fairy godmother and amaze my little cozy coven of authors. I rarely see any of them more than once a year, and it's so important to me to let them know how much I care about them, not only as authors but also as people. Publishing can be so impersonal, especially now that all the houses are being gobbled up by vast corporations." Her eyes filled with tears as she bent down and hugged Dilys. "Some talents continue to shine, and we'll never forget them. Dilys's first book set records in all the mystery bookstores in America."

Dilys remained dry-eyed. "Then why can't bookstores order it?"

"I'm sure they can," Roxanne said, straightening up. "The last time you called, I checked with the sales department. Several thousand copies are in the warehouse. I'm afraid you overestimate the booksellers' enthusiasm just a little."

"Does anyone work in this warehouse," asked Dilys, "or is it just a dim building filled with boxes of books that will never again see the light of day, much less a shelf in a bookstore? I was making nice semi-annual royalties off the paperback sales of my books, Roxanne. Now booksellers are telling me that they can't get the books." She looked at me. "Did you have any problems ordering my backlist, Claire? Be truthful."

Despite my better intentions, I began to squirm as Roxanne turned to stare at me. "Well, I was told your first was out-of-print and your second was on backorder. I was going through a distributor rather than Paradigm, however."

"There you have it," said Roxanne, as if proving a point. "Why don't we just kick back and enjoy the party, Dilys? Tomorrow we'll go over all this and arrive at an understanding."

"I'm quite sure we shall arrive at *something*," Dilys said pointedly as she went around me and down the hall toward the staircase.

Roxanne laughed. "Dilys is such a gem, isn't she? I absolutely melt whenever I hear her marvelous accent. One would think after twenty years in the Midwest that it might have lost its edge, but it's her way of clinging to home and her quaint ways. I think I'd better find a glass of wine and go back to Allegra before she passes out on the sofa. I do worry about her. She's hardly a scarred veteran like Laureen or Sherry Lynne, or Dilys, for that matter. One of the reasons I was so enthusiastic about taking her on was her lack of guile. Most authors are demanding and cantankerous, but a few are ripe to be molded, taught, brought into focus like modern-day Pygmalions. She listened to me and learned, which is why she's on the best-seller lists. Of course, being photogenic and personable helps, too. Take an author like"—her voice dropped to a whisper—"Walter Dahl over there in the corner. Given the chance, he would berate every personality on every morning talk show. He would alienate potential readers and provoke reviewers into utilizing snake venom to write about his books."

I looked at Walter, who was glaring at us. "Surely content matters more than personality?"

"Surely," she said.

As she left in search of the perfect Chardonnay, I noted that the rain had stopped. I also noted that Laureen had Ammie Threety in tow as they went out the back door to the garden. If Laureen wished to hear the evolution of what must have become convoluted prose over the last ten years, so be it. Neither required the assistance of Bo Peep.

Lily was busy uncorking wine for the more dedicated registrants, who appeared to be having a lovely time debating the merits of Dorothy L. Sayers and Agatha Christie versus Sir Arthur Conan Doyle and Mickey Spillane. The decibel level was high, but well within the boundaries established by the Farberville city directors and enforced by the city's finest.

After a savage mental battle, I managed not to envision a particular member of said finest. Get through the weekend, I lectured myself as I pasted on a smile that most likely would have frightened small children. I could deal with it on Monday morning, when I would be calm and fresh and sane—and totaling credit card receipts with an inane grin on my face.

"Excuse me," said a petite woman in skintight jeans and a translucent blouse. "Have you seen Ammie Threety? She was talking to Ms. Parks a minute ago, but when I came back from the can, they were gone."

"They went out into the garden," I said, pleased to have a straightforward answer to a simple question.

"Great," the woman replied. "I have to be at work at seven o'clock tomorrow morning. Ammie'll kill me if I drag her away, but I got to get home. We live in Hasty, about twenty miles from here. Our library's not more than a room at city hall, but Ammie's there most every week, checking out armloads of books. She knows more about books than most folks in Hasty know about eviscerating chickens—and that's saying a lot. Now she's out there talking to one of her most favorite authors. I can't just make her leave, can I?"

I remembered the glow on Ammie's face when Laureen had touched her. "Did you drive in together?"

"No," the woman said, chewing on her purple lipstick as she looked at the door to the garden. "I didn't get off work until four, so I met her like we agreed at a diner south of town. Her car's still there. I don't know what to do. If I make her leave just when she's spilling out her heart to a real writer, she'll never forgive me. On the other hand, I've got a husband, kids, and my ma, all expecting supper. I've gotta run three loads of laundry before I go to bed. What do you think I ought to do?"

Having not experienced a crisis in at least five minutes, I smiled benignly. "I'll make sure someone gives Ammie a ride to her car. Go home with a clear conscience."

"If you say so," the woman said uncertainly. "Ammie doesn't drink too much or anything, but she doesn't like to drive at night. I told her she could follow me home. I don't want her to be pissed at me."

"I'll share your concern with her, and I will personally make sure she's transported to her car and capable of driving herself home."

"Okay," the woman said. "Just don't let her think I dumped on her. I'd like to hang around, but, you know—kids, laundry, that stuff. Tell her I'll call her Monday. Maybe she'll have sold her book by then. She's been writing it ever since she went to college."

"Maybe," I said with an insincere chuckle. Six hundred

pages, reworked for ten years, were not apt to be publishable. Then again, she had the link to Roxanne Small, who might, by the grace of obscure publishing deities, read Ammie's efforts.

The loveliest aspect was that I really didn't care. My only concern was to keep the conference simmering at a reasonable temperature until the next evening, when Dr. Shackley would seize the podium and I could fade into the azaleas. Rid myself of the unwelcome cat. Suggest that Lily put her brochure in an anatomically-inappropriate place. Pour myself a glass of scotch. Concoct blisteringly clever things to say to a certain person. Write an anonymous letter to the CIA—or should that be the supposedly no longer existent KGB?—suggesting that not all visitors to St. Petersburg were guileless tourists.

Life was looking up, or so I thought.

As Laureen Parks was so fond of writing in her sixty-odd books, "Had I but known." I should have had it tattooed across some aspect of my anatomy.

My brain, for example.

CHAPTER

5

I was considering how best to arrange to get Ammie to her car when Walter approached me in a manner not unlike a Scud missile in the throes of a bad hair day. "That was Roxanne Small, wasn't it?" he said. "I've seen her photo in *Publishers Weekly,* so there's no point in denying it. She looks much older in person, as well as haggard. It's obvious she has a sexually-transmitted disease. The Thurber Farber Foundation should provide vaccinations on the house."

"Mr. Dahl," I said coldly, "that was indeed Roxanne Small, and I have no interest in discussing the status of her health. Let's talk about your abrupt departure from the airport. Common courtesy might have dictated that you inform—"

"I do not subscribe to any common cause, including one that might dictate the need for an apology. A car was to be sent for me. I was informed that something more similar to a public transit vehicle had appeared. I took a cab." He pulled a slip of paper out of his pocket and handed it to me. "Here's the receipt. I expect to be reimbursed. What's Roxanne Small doing here? I was never warned about her participation in this banal little gathering. I would have declined to attend. She is a beastly woman who undoubtedly devours her young at birth. I would not be surprised to learn that's been her primary source of food for the last thirty years."

"Gracious me," I said, politely omitting the fact Roxanne was not the first person at the conference to evoke this desire to flee. "Shall I notify the protein police?"

Walter aimed a finger at me. "You know what I meant. Why wasn't I informed?"

"She dropped in to visit her authors. The other four seem to have some sort of relationship with her, past or present." I thought for a moment. "You're published by White Oakleaf Press, aren't you? I had a very difficult time getting your books. I finally had to order directly, but I wasn't at all confident I'd get them until a few days ago."

"White Oakleaf is a highly-regarded literary press," said Walter. "They are not accustomed to handling what I assume was a small order from a nonentity of a bookstore in an obscure state."

"You live in Wyoming, yes? I wonder how many people present could find Wyoming on a map. Would you care to make a wager?"

"This is hardly a moment for gauche attempts at levity," he

muttered, glowering at the hallway that led to the front of the inn. "I will require a flight out tonight. Get me as far as Denver and I'll make arrangements from there."

I have to admit I was baffled. "What's the problem? Roxanne Small isn't your editor."

"And she never will be. The woman is insufferable. Shall I call the airline or will you?"

"If you choose to leave, you do so at your own expense," I said. "The Thurber Farber Foundation will not pay expenses and an honorarium to an author who fails to participate in the conference because of some unforeseen personality clash. Call whomever you wish. The taxi cab's telephone number is likely to be on the receipt you just gave me. Let me give it back to you. You'll need it if you intend to write all this off as a business expense. We'll bill you for the airline ticket."

After a moment of silence, he said. "I may be inclined to reconsider after a decent night's sleep, although the wallpaper in my room is shrieking in botanical ecstasy. Petunias are achieving orgasm as we speak."

"We have no reason to continue this conversation. Retreat upstairs and regard the petunias with voyeuristic relish, or head for the airport. The conference will go on with or without you."

"You are a veritable Boadicea, Ms. Malloy. Is your brassiere made of leather?"

If I'd had a sword in hand, I would have whacked him hard enough to send the goatee flying off his chin. "We would prefer that you participate tomorrow, but I'm not in the mood to play nursemaid to ill-tempered toddlers."

He stalked away, leaving me free to mingle with the registered attendees, which is all I did for the next hour. They seemed to be a literate and articulate bunch, well versed in mystery fiction. Around three-quarters were women, a preponderance of them librarians and teachers. I had a feeling that the panels the following day would be lively as soon as I opened them up for questioning—which might happen within minutes.

Eventually, I was cornered by a woman, her demeanor as drab as her clothing, who confided in a terrified whisper that she was Earlene of steering committee notoriety. "Isn't this terrible about Sally?" she said as if sharing a dark secret. "She's such a wonderful person. If anyone deserves sainthood, it's Sally Fromberger. If I were Catholic, I'd call the pope. Well, and if I had his number. He's most likely unlisted."

"I know she put a lot of work into planning the conference," I responded tactfully. "It's a shame she has to miss it."

"Registration was supposed to take place in the hallway before the reception, but no one thought to bring the box. I'll handle it myself in the morning before the first session. After that, everyone will have a badge and a packet with a program book. Do you need someone to sell books while you're moderating the panels?"

I considered her question. "I don't think so. My daughter and her friend can keep an eye on the stock when I'm not present. What I really need is someone to drive one of our attendees to her car when she comes in from the garden in a few minutes. Is there any chance you might be able to do it?"

Earlene seemed pleased with the possibility of a contribution to the cause that surpassed providing nametags. "You'll point her out to me?"

"Oh, yes," I said, glancing at the back door. "In the meantime, you might want to start dropping hints that the reception is winding down. The wine's pretty much gone, and I don't trust Lily Twiller not to burst out of the kitchen with a shotgun and order everyone off the premises."

Earlene's eyes bulged like those of a bullfrog caught in the beam of a flashlight. "She wouldn't do that, would she? The Thurber Farber Foundation would not look kindly on us if the conference participants were threatened with physical harm. Should I sneak away and call Sally? She'll know what to do."

"I was exaggerating, Earlene. Lily undoubtedly is packing nothing more lethal than a carrot stick, and her bullets are undoubtedly of organic origin."

"I get it," she said, winking slyly at me. She raised her voice. "Would you look at the time? I for one don't want to be groggy in the morning when the first panel begins at nine o'clock sharp. We need a good night's sleep so we'll feel perky and ready to ask insightful questions. It's all I can do to keep my eyes open."

In that it was seven o'clock, no one else seemed to share her desire to tumble into bed. The message was received, however, and the topic of conversation shifted from mystery fiction to where best to have dinner and perhaps another drink or two.

Sherry Lynne joined me. "Did I catch a glimpse of Roxanne Small—or am I too worried about Wimple to think clearly?"

"Wimple is fine, and yes, that was Roxanne. It seems she went to grad school at Farber College and thought it would be amusing to surprise her authors while they're in town. She's staying here at the inn, so she must have made plans a while back. She's your editor, isn't she?"

"Yes," said Sherry Lynne. "I guess I'd better find her and thank her for coming all this way. She's a very busy woman; her assistant was telling me just the other day on the telephone about all the demands on her time. She's built up quite a large stable of mystery writers. If you get along well with her, she can do wonders with the marketing and sales of your book."

"Like Allegra's, for instance?"

Sherry Lynne shrugged. "Has she gone upstairs?"

"Try the front room on the right," I said. After Sherry Lynne left, I began deftly steering people down the hall like a wagon master in a fifties' television series. Once the room was cleared, I tracked down Lily, who was in the kitchen gazing despondently at a vast array of bottles, wadded napkins, and lipstick-smudged wine glasses.

"This is not what I expected," she said.

"Nor is it what I expected," I countered without sympathy. "Based on the written agreement, you're providing a light supper to the authors. I should think most of them are ready for something. Soup and a sandwich should be adequate. They'll expect something heartier in the morning, along the lines of bacon, sausage, eggs, grits, biscuits, toast, whatever."

Lily shuddered. "The Azalea Inn is strictly vegetarian. I serve seasonal fruit from the farmers' market, wheat breads, and tofu and onion tarts."

"I don't much care if you serve boiled hats. Just feed the authors tonight and in the morning. Be prepared to feed one hundred people tomorrow at seven o'clock, because that's how many tickets have been sold. If you want to discuss the menu, call Sally at the hospital. All she's doing is having things dripped into her. I, on the other hand, am going home."

As I sailed out of the kitchen, Laureen and Ammie were

coming through the back door. I caught Earlene's eye and gestured accordingly.

I then went down the hall and into the sitting room, where I found Allegra, Dilys, Sherry Lynne, and Roxanne. Everyone seemed reasonably comfortable. I assured them that a supper of sorts would be provided and that drivers would be on hand in the morning to shuttle them to Old Main for the panels and back to the inn for breaks as they wished. I did not mention tofu, in that I myself find the concept alarming. I was trying to remember where I'd stashed my purse when Ammie tiptoed into the room.

"It was nice to see you again," she said to Roxanne. "Maybe next time you come we can have lunch or something and talk about the good old days. Well, I don't actually know if that's what they were for you, but they sure were for me. When I get home, I'm gonna dig out all my old notebooks and stories, even the ones you gave me bad grades on. Maybe I'll write something new and send it to you."

Roxanne patted the sofa cushion. "Sit down for a few minutes, Ammie, and we'll have some coffee and a nice talk. Would anyone else like a cup?"

Sherry Lynne shook her head. Allegra mentioned that a glass of wine sounded better; Dilys concurred and followed her out of the room, hiccuping in a manner unsuited to a modern-day Emily Brontë. Although I was desperate to go home, change into a robe, and pour myself an inch or two of scotch, I told Roxanne I'd speak to Lily about coffee.

When I came out of the sitting room, I found Earlene sitting on the bottom step of the staircase.

"Why don't you join everyone else?" I said.

"It'd be like sticking pins in balloons. At a distance, they're all glamorous and wonderful and witty. I'd just as soon let them stay that way. Tell Ammie that I'm perfectly happy to wait out here for her."

I wondered how many minor pops I'd heard over the course of the day. More than a few, I surmised as I went back to the kitchen and asked Lily to start a pot of coffee. She was in the midst of explaining why the Azalea Inn was a caffeine-free environment as I went out to the sunroom.

Laureen, Dilys, and Allegra were snickering madly as they examined wine bottles.

"Do all of you know each other?" I asked.

"From one event or another," Laureen said. "This is an incestuous business, dear Claire. Publicists, editors, and assistants are constantly shifting houses. We've all experienced the same people—the good, the ignorant, and the flat-out incompetent. I've had the same publicist at three competing houses. She's all of twenty-seven now, but very well trained. She knows that I travel first-class, never appear before ten in the morning, and require escorts who allow me to smoke."

"The first panel's at nine," I said. "I don't have a program, but I believe it's on the evolution of the amateur sleuth."

"And I'm sure you will lead a spirited discussion," Laureen said blithely. "If not, my grand appearance at ten will liven things up."

"Three inches of rosé," said Allegra as she snatched up a bottle. "I'll share."

"Half a bottle of Chablis and I won't," said Dilys, clasping a bottle to her bosom. "Bedtime bliss. It's my only solace these days."

Laureen frowned at her. "Are things not any better at home, Dilys? I thought the bypass surgery . . . ?"

"Denton's doctor told him not to worry," Dilys said, her eyes welling with tears, "but he's still sleeping in another bedroom. Being downsized at fifty is far from humorous. Denton can't even find a job as a bookkeeper. We've been surviving on my royalties for two years, but now those have dried up. In my idle moments, I speculate on how challenging it would be to break into this mystical warehouse and liberate my backlist. Don't mention my name if you see a story about a terrorist with a Tottingham accent."

"Is that what it is?" said Laureen, kissing Dilys on the cheek. "I knew there was something about you that makes me dote on you. It must be your accent."

"Not my undeniable wit?"

"No one can ever surpass the flawlessness of your prose, my darling, or your exquisite satiric touch. Roxanne has no excuse to bury your backlist as she's done. Have you spoken to your agent?"

"I'm new at this," Allegra said, "but it does sound as though your agent—"

"May he rest in pieces," Dilys said, then giggled as befitting someone taking swigs of wine from the bottle. "He went camping in Canada last month and had a fatal encounter with a grizzly bear. His agency is in disarray, for obvious reasons, and his widow has not yet decided what to do. Legally, I'm caught up in the quagmire." She took another gulp. "Too much to bear, I suppose, unless, of course, he bared himself to the bear in order to retain foreign rights, in which case he could barely hope to escape intact."

I regret to report that Dilys, Laureen, Allegra, and I all started snorting as we struggled to pretend we weren't laughing. There was nothing humorous about being killed by a bear. Dilys's lilting accent made it all sound like a lovely little fairy tale, however; I presumed none of us were imagining any sort of pain and violence. Then again, I reminded myself as I regained control, these women's incomes depended on murder most foul.

Lily came out of the kitchen, holding a tray with a coffee carafe and several cups. "I'm heating the lentil soup," she said as she thrust it into my hands. "Supper should be ready shortly."

We all went back up the hall to the front room, where Roxanne and Ammie were in a rather uninteresting conversation about people they'd known ten years ago. I might have recognized a few names had they been professors, but they seemed to be Ammie's classmates. I stepped around Sherry Lynne, who seemed to be dozing, and set down the tray.

"Earlene's ready when you are," I said to Ammie.

"I don't mind waiting," called the designated driver. "I'm really very comfortable."

Roxanne raised perfectly-shaped eyebrows. "Shouldn't we invite her to join us?"

I shook my head. "She'd rather idolize the authors from afar. She's afraid she'll see warts and wrinkles if she gets too close."

"If she gets *too* close," Allegra said, "she might catch a glimpse of my butterfly tattoo."

Sherry Lynne's eyes flew open. "I assume you're joking. Tattoo parlors are a significant source of AIDS."

Roxanne poured coffee into a cup and handed it to Ammie. "Lighten up, Sherry Lynne. This new generation of authors is less bound by convention. The only cat in Allegra's book is the one skinned by the serial killer. The cozy tide is ebbing. Today's readers want realism, not tea and fishpaste sandwiches." She patted Dilys's knee. "As a child, you never really ate them, did you? They sound so nasty."

Dilys sighed wistfully. "As a child, I was mad for them, along with hot scones and strawberry jam."

Laureen poured herself a cup of coffee. "When I'm in London, I always zero in on cream cakes."

All this discussion of food, be it fishpaste or cream cakes, was reminding me that I hadn't found so much as a mouse-sized morsel of cheese on arrival at the Azalea Inn. I wasn't sure I'd had lunch, for that matter.

"If everything is satisfactory, I'm off," I said as I stood up. "I'll see all of you in the morning for our panel at nine. I had very little warning that I would be called on to moderate and am woefully unprepared, but I assume you know the drill."

No one offered a counter-proposal. I went into the hallway and nodded to Earlene, who seemed to have taken permanent possession of the second step, waved at Lily, who was coming toward the sitting room with a tray of soup bowls and a platter of sandwiches, and continued outside. The rain had started once again, but with only a gentle cadence. I debated whether or not to go by the grocery store, then accepted the reality that I could not meet Sherry Lynne's soulful gaze in the morning if I couldn't swear with pained honesty that Wimple had been cared for as promised. I stopped and shopped.

In that the creature was locked in the enclosed porch at the top of the stairs that led up from the garage to the kitchen, I parked in front of the duplex and dodged raindrops to the front door. It swung open before I could dig out my key.

"Mrs. Malloy," said the emaciated and perpetually gloomy musicology graduate student renting the downstairs apartment, "we have a situation. I don't want to call the landlord, but I need to study. The noise is intolerable."

I was tempted to suggest he needed to study nutrition instead of Bach, but merely smiled and said, "Is my daughter playing her stereo too loudly? I'll have her turn it down."

"It sounds as though she's sacrificing animals in a satanic ritual."

Before I could think of a response, we both heard an unearthly sound that hinted not only of bloodshed, but of primal horror and pain.

"We're looking after a cat," I said with a nervous chuckle.

"What is she doing to it?" he countered. "Maybe I ought to call an animal rights group. It sounds as if it's being disemboweled on the dining room table."

"I'll take care of it," I assured him as I hurried upstairs. I unlocked the door and went inside. The dining room table was bereft of entrails and other nasty things, and the noise was emanating from the porch off the kitchen. I peeked through the glass panel. Wimple's back was arched and he was obviously outraged by his incarceration, if his protests were to be interpreted thusly.

Caron was in her room, sitting cross-legged on her bed with the telephone receiver glued to one ear. "Mother," she said, looking up with a withering glare, "do you mind? Inez is telling me about the Latin Club banquet. Angela Ridinn's toga came unpinned in the middle of the skit about Cleopatra and Anthony, and from the consensus, there was no doubt the asp would have committed suicide."

"Do you not hear the cat?"

"I gave it a can of tuna fish and a bowl of water. What else was I supposed to do?"

"Did you provide a can opener?"

Caron told Inez to wait, then put down the receiver. "I opened the can and stuck it on the porch at great personal risk. I thought about reading it a bedtime story, but I couldn't put my hands on a copy of *The Owl and the Pussycat*. My nose was running and my eyes were itching; my face was pea green by the time I slammed the door."

I froze as another yowl curdled its way through the apartment. "We have to do something."

"I was hired to drive authors, not forcefeed a cat. If Inez hadn't bungled everything, I would have made twenty-one dollars today. Instead, all I did was walk up a really long hill in stifling heat to find out that I could have stayed in study hall and earned an equal amount of money. I was so hoping to buy a Ferrari on Monday."

Two years until I could pack her off to college, I reminded myself as I closed her door. Or perhaps I could surreptitiously sign her up for the Peace Corps and arrange for an assignment to a country in which headhunting was still a popular sport. Or leave her in a basket at the door of a convent in a newly autonomized country such as Azerbijan—sans passport.

Another yowl sent me into the kitchen. I opened a can of gourmet cat food, dumped it in a very nice china bowl, and eased open the door. "Here we go, Wimple," I said soothingly. "*Paté de foie de souris.*"

That's mouse liver paste, for those who have not sampled the delicacies of Paris.

I closed the door just as the cat sprang, claws primed to effect significant damage on my aristocratic facial features. I then poured kitty litter in a plastic dishpan, made sure the cat was gulping down its dinner, and slid the box into the porch.

I showered, put on my robe, and was lightheartedly dealing with food and drink when the doorbell rang. After a few seconds of thought, I realized there was absolutely no one with whom I wished to deal. The doorbell rang again—and again, and again. Wimple, who'd been relatively peaceful, resumed his remonstrations. Caron protested from her bedroom. The downstairs tenant thumped on his ceiling with what I hoped was a broom rather than an automatic weapon. It was only a matter of minutes before the sorority girls from next door showed up to shriek at me (that being, as far as I could tell, their sole means of communication).

"Oh, all right," I muttered as I went down the steps to open the door. Bad call.

Peter was turning on all his charm, his eyes ever so sticky-sweet and his expression fraught with contrition. "Can we talk?" he said as he came into the foyer.

"We have nothing to talk about."

"Yes, you do!" yelled the downstairs tenant. "Otherwise, he wouldn't be ringing the doorbell as though composing a symphony in E-flat!"

"I suppose I was leaning on the doorbell," he murmured, brushing past me on his way upstairs.

I had little choice but to follow him. I was contemplating which items of cutlery in the kitchen might be most lethal as I closed my door. "What gives you the right to barge in here like this, Peter? I told you that I didn't want to see you. I may not be a priority player in this sick ménage à trois, but I still have a few rights. One of them is whether or not I choose to hear the details. I choose not to hear them. Has it occurred to you that I'm a medievalist? The next time you lean on the doorbell, you can expect boiling oil dumped off the balcony. Does that cover it?"

"Ah, so you got my flowers."

I grabbed the vase and headed for the kitchen. "And they're going into the garbage disposal."

"Your garbage disposal died three years ago."

"So they're going into the trash," I said. "Just leave, okay?"

"Not okay. Have you got any beer?"

I noted the profound silence from Caron's room as I stopped in the middle of the kitchen. I banged down the vase and returned to the living room, where I found him on the sofa, his feet on the coffee table, his smile meant to be beguiling.

I was not beguiled. "If I call 911, will they come get you?" I asked as I sat down in a chair across the room. "Dare I hope for a SWAT team?"

"Will you please listen to me?"

"Why should I?"

"Because," he said "I love you. I want to marry you. I want you, Caron, and me to be a family. I want us to live together, deal with whatever happens, and after Caron goes on her way, get old and constipated and gray and disabled together."

"With adjoining plots in the cemetery? What if our karma doesn't correspond, and you come back as a cockroach? Is that part of the deal? Will I have to scurry around cabinets, too?"

"You are in a mood, aren't you?"

"No, Peter, I'm not in a mood, or even what you'd like to describe as a jealous snit. You just spent three months with your ex-wife. In that you worked out all the details of the divorce ten years ago, I can only assume you were working out some entirely new ones."

"Any chance of that beer?" he said, grinning in what struck me as gauche fashion.

Since Caron undoubtedly had her ear glued to her bedroom door, I nodded and went into the kitchen. "All right," I said as I returned with a beer and my glass of scotch, "but you have precisely five minutes. I set the microwave. At the sound of the ding, you will get up and leave, your explanations half-thawed or otherwise. Got it?"

Peter nodded. "It may take a few more minutes. Leslie wants to have a baby."

"Female imperative," I said, although my throat was tightening and most of my organs were shutting down. I was pleased to see that Peter was beginning to perspire.

"I guess so. In any case, she thinks that she and I present a very strong gene pool. No need of chlorine, so to speak. Neither of us has a family history of heart disease, diabetes, or cancer. Not everyone on each side has been short-listed for a Pulitzer, but there's a decent scattering of doctors and lawyers."

"Then what's the problem? Buy a bungalow in the suburbs of Connecticut and procreate to your heart's content. Oh, and buy a swing set while you're at it. Very important to gross motor development. Maybe one day you can be president of the PTA. Please don't ask me to be godmother, though. I'm entirely too busy these days."

"Claire."

"That is my name," I said as I plucked the bottle out of his hand and opened the front door. "If you don't mind, I have a difficult day in front of me. Go home and call Leslie—unless, of course, she's at your house, waiting for you to commence activity. She doesn't sound like the sort of woman to greet you in flannel pajamas and face cream. Good night, Peter. If we meet anytime soon, it will not be at my instigation."

"Leslie and I are not going to remarry."

"Then I shall be spared the necessity of finding an appropriate wedding present. Cobras are expensive and hard to wrap. Good night."

Peter stood up. "It's the genetic thing. It has nothing to do with my feelings toward you."

I willed my lips not to so much as quiver. "Congratulations on your impending fatherhood. I'm sure you'll make a wonderful Little League coach. Will you please leave?"

The moment the door closed, I collapsed on the sofa and grabbed the telephone. "Luanne," I shrieked when she answered. "What have I done? What has he done? What am I supposed to do about what he has or hasn't done? Has he really done it? We are not talking petrie dishes here."

Luanne took a minute to assimilate all this, then sighed and said, "Would you care to elaborate?"

CHAPTER

6

I was not in the best of moods the next morning as I went into Old Main and down the hall to Room 130. The door was locked, to my chagrin but not my surprise.

Earlene was seated behind a card table at the far end of the hallway, passing out packets to a line of conference attendees. "The panel's in the room behind me," she said as I approached. "None of the authors have shown up yet, but I guess they'll be along."

"Caron's on her way to the Azalea Inn," I said. "Not everyone can squeeze into the car at one time, but it's only a three-minute drive. Do you have the key to the room where the signings are supposed to take place?"

She gave me a stricken look. "No, but maybe Sally knows where to find one. If you'll take over registration, I can call her."

"That's not necessary," I said in the tempered voice of a mild-mannered bookseller whose ex-lover was likely to be in the process of inseminating his ex-wife out of exaggerated concern for the genetic health of the next generation. "Let's assume that someone will appear to unlock the door between now and the first break." It occurred to me that the person responsible to do so might be Arnie, in which case I might as well ask Earlene to call Sally and find out how best to locate a crow bar.

I was pinning on my badge when Sherry Lynne, Allegra, and Dilys came down the hall. "Is the inn comfortable?" I asked.

Sherry Lynne grabbed my arm. "How's Wimple? Is he eating?"

"He was a bit distressed last night, but he settled in," I said. "He's most certainly eating."

Dilys raised her eyebrows. "You ought to buy a child next time you're at a pet store, Sherry Lynne. They're cheaper to feed and better at expressing their sources of dissatisfaction. They're not terribly good at catching mice, but they can be trained to clean their own litter boxes. Most of them, anyway."

"Oh, no," Allegra said with a groan, "please don't pull out photos of your grandchildren again."

"They are particularly attractive," Dilys said to me. "Wilmont's head is on the large side, but the pediatrician says this indicates superior intelligence."

"Wilmont is walking at the remarkable age of seventeen months," Allegra added. "If he ever starts talking, it undoubtedly will be in fluent French."

Dilys gave her an icy look, then turned around to speak to fans carrying armloads of her books. Sherry Lynne was surrounded as well by fans with shopping bags filled with her backlist. Allegra waited for a moment, then went into the ladies' room.

A few minutes later Walter and Roxanne came down the hall. Neither had visible claw marks, but I gathered the three-minute ride had not been amiable. Caron did not appear in their wake; odds were she had crawled under the car and was begging pedestrians to release the emergency brake.

"Roxanne," I said, "I hope you'll contribute to the discussion."

"Of course I will, Sally," she said as she squeezed my hands. "I want to do everything I can to make Farber College's first mystery conference successful. The reception last night was delightful, and I so enjoyed the lentil soup and sprout sandwiches. My system will be exuberant by tomorrow."

"While mine shall be authenticating an entirely new definition of writer's block," Walter said as he went into the seminar room.

Despite the fact it was most clearly none of my business (which has never stopped me yet), I was about to ask Roxanne about Walter when I saw Jorgeson tromping down the hall. This was not good, in that Jorgeson is Peter's minion and never drops by with a bouquet of flowers and a free movie pass. He and Peter focus on criminal investigations, not fraternity pranks and parking tickets. The possibility that something dire had happened to Peter flitted across my consciousness but was not allowed to light.

"What's up?" I asked him as we moved into a stairwell.

"Bad news," he said. "One of the people signed up to be here was killed last night. Most likely it was an accident, Ms. Malloy, but we have to ask. You know how it is."

"I suppose I do," I said as I leaned against the wall.

He took out a notebook. "Her name was Amelia Threety. Age thirty, unmarried, ran a hardware store in Hasty. She had a car wreck last night on the highway. A truck driver stopped and tried to help, but there wasn't much he could do. She died before the ambulance got there."

"Oh, God," I said, sinking onto the floor.

"You saw her last night?"

"Yes. She was burbling with enthusiasm over her college days. She'd found the inspiration to go home and rededicate herself to becoming a writer. She may not have been the brightest star in the constellation, but she was so imbued with optimism." I wiped my eyes. "What happened?"

"According to the truck driver, she missed a curve, ran off the road, and smacked into a tree. No one was following too closely, and no one was coming from the other direction with headlights that might have momentarily blinded her."

"So why are you here?"

"We understand she was at a wine and cheese reception last night for this conference."

"At the Azalea Inn," I said, nodding. "I saw her with a glass of wine early in the evening, but when I left, she was having coffee with the authors and an old friend of hers. I had no sense she'd been drinking too much."

"The medical examiner ran a blood alcohol test, and it was well under the limit. Thing is, he also did a basic drug screen, and there was some kind of barbiturate in her system that might have interacted with as little as one glass of wine. The sheriff's deputies talked to her parents, and they swear she wouldn't so much as take an aspirin unless she was in bed with the flu and running a temperature. Parents don't always know what their children do, but the sheriff asked us to look into her activities last night." Jorgeson's bulldog jowls sagged. "And there was your name, Ms. Malloy. When I die and go to heaven, is Saint Peter gonna tell me I have to wait on a bench outside until you meddle into the cause of death?"

Both of us wished he had not uttered Peter's name, but we did our best to ignore it. "Most likely, Jorgeson," I said briskly, standing up. "The person you should speak to is Earlene, whose last name I don't know but whose whereabouts I do. She agreed to take Ammie to her car after the reception."

"Speaking of Peter . . ."

"Unfortunately."

"The lieutenant said he was going to talk to you."

"He came by my apartment last night." After a short battle, my self-respect succumbed to baser instincts. "Do you know anything about the lovely Leslie? Is she in Farberville buying a layette? Shall I send a silver spoon?"

"I don't know what's going on, Ms. Malloy. All I know is the lieutenant's moping around the office and mumbling to himself like a drunk. He's more miserable than the guys we find living in makeshift tents at the edge of town."

I held back a smug smile. "I suggest that you have a word with Earlene, who may well have been the last person to speak to Ammie. Perhaps Ammie asked her for a pill to counteract cold or allergy symptoms. Pharmacology is not my area of expertise."

He gave me a rueful look. "And mine's not counselling."

I impulsively leaned forward and kissed his cheek. "You're a sweet man, Jorgeson. One of these days I may decide to call you by your first name. What does your wife call you?"

His face turned red. "That, Ms. Malloy, is between her and me."

Rather than embarrass him by pressing for details, I went out to the registration table. "Earlene," I said, "someone needs to handle this while I have a word with you. Are there any other committee members here?"

"I'll do it," said a woman in wire-rimmed glasses and a broad-brimmed flannel hat. "It can't be harder than checking out books after story hour. The beasties are always drooling on their library cards, if not chewing on them."

Earlene reluctantly allowed me to pull her into the stairwell, where I told her as gently as I could about Ammie. She sat down on a step and bowed her head for a long while, then looked up.

"I feel just awful," she said. "If I'd for one second thought she shouldn't drive herself, I would have taken her home. She seemed fine, though. She thanked me for taking her to her car, said something about how much she'd enjoyed the reception, and offered to volunteer today if we needed anyone. The last thing she said to me was that next year she'd sign up for a committee and help however she could. I don't know what we should do, Claire."

I gave her a tissue from my purse. "Well, we're not going to call Sally. She's dealing with enough stress as it is." I glanced back at Jorgeson. "I should tell the people who were having coffee with Ammie last night. Is that a problem?"

He shook his head. "It was on the local television news this morning. What I'd like to know is if anyone gave her something that might have caused the reaction. It was most likely done as a kind gesture. The only reason I've been assigned is to clear up the details. Once we find the source of the barbiturate, the matter will be closed."

"I didn't give her a pill," Earlene said, beginning to sniffle. "If she'd asked, I might have checked to see if I had anything, but she didn't say a word. She was so happy, Claire."

"I know," I said in an ineffectual attempt to comfort her. "Why don't you take a walk? Registration's under control."

Jorgeson and I watched her go out the door at the end of the hall. I glanced at my watch, then said, "Those who had coffee with Ammie are in the panel room, but so are a hundred people who've paid to listen to them speak. Is there any chance you can come back at eleven?"

"I don't see why not, Ms. Malloy."

"They have an hour and a half break before the luncheon. I'll ask them to wait here so that you can talk with them."

I went into the seminar room. The authors, at this point without Laureen, had taken seats at the table in the front of the room. Dilys and Allegra were chatting. Sherry Lynne was staring at her folded hands, possibly uttering a quiet prayer for Wimple's well-being or for Dimple and Doolittle, cruelly abandoned for the weekend, although no doubt boarded at an establishment more expensive than the Azalea Inn (or possibly the Ritz-Carlton). Walter was arguing with a woman in the front row, who seemed ready to leap to her feet and thump him with her book bag.

As reluctant as I was to interrupt a promising scenario, I

went behind them and said, "I have some sad news. Ammie was killed in a car wreck on her way home last night. The attendees have already spent money to travel here and stay in hotels, so there's no way we can cancel the conference. I'll make the announcement, ask for a moment of silence, and then we'll proceed as planned. Is this all right with everybody?"

I'd been expecting a show of emotion, but they all nodded and resumed what they'd been doing. I looked out at those seated in the audience and at those coming through the door with their packets and badges. Roxanne deserved to be told privately, but she wasn't in the room. The woman who'd worried about leaving early the previous evening wasn't there, either, but she'd mentioned getting up early to go to work, possibly in a situation that involved deeply distressed poultry. She'd probably been there for the free wine.

At nine o'clock, I took my position behind the podium and made the announcement. Varying degrees of grief crossed the audience's faces, and a few tissues were taken out to wipe away tears. I stressed that the police were investigating it as an accident, gazed at the grainy wood of the podium for a minute, then cleared my throat and asked the panelists to voice their opinions about amateur sleuths.

An hour later, no one at the table had actually descended to the level of physical savagery, although Dilys had accused Walter of pomposity, Sherry Lynne had scolded Allegra for gratuitous violence against defenseless creatures, Walter had used the word "insipid" eleven times and "fatuous" eight times, and Allegra was clicking her pen in a most ominous fashion. Members of the audience had attempted to ask questions, but they'd been drowned out by the arguments among the authors.

The door banged open and Laureen came into the room. "Darlings," she said as she came forward, "you are babbling like the mob in *A Tale of Two Cities*. If a guillotine needs to be brought into the room, I'm sure Claire will arrange it. In the meantime, let's do stay on topic." She sat down in the chair left vacant for her and beamed at the audience. "The amateur sleuth dates back well before the Golden Age of British mystery fiction, but did not really achieve significant popularity until the advent of the contemporary gothic heroine novels. In my first novel, written quite a few years ago, I introduced a plucky young woman willing to defend her virtue and her inheritance. In order to do so, she was required to face peril with strength and sensibilities."

Laureen managed to retain control for the next hour, reducing her colleagues to mute glowers. I was delighted to sit back and watch as she ran the show with the expertise of a besequinned Las Vegas emcee. We may have lacked albino tigers and nubile women wearing little other than feathers, but the threat of bloodshed evaporated. At eleven, she called the session to a close and reminded everyone that a luncheon would be provided at the student union ballroom.

"Wait!" I said, leaping up. "These delightful authors will be available to sign their books in room one-thirty in five minutes."

Earlene waved from the back of the room. "I just checked and it's still locked. Maybe we can have the signing after the second session."

A woman in the second row stood up. "Will you sign the ones we brought with us? I've got every book Ms. Parks wrote, all the way back to *The Maze at the Manor*."

I gestured at the audience to go for it, then caught up with Earlene before she could find a telephone. "I'll call maintenance," I said. "We'll have books available for sale before and after the second session. If the authors attempt to leave the room, please mention that Sergeant Jorgeson will be here shortly to have a word with them about last night. Afterwards, Caron and Inez will be outside should anyone prefer to be driven to the student union rather than stroll over there."

I left Earlene poised to tackle any of the authors who tried to flee, and went up the staircase to the English department office. I had expected to find it locked, so I was a bit surprised to find the secretary clicking away on her keyboard.

"Am I disturbing you?" I said.

"Why would barging in and asking me a stupid question disturb me? The only reason I would come into the office on a Saturday morning is to make out my Christmas wish list. I would never come in just because Dr. Shackley called and told me he wants verification of references of all the applicants for teaching assistantships for the fall semester on his desk first thing Monday morning. If that's what I was doing, you would be disturbing me."

"May I please use your telephone?"

She hit a couple of keys. "Be my guest. I'm torn between a Bentley and a Rolls Royce. I'll have to think about it while I go pee."

Wondering who had the courage to cohabitate with her, I waited until the door closed, then called the maintenance extension. No one answered. There had to be an emergency number for weekend crises, I told myself, and the loss of significant book sales was certainly more critical than a mere explosion in a chemistry lab. I called the college operator and politely requested the emergency number.

"I do not have that number," intoned the operator.

"There has to be one. What if the elevators in one of the dorms quit operating? No one could expect the residents to walk up to the ninth floor for two days."

"Which dorm is experiencing this problem?"

"None of them. That was hypothetical."

"Hypothetically, which dorm is experiencing this problem?"

"What difference does it make?" I said, trying to remain calm. "Let's say the freshman girls' dorm, okay?"

"We no longer segregate students by gender due to federal statutes forbidding discrimination by race, creed, color, national origin, age, or sex."

"Pick a dorm, any dorm. If a crisis arose, whom would you call?"

"What is the address of this hypothetical dorm?"

I banged down the receiver. I had a feeling the department secretary would not take up my cause, so I went down to the first floor. Jorgeson was heading into the seminar room. I followed him.

The remaining attendees had the last of their books signed and filed out. Jorgeson smiled as he sat down on a chair in the first row. "Nobody should be concerned about this investigation."

"Investigation?" Laureen echoed.

I realized she'd missed the original announcement. "Ammie was killed in a car wreck last night," I said.

"That sweet little thing?" Laureen said, turning pale and

snatching up a program book to fan herself. "This is tragic. It was possible she had developed a workable story despite a number of irrelevant subplots. I told her that I would help her to shape her manuscript into something that might be submitted for publication, and that I would ask my agent to represent it. She very well could have been getting a higher advance than I next year."

"Ammie Threety?" I said.

Laureen put down the program book. "She had some very fascinating concepts for plots. Whether or not she could have put the words on the page is irrelevant now. If you don't mind, I'd like to go back to the inn until the luncheon."

Jorgeson cleared his throat. "I'll be as quick as possible, ma'am. Ammie took some kind of drug that would have acted within half an hour of ingestion, which implies she took it just before she left the inn. Did she ask any of you for a cold tablet or pain pill?"

Walter rocked back in his chair. "I never so much as spoke to her."

"Yes, you did," Dilys said. "I noticed the two of you over in the corner. From her expression I gathered you were being very cross with her."

"The mousy little thing with the heavy thighs?" said Walter. "For some reason, she thought I might be interested in the book she's been writing for the last decade. I can assure you that I was not. She looked like the sort to include recipes for biscuits and black-eyed peas and whatever else people around here eat."

I gave him a steely look. "What do people in Wyoming eat—roadkill?"

"Ms. Malloy," said Jorgeson, "I'll handle this. The rest of you had coffee with her?"

Laureen nodded. "Some of us had wine, and I believe Sherry Lynne was drinking club soda. Roxanne insisted that Ammie have a bowl of soup and a sandwich. The woman who owns the inn did not look pleased, but complied. Around eight-thirty, Ammie left. We exchanged publishing gossip for another hour, then went upstairs. If people were creeping around after midnight, I did not hear them."

"Why would they do that?" Jorgeson asked in a thoroughly bewildered voice.

Dilys smiled sweetly. "Standard country house behavior, Constable. All we lacked was a butler and a blizzard."

"Although," Sherry Lynne contributed, "Lily would make a fine Mrs. DeWinter, don't you think? I'm sure she has a closet filled with diaphanous white gowns. Who knows what's buried in the basement or tucked away in the attic?"

Laureen caught Dilys's hand. "The brochure claims the house was once a haven for runaway slaves. What if some poor girl who'd been raped by her master gave birth while stopping there? The baby died, and the girl returns every night at midnight to search for it."

"No, no, no," said Dilys. "After she gave birth, she realized the wee thing could never withstand the arduous trip north in the swirling snow. She smothered it."

"And threw the body in the cistern in the garden," said Sherry Lynne. "That would explain why Wimple was so uneasy when we were out there yesterday afternoon. He sensed the presence of a tormented soul."

Joan Hess

Jorgeson pulled out his notebook and a pencil. "There's a body in the cistern?"

"I say it's in the cellar," said Dilys. "Less risky."

Walter stood up. "Sergeant Jorgeson, you are the stereotypic bumbling police officer off the pages of the frivolous fiction written by these authors. They write it because it's all they're capable of, and the public buys it out of ignorance that results from the lamentable state of public education. Edgar Allen Poe would have allowed the raven to peck out his eyes before he would have written a story about a cat that discovers clues or a mindless virgin who agrees to assignations on the moors." He looked down the table at Allegra. "Or a young woman who has a law degree from Harvard but lacks the perspicacity to notice the man with whom she goes hiking in the mountains has blood under his fingernails and slobbers when speaking of his mother."

Allegra gave him a haughty look. "At least my book has a plot. I picked up one of yours, and tossed it aside after ten pages. Perhaps Ammie was listening to one on tape and fell asleep at the wheel."

"My books are not easily accessible to denizens of white trash trailer parks or fleshy matrons sprawled on beach towels at Coney Island. I write literature, not mindless whodunits with cardboard characters and words of no more than two syllables. My novels are thematic. If I were to say the word 'symbol,' the only thing to come into your minds would be metallic platters."

"And," Dilys cooed, "I'd imagine them squashing your head. We can call it 'Dahl's Unfinished Symphony.'"

"Enough!" snapped Jorgeson. "If any of you remembers

98

anything of importance, call me. On second thought, tell Ms. Malloy and she can call me."

After he'd stomped out the door, harrumphing under his breath, I waggled my finger at the panelists. "This conference is supposed to be a celebration of the mystery novel, not a trap-shooting competition. When we resume after lunch, I would appreciate it if you could focus on an aspect that interests you. If you so much as allude to an attending author's particular sub-genre in a snide way, I will cut you off in mid-word and move on to the next speaker."

I took a deep breath, aware I was lecturing some of the most renowned practitioners in the field. "Caron and Inez are out in front of the building. Sherry Lynne, if you'd like to visit Wimple for a few minutes, Inez will go with you."

Walter curled his lip at me. "I am more than capable of finding the student union without a Sherpa in blue jeans and sneakers. I shall be there promptly at twelve-thirty for a meal that most likely will include chicken salad, brown lettuce, and doughy rolls."

As he headed for the door, the others began to tuck pens and notes into their handbags. Laureen, Allegra, and Dilys agreed that they would like to return to the inn for the next hour. Sherry Lynne decided to look in on Wimple, then announced the necessity of a brief detour by the ladies' room.

"Has anybody seen Roxanne in the last two hours?" I asked as we walked up the aisle between the folding chairs.

"No," said Sherry Lynne, "but this morning at breakfast she said she wanted to go to some of her old haunts."

Dilys sniffed. "An excellent choice of words."

"Did she mention any place specific?" I said, wincing.

Allegra held open the door for us. "I believe she taught classes in this building and in another building across the campus. She thought she might drop by the library and see if she still knows anyone. She's aware of the luncheon, though."

"Okay," I said, wondering why she hadn't attended the panel.

"I am distressed about Ammie," Laureen said as we went out to the sidewalk. "So very young. Does that police officer truly have reason to look into what happened? The highway was wet and it was quite dark by the time Ammie and that peculiar woman left. She might have been driving too fast in hopes of getting home before the rain started up again."

"The drug in her system may have caused her to doze off. No one involved in the conference seems to have given her anything, however, so I presume we've heard the last of it. I'd like to find Roxanne and tell her before she hears people chattering about it at the luncheon."

Caron and Inez were perched on the hood of the car, discreetly watching college boys walk by. No one appeared to notice them, which may have contributed to their slumped shoulders and sulky scowls.

"Have you seen Roxanne Small lately?" I asked them as Dilys, Laureen, and Allegra climbed into the car. "She's the blond-haired woman who rode here with Walter this morning."

"She probably's at the nearest pawn shop buying an Uzi," Caron said. "He's probably doing the same at another shop around the corner. These people are dangerous, Mother. The women talked all the way here about poisonous plants in the garden behind the inn and how to grind up the leaves and make herbal teas. If one of them offers me a cup of any beverage, including water, I will Totally Freak."

"Me, too," Inez said, her nose twitching in alarm.

"I think you're safe," I said. "Caron, take them to the inn for about an hour. Inez, wait here for Sherry Lynne. She would like to visit Wimple, and it's probably easier to walk than jam six bodies in the car."

Caron sighed. "And what are you going to do?"

"I'm going to the football stadium."

"Trying out for the team?"

"Something like that," I said, then headed up the sidewalk that went past the library, the law school, the administration building, and eventually to the stadium. The thought of being obliged to climb the bleacher steps to the row of skyboxes was somewhat less appealing than a cup of foxglove tea, but I could see no other option. Maintenance was obviously a weekday operation, with no disasters allowed after happy hour on Friday. If Arnie was not in residence (or, equally likely, refused to open the door), I would be reduced to calling campus security to report the presence of a squatter in the president's skybox. The way things were going, camera crews from the local television stations would show up, and Peter and Leslie would be snickering at me over martinis during the six o'clock news.

Vodka martinis, that was. Stirred, not shaken.

CHAPTER

7

One of my least favorite activities is perspiring; it's followed closely by strenuous breathing, with mottling a distant third. Well, there may have been some intimate moments when such things seemed an appropriate state of affairs, but hiking across the campus was not one of them—and I will not elaborate.

I cut across the administration building parking lot and turned down the hill toward the football stadium. It rose from the asphalt like a metallic soup tureen. On the west side, a tier of windowed skyboxes divided the bleachers below from those bumping the stratosphere, which were charmingly nicknamed the "nosebleed section."

On weekdays, the stadium parking lot is filled with vehicles of endless variety, although those from the more expensive end of the spectrum were apt to be parked at the lots adjoining houses bearing Greeks. Now it was pretty much empty. I arrived at a chainlink fence that was padlocked. Scaling it would not be decorous, especially if I were confronted by a campus cop while my rump was exposed to hither and yon.

I continued around the corner and along a sidewalk. Gates, all padlocked, were designated with signs identifying the sections to which the ramps led. I was feeling a bit discouraged when I found a gate without a padlock. There was not a sign designating it as "Arnie's Private Entrance," but I had a feeling it was.

I glanced over my shoulder in true criminal fashion, then slipped inside and ducked into a concrete tunnel. I knew where the skyboxes were—approximately twenty feet above me—but I had no idea how to get to them. I went to the end of the tunnel and peeked out at a vast green expanse of plastic grass with symmetrical white lines in some sort of pattern that no doubt had significance to the game. Like Rocky (the boxer, not the buck-toothed flying squirrel), I could stand in the middle of the field and bellow Arnie's name, but prudence overruled whimsy and I went back up the tunnel.

After a while, I found a set of double doors with a sign forbidding entrance by anyone without a pass. The doors were closed, but not padlocked. I walked up what seemed like an endless flight of concrete steps to a corridor, one side exposed to the street—and to all who walked or drove by—and the other side lined with doors.

"Arnie," I muttered as I prowled down the corridor, "come

out, come out, wherever you are." There were small brass plaques on some of the doors, proclaiming corporate ownership of the best seats in the stadium. Students were welcome to sit on plywood benches in the adjoining county (or time zone). Go, team, go.

The president's box had a somewhat flashier plaque, although of a generic sort. I was about to knock on the door when a black woman with layers of tattered clothing came down the corridor, squeezed past me, and went into the next skybox. While was pondering this, a ferrety man dressed in a camouflage jacket, a knitted skull cap, and sunglasses came out of yet another door and scurried toward the far end of the corridor as if pursued by demons yelping at his heels.

It was fairly obvious what was going on. I knocked on the door, waited a few seconds, then pounced on it with my fist. "Arnie Riggles!" I said as loudly as I dared, considering my visibility. "Open up right now or your scrawny buttocks will end up with stripes just like the faux-grass in the stadium. Do you know what one up the middle of your back would make you resemble?"

The black woman stuck her head out her door. "He ain't here. I heard him leave last night, and he hasn't come back, far as I can tell. His television's always blazing when he's here. I don't know why that boy listens to the news the way he does. It don't have anything to do with the likes of us."

"Do you have any idea where he was going?"

"This ain't a sorority house, honey.' She closed her door.

Wondering how many of the three dozen skyboxes were inhabited and how much rent Arnie was collecting from the heretofore homeless, I retraced my way across the parking lot and up the hill to the administration building. Somewhere on the campus was the maintenance office, and inside it, several people with all the charm and acumen of Arnie. They might be watching whichever sport was dominant on TV and drinking beer, but surely one of them would have a key to Room 130.

I rattled the doors of the administration building. Sorry, Monday through Friday, eight to five o'clock. I was desperate enough to gaze speculatively at a dorm only a block away, but I had no idea how to disable an elevator. Starting a fire in a laundry room seemed extreme.

I was envisioning myself returning a couple of thousand dollars worth of books as I started for the student union. I'd get full credit, but I'd be obliged to pay shipping. Sally's conference was going to cost me a substantial amount of cash—cash I didn't have. The Thurber Farber Endowment for the Arts was not likely to reimburse me.

The luncheon would not start for another half hour. I sank down in the grass and tried to think. Since Arnie was not at the skybox, there was no point in sending in campus security (excluding petty vengeance, which, frankly, was an attractive idea). Could a locksmith be persuaded to tackle a door on university property on the say-so of a frantic woman with no legitimate ties to the campus beyond a plastic-coated conference badge? If I threw myself on the floor in front of the English department secretary, would she relent? Was it possible the unseen Dr. Shackley might have a key? Had any of the designer-clad students ambling by made a passing grade in Burglary 101?

"Mrs. Malloy!"

Startled, I looked up at Inez, who was running toward me

like a newborn colt, her knees wobbling and her eyes wide with panic. She collapsed a few feet away from me, wheezing in an alarming way. "The most terrible thing" —she gasped—"terrible! I didn't know what to do! Then I remembered you said something about the stadium." She broke off, clutching her diaphragm as she struggled to catch her breath. "I ran all the way."

"That I can see," I said in what I hoped was a comforting voice. "It can't be all that terrible. I haven't heard any sirens or seen clouds of black smoke."

"Not yet," she said as she struggled to sit up. She pulled off her glasses and dried them on her shirttail, then replaced them on her nose and gave me a look she'd obviously learned from Caron, the master of lingual capital letters, and bespoke of the Propinquity of Doom. "I took Sherry Lynne to your apartment so she could see that the cat was okay. She was real nice about having to walk. I got out the key you keep hidden under that flowerpot, and we went upstairs. It was awful."

"Did that damn cat get into the apartment and shred all the upholstery?"

"Worse."

"Please don't tell me it staked out its territory in a particularly pungent way. If it pissed in the furnace vent, we'll be gagging until Christmas—assuming I'm not evicted on Monday."

"Oh, Mrs. Malloy, when I saw Sherry Lynne's face, I could have died on the spot. She thinks it was all Caron's fault, but I'm sure it isn't. I feel awful, just like the prosecutor in *Courting Disaster* when she finds the bones in the shed—"

"Bones?" I squeaked, recalling the downstairs tenant's outrage the previous evening. Surely not.

"It was her sister. The serial killer had been stalking her in order to—"

I grabbed Inez's shoulders and squeezed them until she lapsed into silence. "You are hot, you are winded, and you are upset. I understand, and I deeply appreciate your effort to find me. Will you please get to the point?"

Inez removed my hands and gave me a solemn look. "The back door to the porch was open. The cat was gone."

"Gone where?"

Even Inez realized this was a truly stupid question. "We don't know, Mrs. Malloy," she said carefully. "Sherry Lynne said she was going to search the alley, then go to the Azalea Inn to see if Wimple might be in the garden. I figured it would be better to find you than to go with her. Caron said something about driving by Rhonda's to see if Louis Wilderberry's car was there. Don't get angry; she'll get the authors to the student union for the lunch thing."

I had no theory how Wimple had unlatched the door, but in Sherry Lynne's books, he played the piano and sent faxes to Europe. A latch would be a piece of codfish cake.

"Compose yourself," I said to Inez, wishing I were a latter-day Fagan who could assign her to stake out the skyboxes. "The luncheon starts in thirty minutes. You need to splash cold water on your face and calm down."

She stood up. "Whatever. Sherry Lynne's really, really upset, though. I told her you'd know what to do. I mean, you've solved all these murders. Finding a cat can't be that hard."

I thought about the neighborhood, replete with bushes and trees and open basement windows, that stretched for blocks around my duplex. I thought about the traffic on Thurber

Street, particularly aggressive on the weekends. I thought about the tens of thousands of readers who'd vicariously adopted Wimple (and his cohorts) as their own. I thought about my glimpse of a glint in Sherry Lynne's eyes. A frosty white glint, as if reflecting off an iceberg in the North Atlantic that might sink us all.

"You're right," I said. "You go on to the room where the luncheon will be held and make sure everything's ready. I'll go see what I can do about the cat."

"You want *me* to make sure everything's ready?" Inez squeaked. "What if it's not? They're not going to pay any attention to a geeky high school kid with grass-stains on her knees."

I smiled grimly at her. "This will be your finest hour, Inez. You have complete authority. If you don't like the color of the napkins or the placement of the centerpieces, tell them to make changes. If you think pickles are better than olives or vice versa, demand a replacement. Anyone who challenges you can call Sally Fromberger at the Farberville Hospital and argue with her. Approximately one hundred people will be having lunch shortly. Go for it."

"I've always hated olives, especially those green ones with pimentos. They look like eyeballs that were dissected years ago and left to ferment on the back shelves in the refrigerator."

"Then you shall have pickles," I said. "Tell the staff to put out whatever kind you prefer. Dill, sweet, whatever. The power lies with you, Inez. Go in there and make sure everything's on schedule. I'll be back."

She did not looked convinced, but obediently trotted toward the student union. I could not bring myself to imagine the ensuing confrontation as I headed for my duplex, where, if nothing else, I could call the Farberville Animal Shelter to inquire about Wimple. Cats were rarely picked up, but it was all I could think to do before I found myself in the presence of Sherry Lynne Blackstone, aka one very unhappy person who had blithely fictionalized the deaths of more than two dozen people, all of whom had been unkind to cats. My benign negligence might not be an adequate defense.

I arrived home in less than five minutes. In her distress, Inez had left the front door unlocked, but very few thieves had their eyes on my cheap television and a VCR that had last played *Star Wars* in a galaxy long, long ago. I opened the kitchen door that led to the porch and ascertained that Wimple was not cowering under a bench or clinging to the ceiling. The outside door was ajar. The gourmet catfood had been eaten. Like Elvis, the cat had left the building.

I went down to the yard, praying I wouldn't encounter Sherry Lynne blundering across backyards in a blind frenzy. What I found nearby was worse: a greasy blue baseball cap that was recognizable—Arnie Riggles's calling card. Odds were that he had not kidnapped Wimple, who would have not come along harmoniously and might well have been responsible for bloodstains on the steps had he been manhandled. No, Arnie had opened the door to the back porch, perhaps in all innocence, and possibly to explain why the door to Room 130 was locked.

Which did nothing to resolve the situation. Excuses are irrelevant. They are seized upon by almost everyone to explain away what can only be described as incompetence. I'd long since lost the wherewithal to tolerate long-winded stories of why that which should have been done had fallen through a crack. Sally Fromberger, bless her anal-retentive soul, knew how to avoid such things—she did them herself. In her case, she might have shared a bit more, but I sympathized with her approach. Leaving Earlene as the second in command would have resulted in us all standing in the street like a flock of sheep.

None of this was producing a cat, however. I headed for the Azalea Inn, bleating Wimple's name every other step. I knew it was futile. I also knew Sherry Lynne would be there, and I would be up a certain crudely named creek sans paddle, life preserver, or even a wimpy excuse (which I myself wouldn't buy without a two-for-one coupon).

My car was not parked in front of the inn, but Inez had mentioned Caron's extracurricular safari. I braced myself for an emotional onslaught, then went inside. The front parlor was uninhabited, as was the sun porch. I went into the kitchen, where I found Lily grimly chopping clumps of green things.

"Basil," she said as if I'd inquired. "Pesto sauce for the pasta. I prefer to mince my hand rather than resort to a food processor. It enhances the flavor."

"Have you seen a large cat?" I asked, eyeing her nervously.

She slammed down the cleaver with enough fervor to send leaves flying into the air like mutilated butterflies. "Have I not made it clear that the Azalea Inn will not tolerate animals, Ms. Malloy? Does this concept confuse you? Shall I make a drawing? The very thought of tobacco smoke has driven me to the edge, but I have done my best to deal with it. You are pushing me. If there is a cat on the premises, I shall bar the inn and put your precious authors on the railroad tracks, in hopes a freight train will flatten them. Any further questions? If not, I would like to focus on the pesto!"

I backed out of the kitchen. I checked the garden, but no

one was sitting on any of the benches or wandering among the azaleas, and Wimple was not, as far as I could tell, stalking squirrels in the foliage. I therefore brilliantly surmised that the authors were in their rooms, entranced by botanical caprices or powdering their noses, so to speak.

I went back inside and sat down on the step that had previously accommodated Earlene, doing my best to force my mind to stop spinning. The cat was out there; Sherry Lynne was up there. Arnie was in cyberspace. My boxes of revenue were sweltering behind locked doors.

I'd pretty much opted for total despair when Earlene came through the front door. "Oh, Claire," she said as she thudded down next to me, "this is a disaster. The panel this morning was . . . well, unpleasant, and I have no doubt this afternoon's will be worse. These authors are so hostile. Our only hope was Roxanne Small, but I doubt we'll see her anytime soon. Sally will be very disappointed with this effort. I truly dread calling her, but I suppose I must."

I grabbed her wrist before she trudged off to do the dirty deed. "You know where Roxanne is?"

"Yes, indeed. I was sitting on a bench doing my best to come to terms with Ammie's death when she came outside. I told her what had happened. She said she wanted to call Ammie's parents, then decided to drive out to the little town to offer her condolences. I was touched by her concern."

"Have you seen her since this conversation?" I asked.

Earlene shook her head. "She never came back to the panel. There's a rental car parked out by the street, though. My best guess is that she's upstairs."

"That seems logical," I said. "None of the authors rented a

car. Maybe I'll have a word with her about this afternoon. If I can deflect some of the discussion toward manuscripts and submissions, I may be able to prevent fisticuffs."

"The guestbook says she's in the Hibiscus Room. She may have felt the need to lie down after visiting Arrmie's family. I know I would have."

"Me, too." I patted her arm, then went upstairs to the second floor. All the rooms were identified with plaques uncannily similar to those on the skybox doors. I knocked on the door of the Hibiscus Room.

There was no reply. Although I expected the door to be locked, I turned the knob and eased into the room. "Roxanne?" I called hesitantly. Everything about the room was tidy except for the schematic abundance of flora on the carpet, the curtains, the wallpaper, the ruffled lampshades, and even the twee collection of potpourri baskets and mint dishes (not to be mistaken under any circumstances for ashtrays). Fresh hibiscuses in a vase dominated the bedside table.

Or should that be "hibisci"?

The bathroom was empty, and there was no indication Roxanne had returned to the room in the aftermath of Lily's bedmaking, vacuuming, dusting, and disinfecting. An open laptop computer sat on a small desk next to a stack of what appeared to be manuscripts.

I went downstairs to the sitting room, found a telephone directory in a drawer, and called the animal shelter. I explained the situation, described the cat, and was informed that none of the current inmates met the criteria. There'd been an incident not too long ago in which a very nasty man had been engaged in selling stolen animals to laboratories. Luckily, he was no longer with us, and I'd seen no stories in the local paper. Arnie's involvement had been peripheral at best. Or at worst, considering the subject, but I doubted he'd found a way to constrain Wimple.

Laureen came into the room and sat down beside me. "I'd like to send flowers to Ammie's family," she said as she lit a cigarette. "From what I gathered, she lived with her parents. Could someone find out their address from her conference registration?"

"I should think so," I said. "That's a kind gesture."

"Oh, I put up a pretense of being a nice person to make my readers happy. My secretary sends out a newsletter several times a year, gabbing about my cats, my rose garden, and my secret family recipes. One of these days I really must read one." She inhaled deeply, then glanced around for an ashtray. None of the fragile china bowls looked promising, so she tapped ashes into her hand. "I felt sorry for the girl. She went to a small, rural high school, but made it through a couple of years of college before family obligations forced her to drop out. She wasn't destined for Harvard Law School, but she would have made an adequate teacher or social worker. Or, with the heavy-handedness of a mentor, even a writer. Exceptionally clever plots can overcome clumsy writing, if one has a dedicated editor. Look at the *New York Times* best-seller list if you doubt me."

"Could she have gotten an editor?" I asked.

Laureen sighed. "Not without help. Roxanne is forever complaining she gets over a hundred manuscripts every week, and that's standard for the industry. They're farmed out to readers, but eventually she herself has to look at those with potential. Two or three of them may get a third read. It's a tough business."

"No kidding," said Allegra as she came into the room. "I just spoke to my publicist. I was hoping to go home tomorrow, but instead I go to New York to do another round of satellite television and radio. The snootiest hotel in the entire city lacks the charm of my one-bedroom condo in Jackson Hole."

"You poor dear," Laureen murmured. "Paradigm House has enslaved you, simply so that you can remain on the best-seller lists for another week or two. It hardly seems fair. Once you get to the deck of the condo, you'll have to spend hours on the phone with your investment broker, trying to decide what to do with all the ill-gotten gains."

Allegra stiffened. "You've made your millions, Laureen. Could it be time for a new generation of mystery writers? Tastes change. Your loyal readers aren't on the corporate fast track; they're on Social Security and Medicare. Dilys's are on medication, and most of Sherry Lynne's are liable to be in nursing homes . . ."

She had enough sense to shut up as Sherry Lynne came into the sitting room. "Claire," she said, "we must speak."

I stood up. "Yes, I'm afraid we should. Why don't we go to the porch?"

"What could have happened to Wimple?" she demanded as we went out the front door. "You assured me time and again that he would be taken care of, but he's gone. He doesn't know this area, nor does he have any idea how to find me. There are movies in which a cat, usually accompanied by a dog or two, traipses across thousands of miles to find its owner, but Wimple lacks that kind of radar."

I resisted the urge to point out that in her books Wimple would have expended only minimal energy to contact a travel agent. Dimple had a passport, for pity's sake. Doolittle meowed in French, German, Italian, and probably Latin.

"I called the shelter," I said, "and they'll watch for him. He knows where the paté and pet carrier are, and he's intelligent enough to return there when he gets tired of exploring the neighborhood. As soon as Caron has taken us to the luncheon, I'll have her go back to the duplex and keep an eye out for him."

Sherry Lynne did not look especially pleased with my optimistic take on the situation. "Cars seem to drive along the alley behind your house at a reckless speed. Wimple is not accustomed to prowling."

No, I thought, he was better versed in yowling. However, as I was preparing more platitudes, Dilys came huffing up the sidewalk, burdened by half a dozen shopping bags.

"I found the most divine little shops just around the corner," she said. "I bought a lovely antique quilt for Wilmont, hand-sewn and made of silk. I was sorely tempted by a crystal figurine of a fairy for my granddaughter Eliza, but she has so many of them already. Is it time for us to get ready for the luncheon? I should like a moment to determine if the beaded vest I bought might go with my ginger and sienna trousers."

I glanced at my watch. "Caron will be here any moment, but she can take some of the others while you decide."

Dilys paused. "Sherry Lynne, is something wrong? You're looking ever so flushed. Should you sit down and put your head between your knees? It's always struck me as a ridiculous posture, but all the American authors seem to find it useful. My mother used to say that nothing was better than a cup of tea to bring one to one's senses."

"I'm fine," Sherry Lynne said. "I've been walking around

the neighborhood, and the heat must be affecting me. You're rather rosy yourself."

"Merely the afterglow of successful shopping," said Dilys. "I'd best trot upstairs and leave my parcels in my room. Do have a sip of water, dear; you look quite dreadful." She glanced at me. "And you, too. We want to look our very best at the luncheon, don't we?"

She went inside before either Sherry Lynne or I could concoct a sufficiently scathing response.

"Have you seen Roxanne?" I asked.

"I have not been looking for Roxanne. I am much more concerned about Wimple."

"I don't know what to do," I admitted. "If Earlene will moderate the panel this afternoon"—I shuddered just a bit— "Caron, Inez, and I will knock on doors in the immediate area. The Kappa Theta Etas have tender hearts, if not sharp minds. Wimple may be happily munching caviar in their dining room, or watching soaps with them."

"Caviar gives him constipation, and he does not care for daytime television," Sherry Lynne said, frowning at me. "It might be best for me to skip the luncheon and afternoon panel in order to continue searching for him. At five o'clock, I'll be obliged to call the police."

I could imagine Jorgeson's reaction. "I'm afraid the police won't do anything except refer you to the animal shelter."

"Wimple is a very valuable cat. My agent insisted that I insure him for fifty thousand dollars."

"You could do that?"

"Betty Grable insured her legs. Enrico Caruso insured his voice. Wimple has as many fans as either of them, and has been featured on the cover of *Cat Fancy* magazine, along with Dimple and Doolittle, of course. I do not play favorites."

"You still may have a difficult time convincing the police to bring in bloodhounds."

"I would never allow that," she said stiffly. "Wimple would be so terrified that he would dash into the street and be run down by some irresponsible college student. I have several photos of him in my suitcase. Perhaps I'll go on the local television news and offer a reward for his safe return."

Which would not reflect well on the conference or the bookseller. I was about to mention as much as Dilys came out to the porch.

"There is a most peculiar message on Roxanne's laptop," she said. "I'm not sure what it means, but it concerns a cat. It reads: 'Ding, Dong, Bell; Pussy's in the Well.' "

Sherry Lynne banged open the screened door and ran through the hallway toward the garden. I wondered if she'd learned to yowl from Wimple, or he from her. Both of them had taken it to an exalted level.

"Oh, my goodness," Dilys said. "Sherry Lynne has seemed to have taken a turn. So what do you think about this vest with my trousers? Is the overall effect a bit too much?"

CHAPTER
8

Allegra was lurking in the hallway, and after a palpably tense second, Laureen joined us from the parlor. "What's going on?" they whispered in unison, if not perfect harmony. Dilys was attempting to explain when Lily barreled out of the kitchen, clutching the cleaver in what might have been a menacing fashion had I not been aware of the pesto plight.

"Ms. Malloy," she hissed, her bloodless lips barely moving, "if that was a cat racing down the hall . . ." The cleaver rose a fraction of an inch. Had she been dressed in a flimsy white prom dress, stained with blood, I would have abandoned all hope and called Stephen King for advice.

"Ding, dong, bell," I said distractedly. "Pussy's in the well."

Lily's cleaver rose another fraction (most of an inch this time). "There's no bell—or well, for that matter."

"And Pussy is not the cat's name," Laureen said as she gulped down a glass of wine. "It's more like Pimple or Pustule or something equally repulsive."

I frowned. "The cat's name is Wimple, and he's been missing since this morning. Sherry Lynne is distraught. He's a major player in her books, as you know."

Laureen's wineglass slipped from her hand. The subsequent shatter resulted in a moment of petrified silence from all of us. "That sort of writing is what's killing all of us," she said with an unsteady laugh. "Does no one savor elegant prose and an old-fashioned, convoluted plot?"

I realized Laureen had found a bottle of wine and had been savoring it for the last half hour. "I need to go out to the garden with Sherry Lynne. It might be better if everyone else waited inside."

"Poor Sherry Lynne," said Allegra as she went past me. Laureen, Dilys, and Lily were on her heels. Walter Dahl came down the stairs, glanced at me, and then headed for the garden, his expression several degrees more condemnatory than mere contempt.

I trailed along for lack of anything else to do (such as buy an airline ticket to Timbukto, which I would charge to Sally Fromberger's personal account). Sherry Lynne was shrieking Wimple's name and batting aside azaleas with such fierceness that Lily was in tears. Laureen and Dilys were doing their best to calm both of them down, while Allegra watched coolly and Walter found a bench to his liking and took out a pipe.

Lily twirled on him like a homicidal ballerina (did I mention the cleaver?). "No smoking in the garden!"

"A pipe is a pipe is a pipe," he replied with a condescending smile. "Considering what I've been obliged to ogle in my room, I'm doing nothing more than taking part in an age-old tradition of post-coital respite."

Laureen managed to immobilize Sherry Lynne, who seemed perilously close to choking up a hair ball. "The lid to the cistern has been moved. You stay right here while I take a peek."

We all stared at the round wooden lid, which had been pulled aside far enough to permit access by what I presumed were unauthorized bodies.

"Why don't I do the peeking?" I suggested.

Sherry Lynne darted around me and looked into the cistern. "Wimple? Are you in there? Just hang on, dear; I'll . . ." Her voice faltered. "Oh, my heavens. It's dark, but it looks like . . . oh, my heavens."

"What?" I gurgled.

"A body."

"A body?" Laureen echoed pensively. "How intriguing. Dilys, your theory about the slave may have been on the mark. I doubt anyone has scrutinized the cistern since the introduction of indoor plumbing."

Sherry Lynne stood up. "It isn't from the Civil War era."

I shouldered her out of the way and took a look. Twenty feet below was something—or someone, but with what appeared to be a halo of blond hair and an outstretched arm of unnatural paleness. "Lily," I said as calmly as I could, "call 911 for an ambulance, and alert them to the reality of the problem. It's impossible to tell if the victim is alive. We'll need the police as well."

Lily gave me a look that implied it was all my fault, which I was quite sure she thought it was, then stomped toward the sun room.

I waved everyone else away. "There's nothing we can do, so let's all just sit down and wait."

"Who could it be?" asked Walter. "A conference attendee who developed self-destructive urges during the panel? One has already driven into a ditch. Will another be knocking back a glass of hemlock at the luncheon? By this evening, shall we expect to find bodies littering the garden like so many snapdragons that have"—he snapped his fingers in case we missed the point—"finally snapped? Should Lily opt for that décor, the poor guest would be kept awake all night."

"You are not amusing, Mr. Dahl," I said. "My best guess is that it's Roxanne."

"What's more, Mr. Dahl, you're a royal pain in the ass," added Laureen. "Claire, perhaps you'd better sit down, too. There's nothing any of us can do until the paramedics arrive."

Sherry Lynne let out a groan. "Could poor Wimple be down there, too? I'd hate to think he might have been . . ."

"Crushed?" Dilys said helpfully. "Splayed beneath a corpse? Seeping blood from the impact?" She took a cigarette from Laureen's purse and lit it as we all stared at her. "Wimple was hefty, but if someone of even moderate body weight were to fall on him—well, it wouldn't be pretty. Cap-splat, so to speak." She took a ladylike puff. "Oh, look there on the wall. Is that a tufted titmouse?"

I blocked Sherry Lynne's attempt to dive into the cistern.

Once I'd settled her on a bench, I took a deep breath. "Roxanne Small is missing, and the body in the cistern has blond hair. Do none of you care that it might be she?"

"Of course we do," Laureen murmured, "and I should think we're all aware of that. Such a nasty shock. The poor creature was a wonderful editor who had a major impact on all of our careers. If she's dead, and I'm assuming that she is, then four of us have been orphaned at Paradigm House, to one degree or another. I, for one, was hoping to discuss the lack of promotion for my upcoming book. With no editorial support, it might as well go directly from the printer to the remainder table—or the shredder."

"And my backlist will remain in the warehouse until the pages turn yellow and crumble into dust," said Dilys, wiping the corner of her eye with a lace-trimmed hankie. "I was so hoping Wilmont might attend Oxford, but now it's out of the question. No punting on the Thames for him, I fear. All he can hope for is rowing on some muddy little creek."

Allegra stood up. "I'd better call my agent."

"Do that," Laureen said sweetly, "and be prepared to kiss the best-seller list goodbye. Without editorial—"

Caron came dashing into the garden. "We've only got five minutes to get to the student union. I can take four of you, and this weird woman named Earlene says she can take the overflow. Come on, everybody, it's time for chicken salad." All she lacked were pom-poms and crew socks.

Dilys stubbed out her cigarette on a flagstone, then brushed it into the woodchips. "Sherry Lynne, are you quite convinced there is no runaway slave in the cistern?"

Laureen made sure Lily had not reappeared, then flicked

her cigarette into the rose bed. "The basement is more likely, dear. We must take a look later this afternoon. What fun to play archaeologists! Do you know anything about carbon dating? Can we purchase a kit?"

"A kit?" Walter said. "Let's do hope it has litmus paper and test tubes. That way we can hope for a passing grade in chemistry."

Caron sank down on the path. "What's going on, Mother? Someone's in the cistern—or in the basement? That doesn't make any sense."

"No," I said flatly, "it doesn't."

"Is it a runaway slave like they said? The body's been there over a hundred and fifty years? We're talking major decomposition."

I tried to pull myself together. "I doubt it. Listen, everyone, there are a hundred attendees waiting for you at the student union. Unless anybody has information to volunteer, why don't you let Caron and Earlene drive you there? I'm sure the police will have questions for you later, but it'll take some time for them to deal with the scene and arrive at an idea of what might have happened. Until then, please don't mention this."

"It's so very intriguing," Dilys said as she stood up. "I've never been in the proximity of a real murder. I must purchase a notebook and pens of different colors."

"Murder?" gasped Caron.

Walter nodded at her. "So very indicative of the moral decay of familial structure and acceptable societal norms."

"Chill," Allegra said. "One more word of four syllables and I issue a bounty—dead or alive. In your case, no one will vote for the latter."

He stuck his pipe in his pocket. "You have no call to make that remark, you slutty flash-in-the-pan. Without Roxanne Small's rather hysterical promotional support, your poorly written, nondescript clone of a best-seller would have sunk like the lump of excretory—"

"You priggish son of a bitch!" Allegra said as she went for his throat, her eyes burning with rage.

Laureen and I caught her. Once we'd pulled her away to a safe distance, I said to Laureen, "Are you capable of moderating the luncheon panel?"

"Of course," she said, "and as the senior member of this farcical troupe, I shall lead the way. Do not think, though, that we will remain here for days on end, waiting for the constables to trudge about their duties. My manuscript is due a week from Thursday. I am leaving tomorrow. I have made arrangements for a limo to pick me up at the airport."

"I'm supposed to be in New York tomorrow," said Allegra. "The *Today* show and a satellite with Larry King."

Dilys smiled unpleasantly. "And aren't you the lucky one? I don't suppose Roxanne will be hosting any of those ghastly in-house parties from the cistern, will she? Then again, I'm sure the wine and cheese have already been arranged."

Walter smiled even more unpleasantly. "An array of New York state Chardonnay and Velveeta? Sardines on saltines? Paté de faux gras?"

Caron might have qualified as a piece of garden statuary. "Mother . . . ?" she whispered.

I realized the red-brick walls were filling with enmity, and suffocation was imminent. "Caron and Earlene are going to take you to the student union for the luncheon, then back to

Old Main for the afternoon panel. Cooperate or kiss your honorariums goodbye. I'll wait here for the police."

To my amazement, all of them except Sherry Lynne trooped toward the back door of the inn. She wiped her eyes, sniffled, and said, "Is Wimple in the well?"

"I don't think so," I said.

"If he is . . . ?"

"Caron will go back to the student union and inform you," I said glibly, not at all sure what the police would dictate. "You just go on. As soon as I have a chance, I'll put a bowl of cat food on the steps and check out the neighborhood."

"Why would that message have been on Roxanne's laptop?"

"It wasn't there when I was in her room."

Sherry Lynne gave me a pitying look. "Did you touch the keyboard? Most laptops switch into sleep mode after a few minutes of being ignored."

"I didn't push anything," I admitted. "I'm not exactly high-tech."

"Why would Roxanne leave that message if she was preparing to throw herself into the cistern? Did she think she was taking the lead role in the drama? Was she taunting me?"

I sat down on the nearest bench. "I don't know, Sherry Lynne. You knew her better than I did. Is that something she would do?"

"She would have skinned her grandmother to push one of her acquisitions onto the best-seller list."

I was staring at her as paramedics and uniformed police officers came into the garden. She went inside, leaving me to face

Jorgeson and Peter Rosen, both steely and barking orders at the unwitting minions.

"Some conference," Jorgeson said as he nervously hovered as though I might swat him with a hydrangea. Super-Cop managed not to notice me. "You ever think it might not be a good thing to bring together a bunch of professional killers?"

"The body's in there," I responded, pointing at the cistern.

The paramedics had brought a ladder. Despite a measurable lack of enthusiasm, two of them descended, confirmed the presence of a body, and requested a litter to be lowered.

Lieutenant Rosen peered down at them. "Are you sure the victim is deceased?"

"One of them," called up the paramedic. "The other's unconscious but still breathing."

"A cat?" I blurted out.

Peter glanced at me, then bent down. "The other is a cat?"

The paramedic's voice echoed in an unearthly manner. "The woman's long gone from what looks like major head trauma, but we might be able to help this second victim. Let's pull him out and get him to the emergency room. No hurry on the other one."

I had an insane vision of Wimple being wheeled away on a gurney, to be resuscitated in the ambulance and later to have surgery while Sherry Lynne watched nervously from the gallery, twisting her hands as tubes and clamps were placed in strategic arteries. Organ transplants might be an option, which would lead to, if nothing else, a tremendously dramatic made-for-TV movie along the lines of "The Six Million Dollar Cat in the Hat."

However, the paramedic had seemed to think it was a guy, as opposed to an obese feline. The uniformed officers lowered a litter, and, when given a signal, hauled it up to the edge of the cistern.

"Arnie," I said with a sigh.

"You know the victim?" Peter said coldly.

"So do you!" I snapped. "You've had him in custody so many times that one of the cells ought to have a plaque over the door. Arnie Riggles, who aspires to be a felon but lacks the wherewithal."

"Mrs. Malloy," he began, "this is not the time—"

The two paramedics came scrambling out of the cistern. "We need to deal with him," one of them said. "The other is strictly the business of the homicide department. Guess that'd be you, Lieutenant Rosen. Have a nice day."

Arnie was whiter than a slice of generic bread, but breathing, and, as far as I could see, free of copious bloodstains. The paramedics transferred him to a gurney and headed for the backsteps of the Azalea Inn.

The uniformed officers stood around the cistern, clearly unwilling to engage in spelunking in the name of law and order. "You think we should call the medical examiner, Lieutenant?" one of them asked.

"I doubt he'll want to take a closer look at the scene. Take photos, then bring up the body."

"But how are we supposed to—"

"A tarp. Do your best not to rearrange her more than necessary."

Jorgeson gazed at me. "You know who this is, Ms. Malloy?"

"I have a pretty good idea."

Peter muttered something rather crude under his breath, then said, "Why shouldn't she, Jorgeson? When did we last find a body with which Ms. Malloy was not keenly acquainted? Were this a Civil War site, I would anticipate that Ms. Malloy could identify all the bodies strewn across the battlefield by name, rank, and serial number."

"This is hardly Antietam," I said stiffly. "The woman in the cistern is likely to be Roxanne Small, an editor from New York. She dropped by at the last minute to surprise her authors."

"Dropped?" Peter said.

I clenched my fists. "A figure of speech, Lieutenant. She did a degree at Farber College, and four of her authors are at the conference."

"And where might they be?"

"At the student union. It was too late to cancel the luncheon."

Peter's deliciously brown eyes widened. "You packed off the potential witnesses to a luncheon? This is a crime scene, after all. We usually prefer to have the opportunity to interview everyone who might know something."

"Fine. Why don't you and your storm troopers go up there and drag them out of the room? Then you can stay and lecture the attendees on the finer points of homicide investigation. Better still, lay out the salient facts and see if anyone can solve the crime before the chocolate mousse is served. Imagine the money your department will save if someone can prove the butler actually did do it."

Peter looked at Jorgeson. "Is Ms. Malloy under the influence of illegal substances?"

"Not that I know," he said. "It's just . . . well, it's just not any of my business. Ms. Malloy, why don't you and me go inside so you can tell me what you know about the deceased? Was she staying here?"

I took his arm. "What a charmingly rational suggestion, Sergeant Jorgeson. Lieutenant Rosen can wait here with the tufted titmice until the body is brought up, then join us in the parlor for herb tea and rice cakes."

Ignoring ominous growls, Jorgeson hustled me inside. "Ms. Malloy," he began plaintively, "I don't want to be involved in this. You and the lieutenant have a lot to work out—or not. I'd as soon get a private security job at the mall as get in the middle of it. He's not my best friend, but we have a long history of working together, sitting surveillance for nights on end, rewriting reports until dawn, chasing down obscure leads, and pounding our heads on our desks. You and me—well, we've had some moments, too. I'm not going to offer any opinions or advice, and I wish you'd leave me out of it."

I squeezed his arm. "Okay, I swear I won't ask you any more questions about the lieutenant's personal life, including the hypothetical proximity of the lovely Leslie and her pedigreed—"

"Ms. Malloy!"

"Jorgeson," I said brightly, "let's sit in the parlor and I'll tell you what little I know. Afterwards, I can direct you to Roxanne's room upstairs. Be sure to push some button on her laptop computer; I don't understand the technology, but it apparently flickers to life and sends messages."

Lily came out of the kitchen, the cleaver still in her hand. "Ms. Malloy, I have dealt with smokers, perfume, hairspray, cheap wine, insults, and at least one cat inside the Azalea Inn. Now it seems I will have to fumigate for murder as well. I am a very high-strung individual, Ms. Malloy. I once attacked a class-mate in kindergarten for breaking my crayons. I stuffed half a Burnt Sienna up his snotty little nose. He was taken to the emer-gency room."

I stepped in front of Jorgeson before he could respond with or without deadly force. "I can order one hundred and twenty Whoppers and send everyone to the park, Lily. Is that what you want? Does your pesto lose its zesto in the freezer overnight?"

"Are you some kind of incubus deployed by the Junior League?" she said, the cleaver wobbling.

"Go back to the kitchen, Lily," I said. "I'm sure Sergeant Jorgeson and Lieutenant Rosen will want to have a word with you later this afternoon."

Jorgeson let out a breath as she retreated into the kitchen. "She's kinda . . . spooky."

I propelled him to the parlor and onto the sofa. "Lily has her pet peeves, as do we all. I myself have always found Russian wolfhounds to be overwrought, anorexic—"

"Ms. Malloy," Jorgeson said with some irritability, "why don't you tell me what you know about this lady in the cistern?"

"Not much, actually. She was, or had been, the editor of the four women authors. Walter Dahl is published by a small press, but he seemed very bitter toward her. She made it clear she did not think highly of him."

"But the women liked her?"

I thought for a moment. "You'd better ask them. There was some veiled hostility, but nothing I can explain. It's a compli-cated business, and my singular role is to order and sell books.

I don't know anything about warehouses, backlists, promotional budgets, book tours, and so forth. I have the impression that Allegra Cruzetti was being well treated, and the others felt they were not."

"Someone would commit murder over a book?"

"I just don't know, Jorgeson. Everybody seemed to have gotten along last night. They may not have painted each others' toenails and cried over old movies, but it seemed to be genial. Roxanne was at Old Main this morning after you told me about Ammie, but she disappeared. She told Earlene she was going to make a condolence call on Ammie's parents. No one seems to have seen her since then."

"Did she go out there?"

I gave him an exasperated look. "How should I know? I was in the auditorium until the break. I didn't see her. For all I know, she went to read resumés at the sperm bank." Ignoring Jorgeson's sigh, I went on. "Walter said he would make his own way to the student union, although he ended up here. Laureen and Allegra came back to the Azalea Inn, presumably to their private rooms, and Dilys shopped on Thurber Street. Sherry Lynne went looking for her cat."

"So none of them has an alibi?"

"None of them has a motive."

"You just said you thought there was some hostility," he reminded me. "Maybe you underestimated it."

I considered this for a moment. "With the exception of Walter, they were all sitting in this room last night, drinking wine, and later having soup, sandwiches, and coffee. There were no reports of hair being yanked or fingernails ripping flesh.

Had there been an incident, I'm quite sure I would have heard about it from Lily one second after I set foot in the inn today."

Jorgeson glanced at the doorway. "What about her?"

"Her name is Lily Twiller and she owns the inn. She was not adequately forewarned about what to expect, and she isn't taking it very well. As far as I know, her only interaction with Roxanne was to allow her to book a room for two nights. If Roxanne was making blackmail demands because she'd discovered the pastel blue towels were manufactured in sweatshops in North Korea, it's your problem, not mine."

"I suppose it is," he said. "So what was Arnie Riggles doing in the well?"

"An excellent question," said Peter as he came into the room. "I thought we were having herb tea and rice cakes. There's nothing more amusing than conducting an investigation over a tea tray."

Jorgeson stiffened. "The medical examiner here, Lieutenant?"

"There's a door at the back of the garden. If the body wasn't out there on a tarp, we could have our party on one of the stone benches. Ms. Malloy may be unaffected by the sight of blood, but it takes away my appetite, even for rice cakes."

"Or borscht?" I asked sweetly.

"Jorgeson, get the registration cards of all the guests staying here and ask the woman in the kitchen to produce proper credentials. As soon as I've finished interrogating Ms. Malloy, I'll want to take a look at the victim's room."

"I find the word 'interrogating' a bit overwrought," I said as Jorgeson fled. "I spent less than an hour with Roxanne last night, and I have no idea where she was earlier today. As for why she ended up in the cistern. . . ." I shrugged most eloquently.

"But you suspected she was, along with Arnie Riggles, and for some obscure reason, the cat that wasn't."

"Do you prefer to continue acting like a jerk, or would you prefer that I tell you what I know?"

Peter crossed his arms. "And of course you just happen to know things."

I crossed mine. "Up to you, Sherlock. I'm not sure how long we can survive on rice cakes, but I'm willing to find out."

After several minutes of silence, in which the only sounds were those of low voices in the garden and the rhythmic cadence of a cleaver pounding a chopping block, I told Peter what I had thus far observed.

Okay, so I may have skipped over a few details. I did, however, suggest he call Sally Fromberger. It would most certainly brighten her day.

CHAPTER
9

So you think Arnie threw himself in the cistern to rescue this missing cat?" Peter asked. "A hero without a cause?"

Overwhelmed with frustration, I sank back. "Whatever. Arnie had minimal involvement. He knew damn well he was supposed to unlock the door of the room at Old Main this morning. He came by my duplex to explain why he hadn't, and then . . ."

"Then what?"

"How should I know? I'd be surprised if he were so gripped with remorse that he attempted suicide. Arnie Riggles is not the type to be haunted by guilt. If he inadvertently set fire to a nursing home, he'd be picking through the site the next morning in order to hold a used denture sale."

"Any idea how we might get in touch with his next of kin?"

"Call Tennessee information and ask for Jack Daniels."

Peter winced. "I was thinking of something more local. Do you happen to have his address?"

"I just described the extent of my interaction with Arnie," I said as I stood up. "Yesterday he carried boxes of books into Old Main and was made aware that he needed to make sure the door was unlocked this morning. I have not laid eyes on him since then. The evidence indicates that he came by my duplex this morning after Caron and I left, and allowed a cat worth fifty thousand dollars to escape into the neighborhood, where it was undoubtedly run down by a Kappa Kappa Killer. I suggest you call the maintenance office for details about Arnie's personal life. If the campus switchboard can't help, try the secretary at the English department. Just leave me out of it—okay? I may have to deal with pesto, but not with you and your sperm count."

"Claire," he said, as if there was anything he could say at this point. He shrugged, as did I. We stared at each other.

Jorgeson appeared in the doorway. "Just heard from the emergency room, Lieutenant," he said. "The Riggles guy is okay, but refuses to offer much information, claiming that he won't talk to anybody but Ms. Malloy here. The woman in the cistern, Roxanne Small, died from injuries resulting from impact. Her body cushioned his fall."

I was very glad I had not ingested any of Lily's tea, since I might have embarrassed myself. "Arnie fell on her?" I squeaked.

"Survival of the fittest," Jorgeson said without emotion. "No indication of a cat, by the way."

"That's good, I guess," I said as I tried to wiggle past him. "Pussy wasn't in the well after all. Just Arnie and Roxanne."

Peter caught my arm just as my knees buckled. "You'd better sit down, Claire. You're not making much sense."

"I am making perfectly good sense," I protested. "Ding, dong, bell; you can go to. . . ."

He looked at Jorgeson. "See if that woman in the kitchen can provide a glass of brandy."

"How thoughtful," I said, "but a bit early in the day. Don't you think we ought to search Roxanne's room?"

His eyebrows rose. "I hate to break it to you, Miss Marple, but police investigations tend to exclude civilians who are snooping around out of idle curiosity. Why don't you wait here until I've determined what further questions I might have? After that, we'll go to the hospital and find out the secrets Arnie wants to share with you and only you."

He stomped out of the parlor, followed by Jorgeson, whose ears were bright red and quivering like rose petals caught in a breeze. I remained on the sofa for a moment, then went out to the porch and glared at the cracked concrete pillars holding up the bridge over the railroad tracks, and at the profusion of weeds on the far side of the street. I was wondering how hard it might be to hop a freight train to France, or at least Topeka, when Caron pulled up in my car.

"What Is Going On?" she said as she joined me. "Did that woman fall in the well? Does this have anything to do with the cat? The door was latched this morning when I left, you know.

I may not have tweaked the creature's whiskers, but I scooted in a can of cat food and a bowl of fresh water before I came here to transport these creepy people, who spend all of their idle moments debating ways to kill people. Allegra Cruzetti listed half a dozen poisons I might slip into Rhonda's next milkshake. Ms. Parks thought drowning might be more cost-effective, while Mr. Dahl favored a blunt instrument or defenestration. Ms. Knoxwood suggested a crochet hook in the ear. I am seriously freaked, Mother."

"I can understand why," I said. "Does the luncheon seem to be going well?"

Caron pulled herself together and managed a shrug. "I dropped them off at the door of the student union. It's not like I could park out front and suggest we all hold hands on the stairwell. The closest parking is about forty miles away, and the oxygen's rumored to be thin. I wish you'd explain."

I sat down on a wicker sofa. "It seems as though the blond woman you brought on your second run this morning ended up at the bottom of the cistern, along with Arnie Riggles, who survived."

"Arnie Riggles?" she said, horrified. "Isn't he the one who—?"

"Yes, and then some. He's not inherently evil, though, and I'm afraid the police may assume he's responsible for what happened to Roxanne Small."

"What's a cistern?"

"Once upon a time, a repository for rainwater."

"What was she doing out by this cistern?"

"A very good question," I said with a sigh. "She's not going to provide any answers, however, and I doubt the authors will be of any use. None of them seems to be grieving over the untimely death of a beloved editor."

Caron rolled her eyes. "There were no bleeding hearts in the car, as far as I could tell. They were discussing an expedition to the basement at midnight. I'm supposed to buy candles and a magnifying glass before I pick them up after the panel. Candles are easy, but I don't have a clue where to find a magnifying glass. I can just imagine myself at Wal-Mart, asking for the forensics aisle. I am not getting paid Nearly Enough for this, Mother."

"Nor am I, since I'm unable to sell any books. I should go over to the hospital and see if Arnie has the key to the bookroom. If not, you'd better start finding ways to fix cat food casseroles, because that's all we may be eating for the rest of the month."

"Excuse me while I throw up."

I held out my hand. "Give me the car key, dear, then go back to the duplex and scout around for the cat. Sherry Lynne does not have big hair, but I suspect she has quite a temper."

She gazed at the line of official vehicles, marked and otherwise. "Is Peter in charge of the investigation?"

"As we speak, he and Doctor Watson are searching the victim's room." I waited until she pulled the key out of her pocket and gave it to me. "Put a bowl of fresh cat food on the top step, then start knocking on doors along the alley and listening for acrophobic meows from treetops. Earlene and Inez can figure out how to get the authors from the student union back to Old Main."

Caron's shoulders were drooping as she went down the walk and around the corner. I sat for a moment, praying for a slow-moving train, then got in my car and drove to the hospital. I presumed I could sail into Arnie's room and ask a few hard questions, but I was informed at the lobby desk that he was allowed no visitors, and that a police officer was stationed by his door.

As intimidated by the pink-haired volunteers as I was by the idea of being gunned down in a hospital corridor, I returned to my car and rested my head on the steering wheel. Roxanne had not come home to Farberville to commit suicide. Push had come to shove, so to speak. Arnie was not likely to have submitted a manuscript in the past and then nursed a grudge when it had been rejected. He certainly had no reason to put his hands on Roxanne's derriere and send her plummeting twenty feet. I was likely to be the only person Arnie feared—and well he should. Now that I thought about it, he was damned lucky to have an armed guard outside his door. At the moment, not even I would scale three floors in the fashion of a sticky-palmed Spider-Man to slither into a room and switch an IV.

Later, maybe.

None of the authors had much of a motive to kill Roxanne, I reminded myself. But were they repressed murderers, as Jorgeson had implied rather bluntly? Plotting murder, pondering method and means, choosing a weapon least likely to be detected, contriving a way to escape accusations—these were daily warm-up exercises. In truth, they seemed to do it at the drop of a hatpin dipped in curare. The announcement of a dead body had been met with academic interest rather than grief. I had a feeling they would all be making notes as they flew out of the Farberville airport, and eighteen months from now I would be reading five novels concerning bodies in the cistern, and in a couple of cases, mummified babies in the basement.

Resentment had been simmering the previous evening, but I'd sensed nothing that might result in murder. Sherry Lynne, Laureen, and Dilys were clearly jealous of Allegra's preferential treatment by Paradigm House, and Walter most certainly bore a grudge; none of this, however, had seemed likely to result in anything more lethal than deftly-flung darts dripping with sarcasm.

The only thing that had happened since then was Ammie Threety's fatal accident.

Earlier in the day Roxanne had said she was going to make a condolence call on Ammie's parents, perhaps out of genuine sadness—or perhaps for another reason. It was possible that she had learned something that had led her to determine the accident hadn't been quite so . . . accidental. She might have discovered a reason to suspect that one of the authors staying at the Azalea Inn was involved. All of them had been in their rooms during the late morning break. When Roxanne returned, had she suggested a private talk in the garden?

I gazed with unfocused eyes at the bland facade of the hospital until I finally remembered the name of the town Ammie had mentioned. It was no more than twenty-five or thirty miles away, which meant I could make a condolence call of my own and return in time to ascertain that the pesto pasta and whatever else Lily intended to serve would be ready for the convention attendees—and that a recently-severed human head would not be a centerpiece, replete with parsley, sage, rosemary, and thyme jutting out of each ear. I had no idea where Lily might find such a thing, but it did not seem beyond her capabilities, should she wish to make a statement, organically-correct or otherwise.

Almost an hour later, I drove across a low-water bridge and saw a bullet-riddled sign boasting of Hasty's population of two hundred and forty-three. The town itself was nothing more than a convenience store, a gas station, a few trailers on cinder blocks, a shabby church, a half-dozen squalid tract houses, and a building identified by a faded sign as "Bobbie Jo's Cafe and Bait Shoppe." The only evidence of life was a raw-boned hound asleep in the middle of the road, where it was likely to be as safe as anyplace else in town.

I went into the café. Four men in their twenties, two with stringy yellow hair and two with stringy brown hair, all apt to have crawled out from under the same rock as Arnie, glanced up at me, then resumed their discussion, which seemed to involve the annihilation of Bambi's kith and kin. The waitress, as raw-boned as the hound and not appreciably more animated, approached the booth with a coffee pot in one hand and a mug in the other.

"You wanna eat?" she asked without enthusiasm. "We're out of the daily special, but you can have a burger and fries. Soup of the day is chicken noodle. The tuna salad platter comes with a slice of tomato and a scoop of cottage cheese."

Wondering if the tuna salad had been prepared with the previous day's unsold bait, I shook my head. "I'm looking for a family named Threety."

"You from the police?"

"No," I said, wondering if I could explain myself in words of no more than two syllables. Conversation had stopped at the nearby table, and I was being regarded with less than admiration. "You heard about their loss?"

"Reckon I did. Ammie was a good girl, my second cousin once removed. We was all hopin' she would finish college and get a good job, but then she had to drop out to run the store on account of her pa's health. My stepbrother Burnett dated her while they were in high school, and he used to tell us how she was always reading books and writing stories. Darn shame what happened to her." She set down the mug and filled it. "Darn shame."

One of the men swaggered came over to the booth as if he was preparing to collect a blue ribbon at the county fair. "I don't recollect you explainin' why you're here."

I took a sip of coffee and tried to ignore the implicit threat in his posture. "Ammie registered for a convention at Farber College, and was at a reception last night. When I heard about the accident, I felt like I should come by and tell her family how sorry we all are."

The waitress gave him a shove. "You go on back and talk about dawgs, Ed. This lady is just being nice, which is something you don't know beans about." She waited until he retreated, then said, "You sure you don't want a hamburger or a tuna salad platter, honey? It won't take five minutes."

"Just directions to the house," I said meekly, keeping an eye on Ed and his cohorts, who were muttering among themselves. I took a dollar bill out of my purse. "Will this cover the coffee?"

"It ain't worth a dime. Go down to where the Ferncliffs lived till their house burned down, and then—"

"I'm afraid I don't know where the Ferncliffs lived. Is it a county road?"

"Not hardly," she said. "Keep an eye out for Hester's House of Curls. Turn left at the next intersection and go about a mile. The Threety place is on the right, just past the pond. You can't miss it."

I've always taken that trite expression as a challenge rather than a reassurance. "Thanks," I murmured, leaving the dollar bill on the table in the obscure hope of ensuring safe passage. "Are Ammie's parents dealing with their loss?"

"What's it to you?" said one of the men. He punctuated his question with a belch, to the amusement of his friends.

The waitress tucked the bill in her pocket. "I'm sure they'd appreciate a visit. Kinfolk are gathering, and the preacher is there, but them hearing about Ammie's last evening is likely to lighten their hearts—assuming you ain't gonna say anything that might distress them."

"Of course not," I said, reacting to the edge in her voice. "By the way, did anyone else come by here today to ask for directions?"

"Not here, but Burnett was telling me about some Yankee woman at the gas station this morning."

"Saw her myself," said one of the rednecks at the table in the middle of the room. "Tight ass."

The man now identified as Ed chuckled. "Damn straight. We don't see many like her around here. Her tits weren't much, but I'd bet my paycheck that—"

"Shut your mouth!" the waitress snapped. "Not one of you peckerwoods would recognize a paycheck if it bit you on the ankle. Unless you want to deal with me, sit still and let this lady be about her business."

"Thanks," I said to her, then went out to my car and continued down the road. Hester's House of Curls was less than imposing, but easy to spot due to a sign with a bleached depiction of a woman with violet hair. I turned onto what soon became a dirt road, passed a pond so covered with muck that even an atheist could have walked across it and scored a miracle, and saw a mailbox with the name Threety spelled out with plastic letters.

A dozen or so cars and trucks were parked in the yard of the farmhouse. Children were shrieking in the adjoining pasture, unmindful of the proximity of tragedy. Feeling as though I should have brought flowers or a covered dish, I went up to the porch and was about to knock when the door opened.

"Come right on in," said an apron-clad woman with wispy brown hair and stained teeth. "Ammie's folks are receiving visitors in the parlor. Will you be staying for lunch?"

"No, but thank you." I came into the entry hall. I presumed that the parlor would be overflowing with sympathizers, but the only two occupants were a very worn, gray-complected couple on the sofa. Neither looked up as I came into the room.

"I'm Claire Malloy," I said as I sat down on a chair across from them. "We're all so sorry about your loss."

The woman blinked at me. "I don't know what's going to happen to us now that Ammie's gone. One of our sons joined the Navy and was killed in some sort of training mishap in California. The other died of cancer just last year. Ammie was all we had left. We never thought we'd outlive our children. They were all supposed to be at our funerals out in the family cemetery behind the orchard. Now all three will be there first."

I leaned forward and squeezed her hand. "I didn't know Ammie well, but she seemed like a vibrant young woman with wonderful dreams."

"She should have got married and started a family," the man said gruffly. "Nobody in these parts needs dreams. Time and again I'd catch her curled up in her room, all weepy over some story in a book. And those notebooks of hers! I told her if I ever caught her scribbling when it was time to get supper started or tend to the animals, I'd burn every last one of them."

I gave myself a moment before I responded. "But she did drop out of college to run your hardware store, didn't she?"

"Reckon so," he admitted.

The woman gave me a trembly smile. "It's so kind of you to come. Would you like some coffee? There's all kinds of salads and casseroles in the kitchen. My sister brought her lemon icebox pie. It's real tasty."

I was painfully aware that I was there under false pretenses, and I almost wished I could disappear into the upholstery like a drip of water on the cushion on which I was seated. "Thank you very much, but I can't stay. I'm a committee member from the mystery convention that Ammie was planning to attend in Farberville, and I need to get back shortly. I was wondering if anyone else from the convention came by."

"You mean that woman from New York?" the man said. "I disremember her name, but she told us how she was Ammie's teacher back in college and just happened to be in Farberville for this thing. Ammie had no business signing up for it. If she hadn't gone into town last night, right now she'd be at the store. She was going to sing a solo at church in the morning. Every evening for the last two weeks I could hear her practicing while she weeded the garden."

"Did the woman from New York say anything else?" I

asked, despite an urge to poke myself in the eye with the nearest sharp object, which in this situation, appropriately enough, was a poker beside the fireplace.

Ammie's mother sniffled. "She promised to do what she could to have Ammie's stories published as a memorial. She said it depended on whether or not they were any good, but she was willing to fix 'em up. She's going to send us a letter after she's had a chance to read them. We could use a little money to help with funeral expenses."

"So she took the notebooks with her?" I asked.

"I showed her up to Ammie's room and left her there. Twenty minutes later she came back downstairs with an armload of them. She was staggering like a three-legged calf when she went out to her car."

"And that was at about eleven?"

"Closer to ten-thirty," the woman said, frowning. "Folks were beginning to arrive, and the preacher wanted to spend some time praying with us and making arrangements for the service. It's going to be tomorrow afternoon. I hope you'll be able to join us."

I looked at them. Neither had noble foreheads or aristocratic noses. Jowls rather than cheekbones defined their faces. Their eyes were clouded. I wanted to fling myself into their arms and promise to operate the hardware store until the time came when Caron (their adopted but nevertheless devoted grandchild) and I stood over their graves and tossed in handfuls of ashes-to-ashes and dust-to-dust.

"Please let me know," I said as I stood up. "I'll make sure you're reimbursed for Ammie's registration. It won't be much, but I hope it helps."

Ammie's father narrowed his eyes. "This woman that came earlier this morning—she ain't stealing Ammie's stories, is she?"

I smiled as tactfully as I could. "Ammie's stories are likely to be more important to you and your family than they might be in terms of literary value. I'll do my best to make sure they're returned to you."

"She coming to the service?"

"I don't think so," I said, then went back out to the porch and down the steps to my car. A mud-splattered white car was parked next to it, and my four new friends from the café were staring at me as I walked across the lawn.

"Too early for the catfish to bite?" I asked as I dug my key out of my purse and unlocked the car door.

Ed sneered. "Who the hell are you?"

"I'm from the FBI. Whenever there's an accident, we conduct an informal investigation. Any illegally-converted guns in your car? Bottle of whiskey in the glove compartment? Plastic bag of marijuana under the seat? Amphetamines rolling around on the mats? Should I be calling for backup?"

"Got your panties in a knot, doncha?" drawled one of the blond *wunderkinder*. "Want me to give you a hand?"

I went over to their car and thumped his head with my knuckles. "The only hand that's involved in this is the one I'll use to rip that pathetic wisp of hair off your chinny-chin-chin. Were you this charming with the woman from New York earlier this morning?"

"The look she gave us was enough to wither our balls," Ed said. "We followed her all the way into Farberville, hoping she'd repent and give Squamus here a chance to achieve his manhood, if you know what I mean, but she—"

"Don't go talking about me," the driver snarled. "I done it with your mother last week, and she squealed louder than either of your sisters."

I hastily intervened. "You followed her into Farberville?"

Ed unclenched his fist and sat back. "We wasn't gonna do anything. She parked in front of some big ol' brick house and darted inside. We waited around, drinking beer and watching the college girls strut along the sidewalk, but then a cop car showed up. There weren't no way Squamus could get it up after that, so we came back here. Any chance you might . . . ?"

"Oh, definitely," I said, smiling. "Why don't all of you boys be at the cemetery in Farberville at midnight? Bring a blanket and a six-pack. My grandmother was buried only yesterday, so the soil at her grave will be nice and soft."

"Sicko!" the driver yelled as the engine roared. The other three occupants expressed equally derogatory parting opinions as the car bounced over a cattle guard and up the road.

To the best of my knowledge, one of my grandmothers was buried in a churchyard in Scotland. The whereabouts of the other was a bit of a mystery.

Roxanne Small's activities were less so. She had made the condolence call, taken Ammie's notebooks and manuscript with her, and had been chased back to the Azalea Inn by a quartet of inbred troglodytes.

I wasn't quite sure why she'd offered to do her best to have Ammie's stories published posthumously. The gesture had been kindly, but not realistic, as Roxanne had well known. It was challenging to think that guilt had kicked in after all these years. Academia was more a stalking than a happy hunting ground; in my limited experience as a graduate student, I'd quickly learned that the trite "publish or perish" gleefully emphasized the latter. One of my professors had resigned to sail around the world after a journal rejected his article deconstructing Chaucer's earlier efforts (which, for the record, no one outside of my seminar has ever been obliged to read).

Ammie was less likely to have produced stories that might compete with *The Canterbury Tales*. Laureen Parks had felt, however, that Ammie's seriously overworked manuscript held some promise. Roxanne Small must have agreed that the potential existed, despite the bleak reality that in most cases, it did not. Anyone willing to churn out a hundred thousand words can write a novel. And anyone with a hacksaw can perform brain surgery.

I replayed my conversation with Ammie's parents, but I could recall nothing they'd said about Roxanne that implied she had learned something, or had found proof that someone currently staying at the Azalea Inn was responsible for Ammie's death. But she must have, and confronted this person in the garden—while backing too close to the cistern.

And then there was Arnie, I thought despondently. Could he have been grappling with Roxanne when she went over the edge of the wall? Weight-wise, it was a fair match.

I was not a happy camper as I drove back to Farberville. I was, considering how distraught I was, damn lucky to have made it intact.

CHAPTER
10

Lily was sitting on the steps of the front porch of the Azalea Inn when I drove up. Her knees were splayed rather crudely, but as far as I could tell, there were no blood splatters on her clothes or a particularly disturbed look in her eyes. This was not to imply I might have proffered an invitation to spend an evening on my sofa with pizza, cheap wine, and video rentals.

"Are the police gone?" I asked.

She gestured at the curb. "Look for yourself."

"Well, I suppose they are," I said lamely. "Did any of them have something significant to say?"

"They stormed around the garden, causing irreparable damage, and then searched Ms. Small's room as if it were a prison cell. One of them had me sign a receipt for a laptop computer. Why would they think I cared? They could have taken her luggage and thrown it off the bridge, or piled it in the alley and set fire to it. This woman brought a curse on the Azalea Inn, as have you, Ms. Malloy. All I've ever wanted to do is create a non-violent ambiance where we can all celebrate nature in an embracing environment. Hypoallergenic soap, healthy meals, cotton sheets with a two-hundred thread count—"

"Can it," I said as I sat down beside her. "Did the police take anything besides the laptop?"

"No. They spent less than half an hour in her room, then told me to leave everything as is until they get in touch with someone. I do hope they're not planning a séance. The last thing I need are diaphanous netherworld creatures who go bump in the night. The azaleas will positively shrivel."

"Why, Lily, is it possible you have a sense of humor?"

"Don't bet on it."

I sat back and looked at her. "I shudder to imagine your past lives. How old are you this round?"

"Thirty-one. In case you were going to ask, which I presume you were, I have a master's degree in art history and seven years of experience as a curator in a museum in Taos. When the Twiller trust informed me that I could have this house, I trampled over all the clay-splattered potters and purveyors of puerile watercolors in my haste to escape. I ran down three tourists clad in khaki shorts and Ray-Bans on my way out of town. I may have outstanding warrants, but I have no regrets."

I sucked in a smile. "You made the decision by yourself? Wasn't that intimidating?"

"I had no choice. All the bikers with the really good tattoos were headed toward California."

"So you came here and opened an inn?"

"And without a clue," she admitted. "I thought I could be a beacon of personal integrity, but all I've done since then is compromise. I even allowed a couple to bring their parrot last month. Birds are filthy creatures, Ms. Malloy. I myself will never sleep in the Hibiscus Room due to the possibility of air-borne diseases. Now I've allowed smoking, and I have no doubt that blasted cat was wandering around before you arrived. I've made an appointment for a double-session with my aromatherapist for tomorrow evening. *They* will all be gone by then, will they not?"

"That's up to the police," I said, dearly hoping she would be proved right. "Were you in the kitchen when Roxanne Small came back this morning?"

Lily nodded. "I'd just finished slicing the scallions when she came in and asked for a cup of coffee. I told her she'd have to settle for tea and offered to bring it to her in the sitting room. Most of my guests understand that this is not a fast-food establishment with a pimply adolescent eagerly awaiting the chance to dunk another batch of frozen french fries in rancid oil."

"Did Ms. Small complain?"

"She said that tea would be fine, then went upstairs. She was not in the parlor ten minutes later when I took in a tray. In that the basil required my immediate attention, I left everything on the table." She glanced at me. "The police officers were brusque. May I assume there's no implication that my herbal blend was a factor?"

This had not occurred to me, although it was possible Lily had been tutored in Taos by a homicidal New Age shaman. "Nothing's been suggested. Have you ever seen the man who was found in the cistern? Could he have been skulking around this morning?"

"Unless his name was Basil Rathbone, I couldn't say. I was chopping. Had there been blood and guts on the cutting board, I most likely would have noticed. I do not have a security guard in the garden. The gate is latched but not locked."

"What about your other guests? They were drifting in about that time, weren't they?"

"Indeed they were," Lily muttered darkly. "The one with the flamboyant hair insisted on making a long-distance call. We finally agreed that she could use the phone in my office, as long as she reversed the charges. She was shrieking about Larry King when I left the room. The one with the English accent thanked me for the tea I'd so thoughtfully left for her. The smoker had the audacity to ask for matches; I suggested that she go outside and find sticks to rub together, preferably on the railroad tracks while a freight train approached. Later, the woman with the cat banged open the kitchen door and demanded to know if I'd chopped up her precious pet and added it to the pesto. I assured her that all of my dishes are strictly vegetarian."

"And the gentleman?"

Her nostrils flaired. "Gentleman? There is no gentleman in residence at the Azalea Inn. If you're referring to that foul-tempered boor, I heard his voice in the sunroom, but I did not scurry out to drop a curtsy and offer to draw him a bath. The only thing he deserves to soak in is a vat of sulfuric acid. I shall cheerfully sacrifice a towel or two."

"Did you notice to whom he was speaking?"

"Most likely God. He seems to feel as though they're peers." She stood up. "I'd better get started on the crescent rolls, unless the supper is to be held elsewhere. If so, the foundation is still going to have to reimburse me for expenses. Stone-ground wheat is not cheap."

I had a feeling that yellow crime scene tape around the cistern would be interpreted as nothing more ominous than artful decoration. "Lieutenant Rosen didn't say anything to suggest as much, did he?"

"He asked me where the hell you were," Lily said with a smirk as she disappeared inside, leaving me to feel like the ninny I was. Caron and Inez were more subtle—or at least more adept in verbal subterfuge. I wouldn't have been surprised if Ms. McLair had appeared on the sidewalk and demanded to know when I intended to turn in my term paper. The topic would not be the intricacies of immaculate conception.

I brooded for a moment, considering certain biological processes beyond my control, then went down to the rental car parked at the curb and peered into it. With the exception of a neatly-folded road map, the seats and floor were pristine. The notebooks that Roxanne had collected at Ammie's house must have been taken inside the inn. According to Lily, the police had not removed them from the Hibiscus Room. Had they been tossed in the cistern, the peculiarity of their presence would have warranted a comment from the paramedics or the investigators.

"Therefore," I mumbled to myself as I returned to the porch and eased open the door. Hoping that Lily was up to her elbows in dough, I glanced around the sitting room, then tiptoed up the creaky staircase.

Roxanne's room was not locked. I looked (okay, snooped) in the closet, under the bed, and in the cabinets in the bathroom. The one suitcase she'd brought was undoubtedly less tidy than when she'd packed it, but there were no notebooks beneath Victoria's sexy secrets and a bottle of gin. The manuscripts on the dresser bore coffee stains and notations in pencil. None of them was thick enough to be Ammie's six-hundred page masterpiece of murder, passion, political conspiracy, alien abductions, sabotage in the Middle East, and whatever else she'd come up with over the last ten years.

So where had Roxanne stashed the notebooks and manuscript she took from Ammie's bedroom? She'd come directly to the Azalea Inn. Aware that she was being followed in a blatantly menacing fashion, she'd hurried inside. The boys from the boondocks had remained out front until the first police car appeared.

Her briefcase and purse had been left on the bed. The former contained only a few letters and faxes regarding manuscripts in production, a galley with the unpromising title of "Celebrate Your Cellulite," and a copy of Allegra's tour schedule, much scribbled upon with telephone numbers, deletions, revisions, and notes to contact various media people. The purse contained loose change, an airplane ticket, a car key with a plastic tag, a worn nail file, a wallet with more cash and credit cards than any one woman needed for a lifetime, and empty gum wrappers.

I went out to the hall. Four of the other doors had botanical plaques; the fifth proved to be a linen closet with nothing more incriminating than pastel towels, blankets, and sheets that would have given Laura Ashley hives. There was no trapdoor in the ceiling that might have led to an attic.

I was trying to decide if I ought to call Sergeant Jorgeson with this rather peculiar observation when I heard footsteps on the stairs. Had I been in a Laureen Parks novel, I would have spotted the heretofore unseen doorway to the turret and dashed up there to hide amidst the spider webs and purple shadows. In a Dilys Knoxwood novel, I would have crouched behind a door, candlestick poised. Allegra Cruzetti's protagonist would have slapped down a restraining order that prevented the perpetrator from setting foot on the second floor of the Azalea Inn, with or without a machete. Walter Dahl's would suggest a session on the couch in the parlor to chat with a few stray subliminal personalities. Sherry Lynne Blackstone's would have merely hissed and darted up a drainpipe to the roof.

Bram Stoker, however, was the author responsible for the dampness on my back and the acceleration of my heartbeat. I looked over my shoulder at the sunlight coming in the window at the end of the hallway ever so tranquilly. Lily Twiller was only a scream away, assuming she was not lost in a meditative catalepsy brought on by stone-ground flour.

Coward that I was, I opened the nearest door, slipped inside, and snatched up the only weapon in sight. I would have held my breath, had I the opportunity.

"Ah," said Walter Dahl as he came inside, "Ms. Malloy, in the Petunia room, with an alarm clock. Is Professor Plum in the bathtub with a bar of scented soap? Shall I anticipate Colonel Mustard in the closet with a mothball, or Miss Scarlet perched on the armoir with a bad attitude?"

I put down the clock. "What are you doing here?"

"That's my suitcase on the dresser. My toothbrush is in the bathroom, as well as my mint-flavored dental floss and electric razor. My well-thumbed copy of Proust is on the table beside the bed, and my slippers beneath it. One might conclude that this is my room."

"I suppose so."

"Note the prevalence of petunias, Ms. Malloy. I fear for my life each time I turn off the light."

I forced a smile. "I heard you coming upstairs, and with all that's happened . . ."

"You assumed the celery was stalking? Lily Twiller is more than capable of restraining her produce."

"Why aren't you at the panel?" I asked.

His eyes slitted. "Ms. Parks has dictated that the afternoon panel will be divided. Ms. Blackstone and that lint-brained Brit are taking the first half. At four o'clock, Ms. Parks, Ms. Cruzetti, and I will take the stage. I tend to find this sort of thing tedious, but in this case, I do anticipate a level playing field."

"Or battle field?" I said, sighing. "Why are all of you so competitive? Not one of you writes more than a book a year. The mystery readers who come into my store buy a bag of books every month."

Dahl regarded me for a moment. "I have a flask of very good scotch in my suitcase, Ms. Malloy. May I offer you a glass while I attempt to explain the realities of the business?"

It was well into the afternoon, and I felt as though I'd spent most of the day in a boot camp in the Louisiana swamps. "Yes, please," I said as I sat down on an expanse of flattened petunias.

"You may have sensed that I did not care for Roxanne Small," he said, returning with glasses from the bathroom. "She is the reason that I had no option but to accept the minimal of-fer from White Oak Press. My publisher is stout-hearted and optimistic, but the key factors in sales are promotion, print run, and distribution."

"What did Roxanne do?"

"Exactly what any boa constrictor does when confronted with a potential meal." He handed me a glass. "Cheers, Ms. Malloy. *De mortuis nil nisi bonum.*"

"Give me a break, Mr. Dahl. You're clearly eager to speak ill of the dead, as well as of anyone else who challenges your narcissistic view of your impact on mystery fiction."

He smiled, although I could hear his teeth grinding like splintered gears. "Went to high school, did we? How admirable, considering the predisposition in this region to be barefoot and pregnant by the onset of puberty."

"Is that an invitation to belt you before I leave?"

"No," he said, "it's a very bad habit I picked up during my years in academia. Shall we discuss Roxanne?"

His tone was level, if not contrite, and his scotch was indeed very good. "An excellent idea," I said.

"Two years ago I submitted a manuscript to Paradigm House. I will confess I was quite naive in matters of popular fiction, having had only a few scholarly works published by university presses, but Paradigm had sent me a galley, requesting a jacket blurb and inviting me to submit my own work to them. When I had a finished product, I wrote a cover letter that described my background and credentials, and enclosed the entire manuscript. Four months later the manuscript was returned, accompanied by a scathing letter of rejection, stating in no uncertain terms that I was an amateurish, pompous twit to have dared take up the editor's precious time with four hundred pages of twaddle. I was advised to bury the manuscript in my yard and not expect grass to grow for seven years. I may be paraphrasing, Ms. Malloy, but that was the gist. Certain phrases were etched on my soul, to be honest, and I shall take them to my grave."

"Ouch," I murmured.

Walter shook his head. "That would have been my response, had it been the end of it. I subsequently learned that Roxanne Small ridiculed me when speaking at writers' conferences, citing me by name and reading aloud from my cover letter. She took passages out of context and encouraged the audiences to bray like the illiterate jackasses they were. She wrote articles that focused on my submission as an example of everything an aspiring author ought not to do if he or she hoped to be published. My name and the name of my college were never omitted. I kept waiting to run across my home address, telephone number, and date of birth in the footnotes. Whatever aspirations I had of receiving tenure, well. . . ."

"Why did she respond so virulently?"

"I have no idea."

I stared at him over the rim of the glass. "I think you do, Mr. Dahl."

He raised his hand, then let it fall away as Laureen Parks swept into the room as if she were clad in a floor-length cape and a diamond tiara. "Ah, Claire," she said, "I was hoping I might find you here. I made a few tiny changes to the afternoon schedule, but I simply cannot allow Mr. Dahl here to continue to badger those two dear women. Dilys was brave during the luncheon, but I saw her shedding tears on her croissant. It was entirely too soggy to be edible. Sherry Lynne agreed to participate in the first half of the panel before she rents a bullhorn and goes looking for that animal of hers. The neighborhood will never be the same."

"None of us will," I said. "Want some scotch?"

She gave me the same dazzling smile I'd been treated to in the garden the previous day. "I would never dream of imposing on Mr. Dahl. Why don't I pop into Roxanne's room and fetch her bottle of gin. She won't be drinking it, will she?"

Walter wiggled his eyebrows. "Perhaps we can arrange for the medical examiner to drain her blood so that you can drink that, too. Surely Lily can be prevailed upon to provide a slice of orange and a maraschino cherry, although I would hesitate to request a perky paper umbrella. We might call it a 'Roxie on the Rocks' or a 'Small Sin.'"

"We shall talk," Laureen said, then went across the hallway and returned with the bottle of gin and a glass she must have taken from the bathroom. "As extraordinarily offensive as you are, Walter, and you have gone well beyond the bounds of anyone I've encountered in decades, I am willing to do what I can to help your career. With your permission, I'll speak to my agent. Roxanne's death will put Paradigm House's mystery imprint in chaos for months, but there are other publishing houses that might be interested—with a bit of prodding, that is."

"Why would you do that?" he asked.

She filled the glass and drained half of it without so much as a wince. "You were not Roxanne's only victim, although she did go after you with a rather amazing vengeance. I was at the Authors Guild symposium when she spoke in January, and I must say—"

"Please don't," he cut in. "I have no doubt what she said, and I have already apprised Ms. Malloy of the situation."

I shrugged. "I had no idea this business was so . . ."

Laureen sat down beside me and patted my knee. "It's a jungle, my sweet Claire, and survival of the fittest can be determined by the whim of the art department or a buyer from a chain bookstore, who, on any given day, is either having great sex with his wife or screaming at a divorce lawyer. A Hollywood celebrity may have a lurid confession out at the same time. A White House pet may be inspired by the muse in time to hit the fall list. All we can hope for is support from our editors."

"You seemed to feel as if Roxanne was letting you down," I said cautiously.

"Had I been swinging through this jungle, she would have chopped off the grapevine and taken pleasure in watching me plummet into a pool of hippopotami." She took a cigarette out of her purse and lit it, then glanced around for an ashtray. "I thought this establishment was smoker-friendly, at least for the weekend."

Walter struggled with a window until it slid upward with a shriek. "You have a vile habit, Ms. Parks."

"You, sir," she replied, "have a vile way with the written word. I actually forced myself to read your first book, and found it worthy of internment in a sandbox—or a litterbox. You accused Allegra of jumping on a bandwagon, but at least it's one that has been hauled out in the last year. Your books are more suited to the middle of the last century, when men wore white suits and women swooned every twenty-eight days because their fathers had rejected them in the formative years."

"Save this for the panel," I said, putting my glass down. "I came upstairs for a reason, and I can use some help. You both have experience concocting ways to dispose of potentially in-criminating evidence."

"How intriguing," Laureen purred. "I do so love a mys-tery."

Walter, who'd been sulking in silence, raised his glass as if offering a toast. "Then why don't you write one?"

"Why don't you?" she said, looking as though she might sling the contents of the dearly departed's gin in his face. "Of course, it would require you to come up with a plot, wouldn't it?"

"And you might need characters that were not clipped out of magazines. Supermodels, by definition, are not the deepest ponds on the farm. Have you ever written about a young woman who did not have raven hair and emerald eyes?"

Laureen crossed her arms. "Have you ever written about one and had a print run over two thousand?"

"Hey, I have raven hair and emerald eyes," said Allegra as she came into the room. "Laureen may not have had me in mind when she began writing, but that doesn't—"

I cut her off. "Gin or scotch?"

"No Zinfandel?"

"Gin or scotch?" I repeated.

She looked at Walter and Laureen. "Gin—and a tranquil-izer gun, if you and I want to get out of here alive."

"So what evidence might we be looking for?" asked Lau-reen. "A smoking gun? A bloody dagger?"

"Definitely gin," Allegra said as she filled a glass and sat down. "Evidence of what?"

I wasn't sure how much I ought to tell them. "Roxanne

went to Ammie's house this morning, and came back here with some notebooks. They're not in her room."

Walter snorted. "Is that why you were searching my room? Do you think I might have strip-searched Roxanne before I threw her in the cistern?"

Laureen took the bottle out of Allegra's hand. "There is only a limited amount of gin in the universe. This has my name on it. The idea of strip-searching Roxanne brings to mind frisking a North Atlantic cod. Cold and slimy, scales glistening, eyes forever rounded, mouth agape."

"Notebooks?" said Allegra, neatly retrieving the bottle from Laureen with only a minor bout of wrestling. "We should be searching for notebooks? Isn't that a bit mundane? I tend to think copies of love letters from JFK or Howard Hughes might be worthy of a search. Ammie Threety's definitive thoughts about life in the wilds, on the other hand. . . ."

Laureen narrowed her eyes. "Notebooks?"

"Roxanne carried them away this morning," I said. "I'm sure they're filled with tedious insights, but her parents might find comfort. Roxanne made some grandiose promises to see that the fiction would be published."

"And they've disappeared?" said Allegra. "You searched Roxanne's room?"

"Have you called in the CIA?" added Walter.

"The FBI, I should think," said Laureen as she refilled her glass.

Allegra smiled ever so smugly. "Never underestimate the ATF in these cases. I can almost hear agents rustling in the garden—unless, of course, it's Sherry Lynne's cat. He could well be typing a confession while he devours a mole or vole."

I stood up. "Has anyone ever told you people how annoying you are? Two women are dead, and a third victim is in the hospital. This is not some ditzy plot in a novel. Dead is dead. It's time for funerals, not jokes."

Laureen drank the remaining gin in a gulp. "You're absolutely right, Claire. We're all being horrid, and we have no excuse. I suggest we find these notebooks so that you can return them to Ammie's parents. I promised her that I would read her manuscript, although I warned her that I would be blunt in my assessment."

"May we presume you've already searched Roxanne's room?" said Walter. "And mine was well?"

"Not yet," I admitted.

"Then why don't I sit here while you do so?"

"Fine," I said. The three watched as I checked all the possibilities. "What about your room, Laureen?" I asked. "Any objections?"

"My dear, were I to hide something, not even the KGB would stumble across it. By all means, let's search my room."

We all ambled down to her room, which was dominated by determined roses. They all once again plunked themselves down and watched me as I crawled under the bed and opened cabinets and drawers. The countertop in the bathroom was littered with vials of prescription drugs, along with various personal items not worthy of mention.

"I never doubted your innocence for a moment," Allegra said to Laureen. "Or, well, not for more than a few minutes. After all, you've killed how many cads over all these years?"

"Eighty-seven," she said as she refilled her glass. "I have not retired, however. Shall we have a look at your room?"

Allegra looked less than enthusiastic at the idea. "I wasn't here when Roxanne came back this morning, and there's no reason to think she would have left anything in my room. I called my agent, then came upstairs and took an aspirin."

"You were downstairs when Sherry Lynne went dashing to the garden," I said.

"I was having tea with Laureen."

Laureen gave her an enigmatic look. "Yes, we were in the parlor, nibbling rice crackers and wondering how far it was to McDonald's. Dilys was shopping, as she is so inclined to do. Sherry Lynne was, of course, having a nervous breakdown, as she is also inclined to do whenever she's concerned about her cats. During the presentation of the Dorothy L. Sayers awards last summer, she made no fewer than a dozen calls to her vet to ascertain that whichever cat it was had successfully coughed up a hairball. I shall never eat angel hair pasta again."

"Not even al dente?" drawled Walter.

"Search my room," Allegra said. "I don't care. This is all so awful and nasty. Roxanne may not have been my best friend, but somebody killed her."

I stood up. "Roxanne Small is dead. She died when she hit the bottom of the cistern. How can you make jokes about it?"

"Jokes?" said Laureen. "I thought we were helping."

"How did you think you might be helping?"

Walter had the decency to flinch, visibly and with some display of contrition, which didn't mean I bought it. "You do understand how distressed we are, Claire. Roxanne was a significant player."

"Did any of you like her?" I asked bluntly.

Laureen sat back. "Like her? Oh, please. You should be

asking about anyone who did not wish her dead, would not have cheerfully shoved her over the wall of the cistern. There may be two or three authors out there who believed in the myth. I would like to think they've been institutionalized. The rest have day jobs."

Allegra shook her head. "Not me. Roxanne was a great editor. She worked with me, nurtured me, encouraged me, brought me along."

"Let's all clap so that Tinkerbell will live," Laureen said, her voice drier than the bottom of her glass.

I felt as if I'd been beckoned to the plate in a World Series game—but without a bat.

CHAPTER
11

Despite an artful array of pricey makeup, scarves, combs, brushes clotted with tangles of black hair, unmatched earrings scattered on the top of the dresser, and the prevalence of magnolia blossoms on the wall and upholstery, the only item worthy of discussion in Allegra's room turned out to be an amethyst broach. Laureen insisted on examining it, then shook her head sadly and pronounced it paste. Allegra begged to differ, claiming it was Victorian and quite valuable. While they squabbled about the authenticity of the filigree and Walter watched with a supercilious expression, I darted into Dilys's room (lilacs), and then Sherry Lynne's (forsythias).

The combatants were in the hall as I emerged. "Empty-handed, I see," Walter said. "Where's all the damning evidence when you need it? A clue, a clue; my kingdom for a clue."

Laureen scrutinized the hall. "Did you look in the linen closet?"

"Sheets and towels," I said, shrugging. "I'd better call the detectives, although they probably won't be interested now that they have a suspect in custody."

"They do?" said Allegra as they swung around to stare at me as if I'd transmuted myself into Queen Victoria herself in order to pass judgment on the broach.

I realized they'd been sent on to the student union before the paramedics arrived. "There was a second body in the cistern. He seems to have—well, fallen on top of Roxanne, and her body provided a cushion of sorts. He was unconscious when they fished him out."

Walter smirked. "Heavens, I hope he was worthy of her, although I myself would have preferred to land on someone with a bit more flesh. Was he a scorned poet from her past? The campus psycho who resides in the sewer pipes beneath the engineering building? A frat boy who'd recently been assigned to read about Medusa and realized this was his opportunity to emulate a Greek hero? I'm sure Roxanne's obituary in *Publishers Weekly* will tactfully omit her familial ties to the Gorgons, but—"

"But," Laureen interrupted, "didn't she have an assistant named Bruce who was fired for shoddy pencil-sharpening? He was always very polite when I spoke with him, but he was justifiably nervous that he might lose his job on any given day. I fear Roxanne would have been mortally offended, and I use the phrase intentionally, had he bounced off of her."

"Bruce committed suicide in a cold-water flat in Brooklyn,"

said Allegra as she finished the gin in her glass. "I think it must be her evil twin. They were joined at birth, after having been obliged to glare at each other in utero for nine months. Major surgery was required to separate them. Now he's hoping she'll be an involuntary organ donor."

Laureen pretended to consider this. "It's not hard to decide which of them received the heart, is it? Perhaps that explains why she was so cold-blooded."

"Or such a blood-sucker," Walter said. "If she is indeed Countess Dracula, we must find a wooden stake and get to the morgue before midnight."

I stopped short of foaming at the mouth, but just barely. "Your collective lack of compassion continues to astound me. Arnie Riggles is a custodian on the campus. He earns minimum wage, but at least he's off welfare and has a job—one that none of you would ever deign to do. Not all of us can be ever-so-witty authors, can we? Somebody has to mop the restroom floors and sweep up the popcorn at the football stadium. The more fortunate are allowed to drive your limos and carry your suitcases to your hotel rooms. The less fortunate stand behind fast food counters and wonder how they'll pay for daycare and antibiotics. They can't afford thatched cottages in St. Mary Mead, much less condos with hot tubs."

"Oh, Claire," Laureen said, squeezing my arm, "I meant no ridicule. My father was a butcher and my mother cleaned houses. The working class has far greater dignity than we ever will."

"Speak for yourself," said Walter, tilting his head so that he could look down his nose at her as though he were a marble general posed atop a prancing steed. "I have risen above the ghetto of genre fiction. My novels are worthy of rigorous analysis by academians and devotees of serious literature. I taught at Harvard before I chose to retreat to an environment more receptive to introspection and spiritual growth. You may feel humbled by your roots, and perhaps you should—it sounds like a dreadfully Dickensian childhood—but I am free of such unbecoming humility. In order to enhance your self-esteem, you might consider writing a novel, and I use the term loosely, in which the heroine does not climb the stairs to investigate bats in the belfrey."

Laureen had replenished the gin in her glass, and she wasted little time in tossing it in his face. "Don't make me kill you, Mr. Dahl. It is not an unpalatable idea."

"With a dagger?" said Allegra. "Our innkeeper is likely to have a paired set, with inlaid pearl handles. Only the best for Mr. Dahl. We'd better do it before the second session is over, though. Afterwards, the line of volunteer co-conspirators will stretch out to the street and around the corner. Dilys can sell tickets for a dollar a plunge, and we'll read about it in the next Miss Palmer novel. I myself will write *Courting Animosity.*"

I had a feeling the second session might require a disarmament treaty to be signed in advance. "Look," I said, "I shouldn't have climbed on that particular soapbox. Arnie's an alcoholic disaster, who, among other sins, has failed to produce the key to the room where I'd hoped to handle the book signing. I'll worry about the missing notebooks later. Please take my car and drive to Old Main, where you should have no difficulty parking. Caron and Inez will be lurking; one of them can bring Sherry Lynne and Dilys back here, then pick you up at five o'clock.

Let's please just get through the rest of the day without this level of acrimony."

Laureen patted my cheek. "You poor thing. Here you are playing Nancy Drew, and no one is taking you seriously. We will toddle off and behave like the professionals we are, and charm the polyester pants off the attendees this afternoon and this evening. It would be nice if you could arrange to sell books at some point, but murder can be pesky." She gave Allegra a nudge toward the staircase, then opened her purse and took out a tissue. "Do dry your face, Mr. Dahl. You look as though you have some tropical disease that is causing your skin to slither. The car key, Claire?"

I handed it to her, and to my amazement, they did toddle off. Acerbic remarks may have drifted behind them as they retreated, but death by dagger was not mentioned within my hearing.

I'd searched all the rooms on the second floor, and I couldn't envision Roxanne methodically shredding hundreds and hundreds of pages and flushing them. Perhaps I really should share this with Farberville's finest, I thought, although I doubted they would find it anything more than the ravings of a most unwelcome meddlesome snoop. Peter's eyes would roll, while Jorgeson's would converge with unhealthy intensity on the nearest inanimate object.

On a brighter note, access to Room 103 might be on Arnie's bedside table at the hospital. With luck, I might be able to remove his key ring, and then relocate the boxes of books to the Azalea Inn before the picnic supper. I wasn't sure how I would do this, but I was ready to carry the books halfway up Mount Everest if that's what it took to sell them.

Once again, however, I was without a car, and the hospital was a good three miles away. Lily might, if pressed, offer me the loan of an ecologically-appropriate bicycle. I could wait for Caron or Inez to bring Sherry Lynne and Dilys back to the inn, but it seemed more likely that Sherry Lynne would opt to search for Wimple. Dilys might inquire about the nearest mall, and either or both chauffeurs would happily accommodate her. It was, after all, Saturday afternoon.

It occurred to me that there was a car out front, albeit one I was not technically authorized to drive. I returned to Roxanne's room, took the key from her purse, and went downstairs. After making sure the notebooks and manuscript were not in the trunk of the car or under a seat, I drove away, feeling as if I were Hertz's worst nightmare.

When I approached the information desk in the lobby of the hospital, I was relieved to see that the shift had changed. "Arnie Riggles?" I said, the epitome of bright-eyed and excessively bushy-tailed optimism.

One of the women punched buttons on a computer. "He's in police custody," she said. "No visitors allowed."

"I'm his sister," I confided. "His little sister. I drove all the way from Tennessee to be with him. I would have been here sooner if I hadn't been obliged to stay till the end of Mama's funeral."

"Your name?"

I moistened my lips. "Jackie Daniels. I've got his Medicaid card, his living will, and his toothbrush. If you'll just tell me his room number, I'll leave them with the officer at the door."

"I don't suppose that would be a problem," she said, then told me the number and directed me to the elevators behind her.

"We all hope your brother recovers, Miss Daniels, and that his . . . predicament with the authorities can be resolved."

"I'm hoping for a coma," I said as I went around the desk and past a gift shop jammed with plush animals, flowers, and helium balloons. I was not tempted.

The police officer sitting in a chair by the door of Arnie's room was broad-chested, hairier than some of Jane Goodall's subjects, and cursed with acne. Had I encountered him in civilian attire, I would have assumed he was Caron's age.

"Next of kin," I announced blithely as I attempted to go inside.

"Wait a minute, ma'am. No visitors."

I had left my scruples in the garden at the Azalea Inn. "My brother, on his death bed, is doomed to lie in bleak solitary confinement as he spirals downward to an eternity of damnation?"

"I was told he's going to recover."

"If your own brother's soul was in peril, would you not insist on kneeling by his bed and praying for his salvation? This country was founded on Christian principles." I gave him a stern look. "Does your mother know you're an atheist?"

"I happen to be a Baptist."

"Well, then," I said, "I should think you'd allow me to read the Bible to my brother while he writhes in anguish. Therein remains the only glimmer of hope to save his soul. 'Yea, though I walk through the valley of the shadow of death, I will fear no evil.'"

The officer managed a weak smile; I was surprised he didn't have braces, or at least a retainer. "He's doing fine, ma'am. Not five minutes ago he was griping about getting chocolate pudding instead of butterscotch."

I wiped away a rather elusive tear. "Our great-grandmother begged for butterscotch pudding just before she died. Arnie was hunkered on the foot of the bed, sobbing his eyes out. He was four years old."

"Hey, why don't you wait here while I call the precinct and clear it? I'll tell them who you are and all, and it should be okay."

"My name is Jackie Daniels," I said sweetly. "Be sure and mention that."

As soon as he started down the corridor, I popped into Arnie's room. He had a pair of black eyes that rivalled a raccoon's, scabbed abrasions on his forehead and chin, and gauze bandages taped across his nose. A swath had been shaved across the forepart of his hair; the stitches reminded me of a zipper. His ensemble was comprised of a hospital gown with the transparency of tissue paper and a formidable plastic neck brace that dictated that for once in his life he keep his chin up.

"You look like hell," I commented as he hastily grabbed the covers, thus depriving me of the joy of ogling his pasty calves and bony knees.

"Senator! I knew you were the sort to visit your constituents in their hour of need. This remote control for the TV is making me crazy. This is a public institution. I pay my income taxes like everybody else, and I expect—"

"You've never paid a dime in income taxes, or even a nickel. I wouldn't be surprised if you've found a way to avoid paying sales tax on a pint of bourbon."

"You didn't happen to bring one, did you?"

"No, Arnie, I did not," I said as I moved away from the

door. "Why didn't you unlock the room in Old Main this morning?"

He turned his face away. "Now that is kinda complicated, Senator. If the truth be known—"

"You won't hear it from him," Peter said as he came into the room. "He spent the night in a locked facility provided by the always accommodating Farberville Police Department. This morning he was arraigned, posted bail, and left in a huff, according to the bailiff." He gazed at me. "Jackie Daniels?"

"At your service, Sherlock. You certainly arrived quickly. Is your hansom cab outside the door?"

Peter did not smile. "I was conferring with the attending physician in the lounge. Now that you're here, Ms. Daniels, perhaps you can persuade your brother to explain in greater detail why he ended up in the cistern with a dead body. We of the Farberville CID seem to be lacking in imagination. Our only theory is that he lost his balance after he pushed her."

"Why would I have done that?" squawked Arnie. "You won't even tell me who she was, for pity's sake! For all I know, she could have been a bleeding-heart liberal and a loyal supporter of the Senator here. I would never harm one of her constituents."

"Does Arnie need a lawyer?" I asked Peter.

"He's been advised of his rights, which is not to imply that anything—and I mean *anything*—he's said has made the least bit of sense and could be used in a court of law. A commitment hearing, maybe."

Arnie managed to sit up. "I am a committed citizen. I have never failed to vote except maybe when I am without legal residence, which has happened on occasion." He glanced warily at me. "You didn't feel obliged to go into that with the lieutenant, did you?"

"No," I said, "and I won't if you'll just provide me with the key to the room in Old Main. Otherwise, the sky's the limit—or should that be the skybox?"

He gestured at a locker. "They put all my clothes and stuff in there. I had my keys earlier, but I'm not real clear about what happened after I went by your apartment."

"Think," Peter said coldly.

I rummaged through Arnie's crud-incrusted clothes while he supposedly thought. I found no massive key ring that permitted ingress to the skyboxes, all of the classrooms and offices on campus, the basement doors of freshmen women's dorms, and whatever else was theoretically secured from the likes of miscreants such as Arnie.

"Hard to say," Arnie said as he ineffectually attempted to scratch his nose through the dressing. "There was something real important that I had to do so the Senator here wouldn't be mad, but it's muddled. Maybe a swallow or two of bourbon might help me remember. Do they have room service here? I'll take a double on the rocks and a side of butterscotch pudding."

Peter stood up. "Ms. Daniels and I will ask at the nurses' station. While you're waiting, Mr. Riggles, I strongly suggest you make an effort to recall your actions this morning. Unless you can come up with something more definitive than this, you'll be charged with homicide and transported from here to the jail. You will not pass 'Go' or collect two hundred dollars, and I can assure you we do not have room service or serve butterscotch pudding." He took my elbow and attempted to hustle me out of the room.

I yanked off his hand. "Do you remember going into the garden behind the Azalea Inn, Arnie?"

Arnie gave Peter a calculating look. "Would that be felony breaking and entering or merely misdemeanor trespassing?"

"What that would be is the least of your worries," said Peter. "You did hear me say 'homicide,' didn't you?"

"To tell the truth, I didn't, Lieutenant Rosen. My ears have been ringing something fierce since I came to in the emergency room. If I weren't so good at reading lips, I wouldn't have been able to follow this conversation at all. I thought you said something about hominy, as in grits."

"Why did you go to my apartment?" I persisted.

Arnie grinned, displaying repellently fuzzy teeth. "I've always liked you, Senator."

"Why the back steps?"

"The front door was locked."

"That makes sense," I conceded. "And the cat?"

Peter once again took my elbow. "Let's not start harping about the cat, Ms. Daniels. There is a body in the morgue, no doubt by this time in a refrigerated drawer. We would like to know why Mr. Riggles pushed her into the cistern."

"I did not!" protested Arnie. He fell back and began to moan as if his skull had imploded from the impact with the pillow. "I can't remember anything except not pushing this lady into the cistern. Of that I'm very sure."

I was too frustrated to rally any resistance as Peter pulled me out to the corridor. "He's lying, obviously," I said, "but I'm not sure about what. If there's a mutant subspecies of humanoids on the planet, Arnie is its spokesperson."

"Claire—if I'm permitted to call you that—is there any chance you might just tend to this mystery convention and allow the Farberville CID to conduct an investigation without your interference? Once we have the physician's permission to stick Arnie behind bars for homicide, I will send out every uniformed officer who's not allergic to cats to poke through the garbage bins in the alley. We'll get search warrants for all the fraternity and sorority houses. We'll put up roadblocks and examine every vehicle that attempts to leave Farberville with a feline hostage in the trunk. A SWAT team will converge on the animal shelter, with assault weapons, bullhorns, and a helicopter or two."

"Does Leslie find this level of sophomoric sarcasm amusing?"

"I couldn't say," he said coolly.

"Am I free to leave?"

"You are free to do as you choose—as long as you stay several miles away from the suspect." He realized he was still holding my elbow and released it with an endearingly boyish blush. "Is this it, Claire? Should I continue making an effort to try to talk any of this over with you?"

"I have a better idea, Peter—if I'm permitted to call you that. Why don't you explain it to Caron? She's had freshman biology, so she knows what happens nine months after the sperm and egg shack up. I suppose she does, anyway; she barely passed the course, and she found that unit a major gross-out, to use her terminology."

I went around him and hurried down the hallway, baring

my teeth at the uniformed officer as he came puffing by, his zits aglow like fairy lights. The elevator took a maddening moment to arrive, but no one attempted to intercept me.

Once I was in the relative safety of Roxanne's rental car, I realized that I had failed to share the information about the missing notebooks and manuscript. Then again, hadn't I been ordered not to interfere? If and when the officiously official team interviewed the authors, it seemed probable that very little of what had transpired the previous evening would be volunteered. Ammie Threety's death had already been dismissed as an accident. The prime suspect in Roxanne Small's death was in custody, sans butterscotch pudding, which meant the nurses, aides, and orderlies on the next shift were in for a hard day's night.

Prevarication (justified, I might add) had taken time. The second panel was apt to be winding down, and all the egomaniacal authors might be roaming the Azalea Inn before I arrived. I looked up at the rows of windows, wondering behind which one Sally Fromberg might be sprawled in bed, watching CNN, sucking up spoonfuls of chocolate pudding, and fantasizing about the exotically mysterious experience she was missing.

Yeah, right.

I drove out of the lot before Peter could emerge. Whatever it was that he thought deserved further discussion escaped me. The idea of him impregnating Leslie, either via a petri dish or the old-fashioned method, had chilled me, perhaps beyond the possibility of a gentle thawing after the fact. Luanne and I had debated it half the night. No matter what understanding he and Leslie had agreed upon, he would be the father, for better or worse, and he would never turn his back on his child. I could not see myself as the stepmother of a fertilized ovum.

After indulging myself with some grumbled expletives, I forced myself to consider the present situation. I was missing three items of significance: the manuscript, the cat, and the key to Room 103. I had no clues where to find the first two, but it occurred to me that there might be an outside chance of finding the third. Arnie had fallen into the cistern, and the paramedics had been less than enthusiastic about spending time at the bottom of the damp, odiferous hole. Arnie's redolence would scarcely have enhanced the ambiance; I myself would have demanded a gas mask, if not full scuba gear.

I drove back to the Azalea Inn. If Dilys and Sherry Lynne were already there, they were upstairs, presumably in their respective rooms. Laureen, Allegra, and Walter would appear within a matter of minutes, and the one hundred attendees in an hour. I thought about stopping by the kitchen to check on Lily, then realized I would be placing myself in danger should she be panicking over rolls that had failed to rise to the occasion.

I tiptoed across the sunroom and went out into the garden. Although the rain had held back all day, dark clouds were moving in as if to spite Sally Fromberger. Lightning flickered beyond Old Main, and after a beat of three, thunder resonated.

The shed at the back of the garden contained rakes, hoes, trowels, flowerpots, bags of fertilizer—and an aluminum ladder. I dragged it out, balanced it on my shoulder, and stepped over the yellow crime scene tape circling the cistern. Selling books was hardly a crime, I told myself virtuously as I pushed aside the wooden cover and eased the ladder into the cistern.

A flashlight would have been convenient, but I had a feeling Lily was of the flickering candle school of detection. Rain began to spatter as I carefully descended the ladder into what might well qualify as the third or fourth ring of the Inferno. Nothing squeaked or hissed or flew into my hair. I was beginning to feel confident despite the increasing rain when the ladder began to shake violently. My foot slipped and I completed my descent in a fraction of a second, landing on my derriere on an uncompromisingly hostile stone surface.

I'm not sure how long it took for me to assess the damage. My breath had been catapulted from my lungs, leaving me wheezing. My tailbone throbbed, but the remainder of my spine seemed functional. One elbow was oozing a warm, sticky substance that was, all things considered, apt to be blood.

I do not bleed gracefully.

Groaning, I sat up and wiggled until I could lean against the wall of the cistern. The bruises on my buttocks might be worthy of depiction in an avant garde gallery in New York; undoubtedly one side or the other would resemble a religious icon. I could become renowned as "Our Lady of the Butt." Pilgrims would flock from all over the world to marvel as I dropped my drawers, and their heartfelt donations would fund Caron's college tuition.

I realized that my head must have hit when I fell. I explored my comely curls and found a bump, not necessarily indicative of a concussion but likely to have realigned a few neurons. Rain was now pelting me, but it did little to sober me up as I gazed bleerily at the ladder, which was rasping upward like a metallic caterpillar. I raised my hand as if to wave goodbye, then sighed and drifted into a senseless scenario of fluttering manuscript pages coated with pesto.

It was much dimmer when I shook myself awake. After a moment to recall what had happened and why I was where I was, I realized that the lid atop the cistern had been scooted back, leaving only a few inches of visible sky. The ladder was gone. The walls were twenty feet high and slimier than the four-month-old bacon in my refrigerator. What had now become steady rain suggested that no one would be chatting on a bench in the garden.

I moved out of the rain, and then despite the obvious futility of it, bellowed "Help!" a few times before subsiding into petulance. Someone would eventually come into the garden and hear my pitiful bleats. The rain might relent at any minute and hordes of attendees would flood into the garden to pollute the stratosphere with second-hand smoke and admire the crime scene tape.

It took me a bit longer to accept that someone had done this to me. The ladder had been pulled up, the heavy lid of the cistern dragged back, deliberately, and with malice aforethought. Was someone hoping I would not be rescued until after dehydration and starvation had resulted in a charmingly grotesque skeleton in the cistern?

It was annoying, and I had no intention of cooperating. There was little I could do at the moment, however, except re-mind myself of why I'd climbed down the blasted ladder to be-gin with. I forced myself to my hands and knees and explored every inch of the floor of the cistern. Arnie's key ring was not there, unless it had been so deeply lodged that it had slipped into the bowels of hell.

I leaned against the wall. Moisture was beading on the stones. Our Lady of the Butt's butt was chilling in a quarter of an inch of water. Cisterns had been built to collect not only rain-water, but also ground seepage. I was in no danger of drowning unless Farberville received an epic deluge, but I had no desire to succumb to a terminal diaper rash.

I had reverted to doze mode when I heard a scritching sound above me. "Hello?" I called. "Is someone there?"

There was no response. I sank back and tried to ignore the dribbles of water that had taken to zigzagging down my back. Parts of my anatomy felt as if moss was forming. If the noise I'd heard was coming from an invasion of rats, I vowed to hold my nose until I fell over dead and could aspire to a more blissful life next time.

A cockroach in a bookstore, perhaps; the ones in mine seemed to be having a fine time and the only thing they did with invoices was to leave droppings on them.

"Wimple!" shrieked a voice.

Even Miss Palmer could have pegged this one. "Help!" I yelled. "Get the ladder."

"You poor creature," said Sherry Lynne. For a moment, I thought she was addressing me, but then she added, "You naughty thing to disappear like that. I've been searching all day for you."

"Has no one been searching for me?" I called.

"Is someone in there, Wimple?"

"Do you believe in trolls, Sherry Lynne? Move the lid and find the ladder!"

The cistern lid slid back, and Sherry Lynne's round face peered over the stone wall. "Claire? What are you doing in there?"

"I'm not waiting for a fourth for bridge. There's a shed at the back of the garden. See if someone thoughtfully replaced the ladder."

"Yes, of course." She vanished, and shortly thereafter lowered the ladder. "I don't understand why you're in there, Claire. It must be terribly uncomfortable."

"No kidding," I said as I crawled carefully up the ladder and stepped into the glorious freshness of the garden. The sky was losing its color, but was a great deal lighter than the bottom of the cistern.

"Whatever were you doing?" demanded Sherry Lynne.

"Would you believe me if I said I was going for a merit badge in spelunking?"

"I don't think so."

"Nor would I," I said, unable to come up with anything else. "At least you've found Wimple. He seems healthy enough."

She nuzzled her face in the cat's ruff. "My boy had a hard day, didn't he? Thank goodness he came back and rescued Claire from that nasty old hole in the ground."

At least the cat hadn't sent up a flare.

CHAPTER
12

Leave the ladder in there." I said to Sherry Lynne. "I doubt the police can find any fingerprints, but they might as well try. And thank you very much. I hadn't gotten around to thinking about what might happen if the person who did this to me returned to more carefully realign the lid—or determine just how easy it is to shoot fish in a barrel, so to speak. I wasn't too far from developing gills."

"Someone was responsible for this?"

"If I had fallen from the top, I'd be destined for the drawer next to Roxanne at the morgue. I was climbing down the ladder when someone shook it. I fell the last few feet. Unless the ladder was possessed, someone was indeed responsible."

Sherry Lynne tightened her clutch on Wimple. "But why were you going into the cistern to begin with, Claire? Didn't the police search it earlier?"

The rain, out of deference to my shivering, had abated. In that the lower half of my body was already soaked, I sat on a wet bench and rolled up my sleeve to examine my elbow. "Yes, but they were more concerned with the bodies. I can't see this cut very well. Is it deep enough to require stitches?"

She averted her eyes. "The sight of blood makes Wimple nauseous. He may bite rather savagely on occasion, but it always makes him uneasy afterwards and he spends hours behind the sofa. Cats are as complex as people, don't you think? Dimple has intimidated every dog in the neighborhood, but never fails to get carsick, and Doolittle sprawls across my keyboard every morning and refuses to budge until I lure him off with his terrycloth mousekin."

"Fascinating," I murmured. "Freud may have missed his calling as a vet."

Wimple's tongue emerged as Sherry Lynne squeezed him even more tightly. "You used the word 'bodies.' Roxanne was not the only victim in the cistern?"

"A local man, employed by the college, seems to have fallen, too. He's in no shape to have a portrait made any time soon, but he'll recover."

"How did he . . . ?"

"The police have been asking him that same question. Thus far he hasn't furnished any answers."

"Did he cause Roxanne's death?"

"I don't know, Sherry Lynne," I said. "Why don't we go inside so I can ask Lily for an icepack?"

Her face assumed the paranoid expression I'd seen the previous day at the airport. "What about Wimple? I am not about
to allow you to take him away again. I can tell from the way he's
trembling that he went through a terrible ordeal today."

"I think his trembling is due to your armlock around his
throat. Take him upstairs as discreetly as you can, and shut him
in the bathroom. Caron will go back to the apartment and get
his carrier, litter box, and some cat food. Lily won't find out until tomorrow, after the deed is done and the two of you are on
the way to the airport. Her reaction is at the bottom of my list
of things to worry about."

"And the identity of the murderer is at the top? If it's not
this man you mentioned, is it one of us? A detective in a rum-
pled suit told us after the luncheon panel to be available for
questioning before the supper."

I looked at my watch, which had kept on ticking. Although
it had seemed as though I'd been in the cistern for the better
part of a week, it was only a quarter past five. "Are the others
here?"

She nodded. "Dilys and I have been back quite a while. She
said she thought she might return to the shop and buy the crystal figurine for her granddaughter. I was so distraught about my
poor kitty that I took an aspirin and lay down. I was awakened
by a conversation between Laureen and Allegra in the hallway
outside my door; from what I could make out, the session was
halted after a fire alarm went off. I took a bath, changed clothes,
and was going to the kitchen to ask for a cup of tea when I saw
Wimple scratching on the lid of the cistern. I could tell from the
crinkle in his brow that it was something more important than
a wounded bird."

"Let me make sure Lily's occupied before you take him upstairs," I said, heading for the back door.

She waited outside while I crept to the kitchen door and pressed my ear against it. Lily's culinary mantra was not for the faint of heart. I gestured for Sherry Lynne to come in, then held my breath until she scurried by me and up the stairs. Wimple's brow was still crinkled, but he appeared to be breathing.

I suppose I should have called Peter, but he and Jorgeson were likely to arrive within the next hour to question the authors. After I told them what had happened, I could expect long-suffering sighs and even a snide suggestion that I had allowed myself to be caught up in a fantasy induced by an overdose of mystery fiction. I was not about to expose my bruises to anyone below the rank of archbishop. And if they did believe me, the authors would be hauled to the station and the supper canceled. Sally would hunt me down in the darkest corner of the Book Depot; Lily would be right behind her, cleaver in hand.

What was increasingly obvious would have gone screaming off the pages of a cozy mystery novel: No one except the five authors, Lily, and the perpetually ill-fated Arnie had been at the inn when Roxanne had taken the fatal dive. The cast of characters had been reduced by one at the time I'd been sabotaged in the cistern. We had no sherry-swilling vicars in the vestibule or sociopathic housekeepers in the west wing. The butler had lost his position a hundred years ago, along with the houseboys and parlormaids. Laureen and Dilys might be convinced a ghost was prowling, but diaphanous entities were more apt to flit across windows than hoist ladders from cisterns.

I considered the layout. Laureen and Allegra had the two rooms overlooking the garden. The window at the far end of the hallway could have provided Walter, Sherry Lynne, or Dilys with an opportunity to watch me begin my foolhardy descent. The window above the sink in the kitchen offered Lily the same opportunity, should her eyes have strayed from the chopping block.

The cat had been recovered. The keys were likely to be lost to posterity, unless some college student had found them in the alley and was at the chemistry lab, brewing up a quantity of illegal drugs, or hunched in front of a computer in the physics building, surfing the Internet for instructions to build a nuclear bomb.

This left only one more item on my list: Ammie's manuscript. If someone had hidden it upstairs, he or she had done so with more cunning than I possessed. The very thought was humbling, and had I not been sitting on an increasingly damp cushion, I would have pondered it at length. My best chance of drying out, however, required a free flow of air.

I rose and looked around the sunroom. The majority of chairs had cushions, but all were too thin to conceal the presence of a thick stack of papers. I checked the drawers of a small writing desk, finding nothing more incriminating than stationery with a logo of the Azalea Inn at the top of the pages. Lily must have taken some degree of pleasure in imagining genteel guests writing letters that extolled the virtues of her hypoallergenic haven. No doubt the pages were made from recycled pulp and the ballpoint pens filled with ink that did not utilize fossil fuel.

There were no promising hiding places in the furniture in the hallway. My heart began to pound as I opened the cabinet doors of the credenza in the parlor, but subsided as I found nothing but a dusty decanter, chipped sherry glasses, and mummified moths. I was on my hands and knees, feeling for a secret drawer beneath it when I heard a noise behind me.

"Goodness," Laureen said from the doorway, "I'm sure none of my heroines was quite so soggy when she searched for clues."

I got to my feet. "The rain, you know."

"Why don't you take a break and come up to my room? I know this convention has been nothing but a series of disasters for you. I'll blow-dry your pants while you have a drink. It's the least I can do, in that I share some responsibility for what's happened."

I realized my thighs were beginning to chafe. "Thanks, I'd appreciate that." I trailed her up the stairs and along the hallway to the Rose Room. "I understand the fire alarm went off during the panel," I said as I sat down on the edge of the bed and removed my shoes, socks, and pants in that order.

"And the sprinklers in the ceiling as well," she said as she went into the bathroom. "I suspect Walter's temper was responsible. All I have is gin."

"Sounds great," I said as I massaged my feet. My toes were as red as the roses coyly winking at me from every available surface. Even the potpourri in a little wicker basket on the bedside table was composed of rose petals. The aroma might have been overpowering had the room not reeked of cigarette smoke. I felt a small prick of sympathy for Lily.

Laureen came out with two glasses of gin and a hairdryer of the caliber Dirty Harry might have packed. She handed me a glass, then took aim at the backside of my pants, which I'd draped over a chair. "Even though I cannot excuse Walter's boorish behavior, I do feel sorry for him. Roxanne seemed to have dedicated herself to destroying his career as a mystery writer."

"As if he had one," said Dilys as she came into the room, then stopped. Her jaw waggled as she took in the situation. She finally regained her composure, as I'm sure her mummy had taught her to do, and said, "Do pardon if I'm interrupting something."

Laureen turned the hairdryer on her. "I've taken Claire hostage and threatened to set her pants on fire if she refuses to divulge the whereabouts of the Star of Farberville. Take one more step and I'll have no choice but to attack your pores."

Dilys wandered past her into the bathroom, then reappeared with a glass of gin. "Do you honestly believe she knows where it is? Five minutes ago I saw Sherry Lynne slinking down the hall with her cat. If the cat swallowed it, we have no choice but dissection. Sherry Lynne will not take kindly to it, and may well decide to dissect us. If we band together, we can take her. Well, I think we can."

"Enough," I said with as much authority as anyone could who was sporting nothing but white cotton panties and bruises below her waist. "Laureen, did you happen to see anyone in the garden after you came back this afternoon?"

"It was raining," she said as she re-aimed her weapon at my pants. "Why would anyone go into the garden?"

"I saw Sherry Lynne," volunteered Dilys. "I was ever so wet when I returned from shopping, and I was hoping Lily might provide me with a cup of cocoa. My mother always gave me cocoa and a biscuit when I walked home from school in the rain. She'd toss a bit of coal on the fire and we'd while away the afternoon reading aloud from *Wuthering Heights*. I was bloody sick of Heathcliff by the time I was old enough to take a secretarial job in London."

"You saw Sherry Lynne?" I prompted her.

"I'd just entered the sunroom when Sherry Lynne went barreling out the door as if the ice cream truck had just come through the gate. I heard no tinkling, though, so I went upstairs to unpack my purchases. I know I shouldn't have, but I bought a silk tie for my husband and a spice rack for my daughter-in-law. Perhaps it will inspire her to do more than prepare fish fingers in the microwave. Wilmont does so love baked beans on toast."

"So you did look out the window," I said to Laureen.

She rearranged my pants and continued wafting the hairdryer across the wet patches. "Only long enough to notice it was raining." Her hand began to bobble. "Dilys, will you please take over?"

"You didn't see anyone?" I persisted.

"I had a headache, as anyone would who had been in the presence of Walter Dahl for more than five minutes. Last week my secretary chanced upon a rare copy of a Theo Bloomer mystery in a used bookstore, and I'd hoped to crawl in bed and read until I had to sparkle yet again. Sparkling on demand is not easy, especially at my age. Then again, it may not be a factor; the book in production at Paradigm House is likely to be my last."

Dilys blinked. "Retiring, are you? Does this mean a few more inches will open up on the bookstore shelves?"

"And according to the proposed promotion budget, I shall sink without leaving a ripple. I'd looked forward to a classy farewell tour, visiting the mystery bookstores that have been so loyal all these years. Now it appears that my eloquence will be wasted on English classes at the local community college." She was quiet for a moment, then managed a smile. "To return to Claire's question, I came downstairs—but not for a cup of cocoa, I can assure you. I'd rallied enough courage to beg Lily for a few ice cubes. I was on the way to the kitchen when I saw you crawling around the parlor."

Dilys gave me a piercing look. "You were crawling around the parlor? I suppose that's no more peculiar than pulling off your pants in Laureen's room. I must say the majority of booksellers I've met over the years are of a sober bent, but they have little choice, considering the uncertainties of their income. Never once has any of them indicated a predisposition to undress in order to impress an author."

"I wasn't crawling around the parlor," I said irritably. "I was searching for something—and it was not the Star of Farberville."

"Then where could it be?" asked Dilys, taking charge of the hairdryer. "If we're going to dissect the cat, I'd appreciate the chance to change clothes. I had several compliments on my new vest."

"There is no Star of Farberville," I growled.

"Ah, well," said Laureen as she settled into an armchair, her hand steadier but her thumb and forefinger making an odd pinching motion, as though she wanted to pluck petals off the upholstery, "then you must have some sort of explanation for your behavior. Heroines must. Genre tradition demands it these days. Twenty years ago I could send them up into the tower, candles clutched in their perspiring palms, but now they seem to need a motive, no matter how contrived."

"I am not anyone's heroine!" I snapped, wishing I was properly dressed so that I could spring to my feet and glower down at her. "I was searching for Ammie's manuscript. What exactly did she say to you about it in the garden?"

"Who?" said Laureen.

"Ammie Threety," I said evenly. "You and she had a long talk in the garden during the reception last night."

Dilys nodded. "Oh, yes, I saw the two of you go outside. If I'd had the courage to ignore the implicit command to grovel at Roxanne's knees, I would have joined you."

Laureen rubbed her temples. "In the garden?"

I wondered how much gin was left in the bottle in the bathroom. Smiling nervously at Dilys, who was now drying my socks, I pulled down my shirttail and went to look. The fifth next to the sink was short only two inches. No empty bottles had been tossed in the wicker wastebasket beside the lavatory.

"Yes, little Ammie," said Laureen as I went back into the bedroom. "She'd written what sounded like a muddled mess. I will admit, however, that it's almost impossible to describe a plot to someone else. I'm forever having to backtrack and mention that, by the way, so-and-so was married to the cad during the war, and that the cousin wasn't really a cousin, but was blackmailing the father for failing to acknowledge his obligation to his demented wife in the asylum. Ammie had the same problem. My brain was numb when we came back inside."

"Yet you thought it had promise," I said, pulling on my damp pants.

"Thrillers are the rage these days. Ammie may have had a round face and sweet brown eyes, but her imagination was quite lurid. Her manuscript would have needed heavy editing, but what I could follow of the plot was intriguing. She was knowledgeable about facial reconstruction, forged identities, and the falsification of court documents. Her information, she told me, came from hours of reading while she sat on a stool behind a dreary store counter."

While all I'd ever done was balance the checkbook, sort through invoices, and when I felt as if I'd earned a respite, read books by the likes of Laureen Parks and Dilys Knoxwood. My few forays into nonfiction involved self-help books extolling me to set goals, meet deadlines, and provide my adolescent with both noncritical acceptance and totalitarian discipline. After a day or two of my muddled attempts, Caron tends to beg to be allowed to live at Inez's house.

But I had yet to learn the ins and outs of facial reconstruction or any of the other things Ammie had so assiduously studied. Next week, I vowed, I would read all the material in the Book Depot involving freak genetic mutations.

"Your socks," Dilys said, tossing them to me as she eyed me with a worried look. "My mother always said that cold feet follow the path to the grave."

I put the socks on, and then my shoes. I would have been pleased if Dilys's sainted mother (or even Heathcliff) had come into the room with a tray of hot cocoa and biscuits, but I was forced to settle for a sip of gin. "Did either of you notice Roxanne in the garden after the morning session?"

Laureen shook her head. "I rested on the bed. The travelling yesterday took its toll."

"And I was shopping," said Dilys. "Did you ever determine who put that peculiar message on Roxanne's laptop?"

"No," I said. "How did you happen to find it? The screen was dark, and it never occurred to me to punch a button."

Dilys went into the bathroom and replenished her glass. "Well," she said as she sat cross-legged on the foot of the bed, her lips pursed, "I've been experiencing a problem with Paradigm House. I am far from computer-literate, but I thought it was possible that Roxanne might have stored sales figures in her files. A green light was blinking, which indicated the machine was still on. I decided it couldn't hurt to give it the old school try. When I saw the message, I rather panicked." She glanced at Laureen. "It immediately brought to mind the novel you wrote about the ghostly messages on the mirror. It was all I could do not to run out of the room, whimpering in terror."

"The mirror was eighteenth century," said Laureen. "The technology was different in those days."

"Why would someone leave that message?" I asked.

Dilys sighed. "I should think it was meant to send us scurrying to the cistern, which we did. If Roxanne intended to commit suicide, she most certainly would have wanted mourners ringing the cistern wall, wailing and sobbing into their hankies as her body was carried up. What would be the point of doing something that dramatic without an appreciative audience?"

I frowned. "But she wouldn't have known about Wimple's disappearance. No one did until after the morning session was over."

"Perhaps," said Dilys, pensively picking at her cuticles,

"she saw the cat on the edge of the cistern. She typed the note, then went outside to save it from certain death. She shoved aside the lid, and when she leaned over to coax Wimple to slither up the wall, lost her balance. This man, no doubt a Good Samaritan, came dashing across the garden, gripped with an inflated sense of heroism, and imprudently decided to rescue her. I find it terribly romantic, if a bit gory. Miss Palmer never leaves the parlor for this very reason."

I was beginning to feel more assertive now that I was dressed decorously. "That doesn't explain why Roxanne would have typed such a whimsical message."

"No," Laureen said pensively, "Roxanne never evinced any sense of humor. If, for some inexplicable reason, she decided to leave a message on the laptop, it would have been to the point and included an unflattering adjective regarding the cat. She had no use for dogs or cats, and if she had possessed an aquarium, it would have contained barracudas."

"That fed exclusively on the digits of midlist authors?" suggested Dilys. "It's not hard to envision her coming home from the office with a pinkie or two, then watching complacently as the surface of the tank roiled until the flesh was stripped and the bones drifted to the bottom."

"More gin, dear?" said Laureen.

I bit my tongue until my outrage subsided. "I feel a pang of sorrow when I read about a car wreck in the newspaper. I come close to crying when the local television news carries a story about a child run down in the street or killed by senseless violence. If one of the spokesmen for the religious right were to suffer a fatal heart attack, I'd wish I had been more tolerant of differing opinions. Roxanne was your editor, for pity's sake! I'm not sure how the relationship went, but I'd think she took you to lunch when you were in New York, and called you on the phone every now and then to keep you informed. Sent you proposed covers, discussed tours and promotion. She might not have ever slept in your respective guest rooms, but . . ."

Laureen looked at Dilys. "When did Roxanne last call you?"

"Let me think. Wilmont had not yet been born, and he's almost four. Roxanne and I did have a honeymoon period, during which she sent flowers and called to tell me how much she loved my latest manuscript. Honey dripped out of the telephone receiver to the extent I'd have to wash my chin when the call was over. Then one day, like Johnny Paper, she ceased to call. I leave queries with her assistant, and if I'm lucky, get a reply in a week or two. I feel as though I've been turned out to pasture to graze on my ever-dwindling backlist." She took a deep breath. "So, Claire, I will not shed a tear at Roxanne's funeral, presuming I bother to attend. She was a vicious woman."

"You're too polite," said Laureen. "Paradigm House had been paying me rather nice advances, but once Roxanne turned on me, my sales dried up—along with my advances. Low print runs, delays in shipping, dreadful covers, confusion with the reps, months before subsequent printings could make their way to the bookstores. Once upon a time I warranted full-page ads in the *New York Times*."

"More than I can say," Dilys said with a sniff. "My agent thinks it will be difficult for me to find a new publisher as long as my backlist is unavailable. Denton had best develop a taste for baked beans. If I don't get higher royalty checks, we'll be eating them straight from the can."

I was trying to think of something to say when a voice from downstairs timidly called my name. "I'd better go see what this is about," I said, then fled with unseemly haste.

Earlene was next to the front door, wringing her hands in a manner Laureen had described in a good three dozen books. "Please don't be too harsh with me," she said as I came down the stairs. Her eyes filled with tears. "I would have called Sally, but I couldn't find a pay phone. I'm sure if you had been there, you would have known exactly what to do."

"What exactly did *you* do?"

"After Walter hurled a pen at Allegra and Laureen poured a pitcher of water on his head, I was afraid that murder might actually come to the campus." She took a handkerchief from her coat pocket and blotted her nose. "I left the room. I was searching for a phone when I saw a smoke detector."

My eyebrows rose. "You set off the fire alarm?"

"I always keep a book of matches in my purse in case of power failure. It never occurred to me that the sprinklers might go off, too."

"You did all that? I'm impressed."

She brightened. "You are? I was so afraid you'd be angry, but I simply couldn't let the panel degenerate into violence. The attendees sounded quite cheerful as they filed out in an orderly fashion, and only Mr. Dahl voiced displeasure." She looked up at me with a certain slyness. "I seemed to have killed two birds with one matchbook. I waited outside until the firemen appeared, then told them I'd noticed smoke coming from beneath the door of the room where your books were stored. They were very annoyed with me after they broke down the door and found nothing."

"Earlene," I said as I came down and hugged her, "that was inspired. If I can just track down Caron and my car, the books will be available for sale at the supper. Five minutes ago I was wondering how much canned baked beans cost."

"My car is out front."

"I shall insist that the steering committee present you with a medal once this ordeal is over," I said.

"That's not necessary," she said modestly as we headed for her car, "but a framed citation might be nice." Once she'd found her car key in the bottom of her dauntingly large purse and we were driving toward Old Main, she said, "In a way, I think everything awful that's happened was Roxanne's fault, from Ammie's accident to the unpleasantness on the panels."

"How could she be responsible for Ammie's accident?"

"Well," she replied, coming to a halt at a stop sign and looking carefully to make sure no Farberville students were driving home after a Saturday afternoon at the pool hall, "her presence got Ammie to thinking about everything she'd written since way back when she was in Roxanne's creative writing class. She was probably so wrapped up in imagining herself a best-selling author that she wasn't paying any attention to the road. I nearly did the same thing myself after I got a letter saying I'd won ten million dollars. It took my husband more than an hour to convince me otherwise."

"And the unpleasantness?"

"It was real hard not to feel the tension once Roxanne arrived. The authors were as subtle as sulky teenagers—with the exception of Walter Dahl, who made no effort to hide his hateful feelings toward her. You should have heard him this afternoon. He pretended he was talking about editors in general, but nobody was fooled. It didn't sit real well with Allegra, and when she started telling how generous her editor was, that's when he threw the pen at her. I guess you could say it went downhill after that."

She parked in a metered space and cut off the engine. "I just wish she hadn't come."

I was beginning to wonder why she had.

CHAPTER

13

The floor of the hallway was tracked with mud, as if a tractor pull had crowned the afternoon's activities. The dampness was pervasive, but at least there was no lingering stench of smoke or scorch marks on the walls. Earlene and I went to Room 103 and looked down at the splintered remains of the door.

"They didn't dilly-dally, did they?" I said.

Earlene shook her head. "They sure didn't. I hope Sally set aside grant money for expediencies."

"Such as wanton destruction of college property?" My fingers crossed that Arnie had not decided that the boxes of books might be worth a few dollars from a fence with a literary bent (so to speak), I went into the room. The boxes were not stacked neatly on the table, but they were all there. A few had been stained by moisture from the sprinklers in the ceiling; I could, if necessary, knock off a couple of dollars on any water-damaged books.

Earlene was clearly proud of the outcome of her ingenuity. "Don't worry about this, Claire. There's a cart that we used for the coffee urn and water pitchers in the panel room. I'll get it and wheel the boxes out to the front stoop, then back my car up to the bottom step. We'll have those books at the Azalea Inn in no time."

"That would be great," I said sincerely. "Do you mind if I go to the second floor for a moment?"

She was already bustling away toward the far end of the hallway, her shoulders squared as though she were preparing to charge down the gangplank of an aircraft carrier and oversee the signing of a peace treaty. I wasn't sure if she fancied herself to be MacArthur, Patton, or Napoleon—or a melding of all three, with a pinch of Ghengis Khan thrown in for good measure.

I went upstairs. The door to the English office was ajar and the stream of words from inside was more apt to be full of Spanish expletives than potential names for a baby. I knocked before I entered.

"Now what?" said the secretary.

"I'm surprised you're still here."

"You're not the only one. I was just adding the last few applicants when the fire alarm resounded so loud I almost wet my pants. I didn't have to, since the sprinklers handled that part and I am now sitting in a puddle that is not, for the first time in several months of incontinence due to erratic pressure on my bladder, my fault. The computer burped, and then the screen went black, taking all my entries for the last hour into some vast cyber-disposal. I am now re-entering them."

"How annoying," I murmured.

"You have a way with words," she said as she resumed typing on the keyboard. "If I were to have such a thing as ten more minutes of uninterrupted time, I could finish, print out the file, dump it on Dr. Shackley's desk, and go home."

"How long does the department keep grad assistantship applications?"

She looked up at me. "Some of them are smudged with dinosaur poop, as if it were any of your concern. I've heard one of the department chairs rejected William Shakespeare's application on account of hints of plagiarism."

"I was hoping I might be able to look at an application from ten years ago."

"No, you are hoping I will get up, take you into the storeroom, and stand around while you thumb through dusty folders. Every time I sneeze, pee will dribble down my legs like tears. You probably think I'm too dumb to understand that this information is confidential. Dream on."

"You wouldn't have to come with me," I said with an inane smile, "and no one would have to know about it."

"Are you thinking you will come up with a reason why I should do anything for you? I could call campus security and let you explain it to them while I finish up and order a pizza on my way out the door. Pineapple and anchovies sound good. I used to order pepperoni, but lately it's been giving me heartburn."

"I could give you a reason, but you most likely wouldn't buy it," I admitted. "A graduate assistant who was here ten years ago was killed today. She came from a highly prestigious school back east. It seems peculiar."

"Very peculiar. Most of the current applicants cannot fill out the forms without using an eraser on every other line. What's so hard about writing down your address and telephone number? It's like nobody ever asked them that before. What's more, half of the transcripts are missing, letters of recommendation are signed in crayon, and they seem to have no idea of proposed areas of study. The expiration date has passed on the cream of this crop."

"All I want to do is glance at the file."

"And all I want is for Dr. Shackley's wife to be beamed aboard the mothership and warped to another solar system." She punched several buttons, and then stood up. "If I were to take a break to buy a candy bar in order to stabilize my blood sugar, I don't suppose Dr. Shackley would ever hear about it. He would never have to find out that I'd left the key on my desk in plain sight, would he?"

"I can't imagine how he would," I said. "It could never be anything more than an oversight."

"Whatever. If I detour by the staff rest room to experience a moment of privacy, then go to the lounge, I should be back in ten minutes." She dropped a key on her desk. "The storeroom's in Dr. Shackley's office, through there. Ten minutes, in case you weren't listening."

I did not think she would take kindly to expressions of gratitude. As soon as she had gone out into the hall, I grabbed the key and went into Dr. Shackley's office. The storeroom had all the charm of a family vault that had been neglected for centuries. Metal file cabinets lined all the walls. Yellowed slips taped on the front of each drawer indicated the year when, in all probability, anyone had last pulled it open. Mindful of the time, I quickly ascertained that Roxanne Pickett's application had been filed twelve years previously, and that she had accepted a teaching assistantship for the following semester. Her grades from Radcliffe were impressive, although she'd received a low grade in physics (hadn't we all?) and withdrawn from a senior thesis course. Her three letters of recommendation were oddly tepid, citing her attention to detail rather than her potential to excel in graduate studies. I had a feeling she'd accepted the offer from Farber College out of desperation rather than fuzzy memories of tire swings in Uncle Bediah's front yard. If Roxanne had developed an urge to find her roots, she would have yanked them up, steamed them, and served them with hollandaise sauce.

I locked the closet, left the key on the secretary's desk, and went downstairs, hoping Earlene had not thrown out her back while moving the boxes of books. Caron and Inez had gone underground for the time being, taking my car with them. I assumed that even between the two of them they lacked financial resources to get much farther than the mall, much less the next county.

Earlene was perched on the trunk of her car, beaming at me like a leprechaun who'd been smoking shamrocks. "I put the cart in the backseat so that we can use it to take the boxes up the sidewalk at the Azalea Inn," she chirped, sans brogue. "I thought about taking the coffee urn as well, but Lily is likely to have one. Shall we go?"

"You stole the cart?" I asked mildly. "Haven't we done enough damage for the day?"

"I merely borrowed the cart, and I'll see that it's returned."

"Of course you will," I said as I got in the car, hoping campus security would not pull in beside us. "We're not going to stop at any gas stations or liquor stores on the way back, are we?"

"Oh, no, I have a full tank." Earlene took her seat behind the wheel. "You were sleuthing, weren't you? How exciting! I was sick with envy when I first read Nancy Drew. I've been wanting a blue roadster ever since, but I was forced to settle for a used Chevrolet. It's just not the same."

"I suppose it lacks the panache," I said. "Do you mind if we swing by my apartment for a minute? If Caron's there, she can help unload the books."

My car was parked out front. I assured Earlene I would only be a minute, then hurried upstairs and let myself into the apartment. I did not require any detective prowess to determine that Caron was home: Soda cans, an empty bag of pretzels, and bread crusts littered the coffee table, and the TV was turned to some channel in which tattooed men with greasy hair lip-synched veiled threats to women clad in chainlink bikinis and salad oil.

Caron's voice drifted out of her room. "You heard me, Rhonda. Allegra has already sold her next book to a big-time studio for like three million dollars, and she promised me a part. Not the lead, of course, but I'll have lines and stuff. While I'm in Hollywood, I'll have a personal hairstylist and makeup artist, as well as a private tutor and a limo to take me to the set every day."

"You need to get off the phone," I said from the doorway.

"Hold on," she said, then covered the receiver with her

hand. "I am in the middle of a conversation, Mother. You're the one who's always harping about how rude it is to interrupt."

"Get off the phone," I repeated. "Otherwise, the next thing I interrupt will involve your life support system in the ICU."

She failed to look terrified, but told Rhonda she would call back and replaced the receiver. "What's the matter now? Does one of your precious authors have a hangnail? Should I call for an ambulance?"

I gave her a wry smile. "After what happened today, that's not very funny."

"I'm sorry." She fumbled through various scraps of notepaper, most of which were buried under cracker and cookie boxes and several more soda cans. It was an impressive beginning for a landfill, considering she couldn't have been home for more than an hour and a half. "You have a message," she said gloomily, "but I can't find it. The gist is that Peter called here from the Azalea Inn about half an hour ago, looking for you. He wasn't pleased when I told him I didn't have a clue where you were. He said if you weren't there pretty soon, he'd issue an APB on you and have you taken to jail for interfering in an official investigation. Can he do that?"

"Yes, indeed. He's done it before, and once he had my car towed off and impounded out of pique. Pique is not attractive in a man of his age, or any man over the age of four, for that matter."

She uncurled her legs and stood up. "So what do you want me to do?" she asked in a tone that suggested I was about to demand an amputation, at best.

"Put the litterbox, the cans of catfood, two plastic bowls, and a can opener in a garbage bag, then let Earlene give you a ride to the inn. The kitty contraband goes to Forsythia Room on the second floor, the boxes of books in Earlene's trunk to the parlor. Should book buyers start arriving early, oblige them. One of the boxes has the gizmo to accept credit cards. You can take checks, or cash if you can handle making change."

Her lower lip jutted out. "I'm supposed to go to a movie at the mall with Inez and Emily. Carrie and a bunch of other girls are going to meet us at Streetcar Pizza afterward so I can tell them all about Allegra Cruzetti and how gorgeous she is. Sally Fromberger said I wouldn't have to do anything this evening, you know. I am trying to have a Life."

"Luckily, your meter is running at seven dollars an hour, which means you'll be able to afford to have a life once this weekend is over. Please do as I ask, and if Peter corners you, tell him I'll be there in less than hour."

She blinked at me. "What are you going to do?"

"I'm going to fix myself a drink and take a lovely, steamy bubble bath. Then I'm going to dust myself with the talcum powder you gave me last Christmas, and put on clean clothes. I may have another drink on the balcony and listen to the Kappa Theta Etas shriek about their plans for the evening—or I may knock on the downstairs tenant's door and ask him to play me a sonata. I shall drape myself across his piano, a rose clutched between my teeth. He'll lose his mind and force me to elope with him to Vienna, where we will buy an estate and raise a family of children with perfect pitch."

"I don't guess I should tell Peter any of that," she said, un-amused.

"You may tell him that I had a telegram from the King of

Siam asking me to teach school in his palace. Please get moving—Earlene's waiting out front."

Once Caron had collected Wimple's essentials and stomped
down the stairs, I made sure all the doors were locked, detoured
through the kitchen for the drink, and retreated to the bathtub
to allow myself a much-deserved break. It had not been an easy
day.

I arranged a inflatable cushion behind my head and sank
back with a blissful sigh. Less than thirty-six hours earlier, I'd
been envisioning myself in the presence of the greatest talents in
the traditional mystery genre. Pearls of wit and wisdom would
have been rolling off their tongues, I might have caught enough
to come away motivated to write the novel that had lingered in
the back of my mind since my undergraduate days.

But the silk purses were sows' ears, I thought with a scowl.
Walter Dahl was another part of the sows' anatomy, the one at
the east end when the sow's snout is pointing west. He certainly
was not as popular as the other four authors. I rarely bothered
to order his books, and after a respectable passage of time, almost always returned them unsold. So why had Sally included
him in Murder Comes to the Campus? I could think of dozens
of more prestigious mystery writers who fit the criterion and
might have accepted her invitation—and generous honorarium.

I utilized my toes to start a trickle of hot water. Laureen,
Sherry Lynne, and Dilys were established masters in the field.
Snaring Allegra had been quite a coup on Sally's part. But why
Walter?

I realized my skin was beginning to tingle, or perhaps sim-
mer. I turned off the hot water before the word "boil" was more

apt, finished my drink and forced myself to get out of the bath. Even as I dried off, applied powder, and dressed, however, I could not stop wondering why Sally had put Walter on her list of illustrious mystery authors.

After fixing a second drink, I went to the living room rather than the balcony above the porch, and sat down on the sofa to call Sally.

"How are you doing?" I said when she answered. "Any idea when you'll be released?"

"I heard."

"Did Earlene call you?"

"Oh yes," Sally said darkly, "as well as Geraldine, Jordan, Kimmie, and Mrs. Whitbread, who's a librarian here in Farberville and a die-hard mystery fan. Dr. Shackley called, too. His wife has a migraine, so they won't be attending the final event this evening. I think we both know what *that* means."

"We do?"

"Without sponsorship in the English department, the Thurber Farber Foundation for the Humanities is hardly likely to give us another grant. It's just as well, I suppose. This entire project has been ill-fated since the day I received word of the grant."

I took a gulp of scotch. "Come on, Sally, Farberville hasn't been experiencing plagues of locusts and frogs for the last six months. Sure, there were glitches with registration and the book room, but Earlene seems to have everything under control."

"There are police officers at the Azalea Inn, investigating a murder. This is not what I imagined when I came up with the whimsical name for the convention. I wish they'd all go away before someone else is killed."

"And tomorrow they will," I said. "I'd like to ask you something, Sally. I can understand why you invited the women authors, but I'm puzzled about Walter Dahl. He's rather obscure."

"I'd never heard of him, to be candid. Since the four authors I really wanted were at Paradigm House, I wrote a letter to the publicity department. The letter I received in response said that the four authors had agreed to participate, and that I might consider providing a broader coverage of the genre by including a literary mystery author such as Walter Dahl. The letter implied that he epitomized that particular aspect, and included the address of his publisher. I was delighted to oblige."

"Who was this letter from?" I asked.

"Someone whose name sounded as if she'd just graduated from high school. Jennifer, Heather, or maybe Brittany."

"But not Roxanne?"

Sally began to snuffle in a familiar yet still distasteful fashion. "Roxanne being the name of the woman found in the cistern earlier today, of course. Just because I'm in the hospital doesn't mean I'm completely ignorant of what's happened. It was on the five o'clock news."

"We're having the book sale this evening," I said, sounding like an aerobics instructor on a cruise ship. "I'll have all the authors sign a book for you."

"I never thought it would turn out like this, Claire," she said, sounding damper with every word. "I thought we would all celebrate the genre, but instead—"

"The picnic supper is at hand. I'm sure someone will let you know how it went. If I don't get to the inn right now, it won't be me because I'll be in jail for the night. Pop a pill, and I'll call you in the morning."

I hung up without giving her the opportunity to respond. I applied fresh makeup, ran a comb through my winsome curls, and stood in front of Caron's full-length mirror to make sure my jacket and trousers were doing their best to make me look ten pounds lighter than someone who ate fettucini alfredo in pricey bistros in New York and borscht with dollops of sour cream in St. Petersburg. Even caviar was not without calories.

Since Caron had failed to leave the car key on the kitchen counter, I decided to walk to the Azalea Inn. I'd just come down the back steps when a voice hissed at me from the bushes. To be more precise, hissed, "Senator!"

"What are you doing, Arnie?" I said with commendable restraint. "Aren't you supposed to be in custody?"

He emerged, dressed in baggy green surgical scrubs. "Some would say that. May I add that nobody ever asked Arnie Riggles how he feels about it? There is only one decent mattress in the Farberville jail, and inevitably there's some four-hundred-pound biker passed out on it. Now that I've grown accustomed to classier decor, I have a true aversion to filthy blankets and lice. You can't blame me, can you? I've been drinking bottled water since the middle of January."

"I didn't know you drank water, Arnie."

"Well, when I brush my teeth." He glanced over his shoulder as a car drove by. "Don't think I missed your sarcasm, Senator. Because of you, I nearly died today. For a while there, I was floating down this tunnel toward a blinding light, fully expecting to find my grandmother with a plate of warm gingersnaps, but then I was snatched back to a gurney in the emergency room. It was very unsettling."

"Arnie," I said, "if you indeed had a grandmother, she would have been much too busy mugging old men in the park to bake cookies. How did you get away?"

Arnie sat down on the bottom step. "It wasn't as hard as you'd think. The policeman at the door was wearing a nametag that said he was L. Flipp. I called the hospital switchboard and had him paged to the front desk, then hustled my butt down the hall and into a linen closet. Green is not my color, but I had no choice. Piece of cake after I put on a mask and grabbed an armful of supplies. Three security guards asked me if I'd seen me, which leads to some complex existential issues we might discuss at a later date. As for now, could you advance me a couple of dollars?"

"So you can take a taxi to your skybox?"

"You ever had hospital food?"

Despite the howls of protest from my conscience, I took out my wallet and waved a five-dollar bill. "This is enough for a hamburger and fries, Arnie, and even a milkshake. Rather than make insincere promises to pay me back, why don't you tell me what happened in the garden behind the Azalea Inn?"

"Yeah, okay." He took the bill, and, after patting himself down, determined he had no pockets and wedged it behind his ear. "It goes back to last night. I was at the Dew Drop Inn, and might have been boasting about how I had keys to the campus, which I am inclined to do with a couple of beers under my belt. This skinny ol' boy offered to buy them, and since I was flat-out broke and running up a tab, I agreed, planning to report them lost Monday morning. Then I started thinking how maybe he shouldn't have the key to that room in Old Main where I'd set the books, as well as certain other keys involving private residences. I was pulling them off when he got all hot and bothered. I had no choice but to whack him upside the head with a beer bottle. I might not have done it if I'd realized he was with some friends."

"So you were arrested for brawling and spent the night in jail?"

"That would be one interpretation. Anyway, the key ring was gone and I went by your apartment this morning to explain, but your front door was locked. When I opened the door at the top of these stairs, this satanic creature streaked by me. I went scrambling after it." He paused to scratch his scalp. "I didn't want you to be even more upset with me, Senator."

I crossed my arms and gave him an icy look. "There is no way I could be *more* upset with you, Arnie. Shall I assume the cat went over the wall into the Azalea Inn garden?"

"Not being a pole vaulter, I went through the gate, thinking I could grab the cat and get it back to your porch before anyone noticed it was gone. It wasn't anywhere to be seen, but then I saw the lid on the cistern was pushed aside. Fearing the worst, I leaned over and made those ridiculous noises people do when trying to convince a cat to cooperate. The cat cooperated by springing on my buttocks, its claws extended like all those gadgets on a Swiss Army knife. That's pretty much all I remember until I regained consciousness. Except for the tunnel, of course, and grandma and her cookies."

"Why won't you tell this to the police?"

He hunched his shoulders. "I didn't want to tell them about the keys. All I'm trying to do is help the homeless by giving them a dry, warm place to sleep. I'm like a social worker, tracking down people who've been sleeping outdoors all winter. The guy in the Tyson box is holding down a job and going to rehab. The woman in the Wal-Mart box is going to have a baby any day now. She's going to name it after me."

"Do you have a trained midwife in another skybox?"

"A landlord can only do so much," he said huffily. He stood up and, with a wary expression, watched as another car drove by. "As much as I've enjoyed our conversation, Senator, this may not be the most prudent place for me to linger. I was thinking I might have a tailgate party in the stadium parking lot to celebrate Memorial Day. Is there any chance I could borrow your tailgate?"

I grabbed the front of his shirt. "Did you see anyone else in the garden?"

"Can't say that I did. If you don't mind, I'd like to go home and relax. It's been one helluva day."

"No kidding." I released him, then watched as he scuttled up the shadowy path between my duplex and the sorority house. Once he was across the street, he could dart from bush to bush all the way across the campus, and he no doubt had an alternative route to the tier of skyboxes that would preclude exposure to any cruising campus cops.

His version of what had taken place pretty well fit what I'd supposed. Wimple was capable of attempted murder, but Arnie was not. Someone else had arranged to speak to Roxanne in the garden, then quite possibly thumped her with a rock and dumped her in the cistern. Any damage to her head would have been attributed to the impact. Coroners tend to find what they're forewarned to find.

Peter was waiting, I reminded myself as I walked down the

street and went through the gate into the garden. Caron would be mortified if I was actually dragged off in manacles, whimpering for a lawyer (and wondering how I'd pay for one). I'd done nothing wrong, mind you, except for possibly not remaining available. I'd told Peter everything I knew, for the most part. If he had no interest in missing cats and manuscripts, it was hardly my responsibility.

"Hey!" bellowed a voice from the patio. "What do you think you're doing?"

"Tiptoeing through the tulips?" I suggested.

"No one is supposed to be out here."

"You're out here."

There was a moment of silence. "Yeah, but the lieutenant told me to make sure nobody goes into the garden."

"Then you should lock the gate," I said primly to the uniformed officer as I went past him and into the sunroom. To my profound dismay, Peter was seated at the desk, interviewing Dilys, who was perched on the wicker throne where Laureen had held court less than twenty-four hours earlier.

She leapt to her feet and came over to squeeze my hands. "Oh, my dear, we've been looking everywhere for you! I was quite sure you were once again in the cistern, but this police officer assured me that you were not. He would not allow me to search the basement. Allegra made some impertinent remarks about the size of the freezer in the pantry off the kitchen, but Lily's been entirely too busy to chop anyone into pieces and wrap the extremities in butcher paper. It would be called butcher paper, wouldn't it? I must make note about it."

"Ms. Malloy," Peter said, sounding a bit frustrated, "is

there a chance you might help Ms. Knoxwood explain her whereabouts today?"

"Ask her to show you her receipts, Lieutenant Rosen. If you'll excuse me, I need to find out if Caron has—"

"I will not excuse you, Ms. Malloy. Ms. Knoxwood, I'll have someone type up your statement and you can sign it in the morning. Thank you for your cooperation." He waited until she left, then came over to me and gripped my shoulder. "You fell in the cistern this afternoon? Did it not occur to you to tell me about this? You might still be out there, unconscious or in too much pain to call for help."

"You are not attractive when you sputter," I said as I disengaged his hand. "May I assume you've spoken to Sherry Lynne Blackstone?"

"If that damn cat—"

"Don't let her hear you say that." I sat down on the wicker chair and gazed at him with all the warmth of Elizabeth II confronting one of her rambunctious offspring. "I intended to tell you when I saw you. It was my impression that someone shook the ladder and then pulled it up, but Farberville is on a fault line. Stranger things have happened during earthquakes. I've already had three offers from the tabloids. The one with the highest bid wants me to swear I saw Jesus's face on the bottom of the cistern lid. I could have, I suppose."

"You might have been seriously injured."

"But I wasn't."

"Obviously," he said in a flat voice. "Would you care to tell me why you decided to climb down into the cistern?"

"I thought it was possible that Arnie's key ring might have

fallen out of his pocket. I've spent all day trying to get inside the room in Old Main where the boxes of books were stored for the convention. Fate intervened."

"Fate does not interest me. Do you have any idea where Arnie is at this moment?"

"Have you checked the cistern lately? It's one of his watering holes, so to speak."

"You did not answer my question, Ms. Malloy. Do you know where Arnie Riggles is?"

"It's my understanding he spends most of his time on campus. You might start there." I arose and beckoned at my nonexistent court lackeys to follow me. "I really must see that Lily has the supper situation under control and Caron has put out the books in the parlor."

He cut me off at the pass. "Someone tried to kill you, dammit!"

"If any of these people had wanted to kill me, I'd be sporting a toe tag. Someone tried to frighten me—and that was a big mistake."

CHAPTER
14

Peter stared at me. "You're determined to prove something to these authors—or to me."

"Don't be absurd," I said with the vastly superior smile of someone recently nominated for a Nobel prize in tact. "If you'll excuse me, I really do need to make sure things are running smoothly. I swear I will not set foot outside the Azalea Inn for the rest of the evening. Roughly one hundred people will be arriving soon. They are anticipating food, drink, conversation, and the opportunity to buy books and have them signed. If you would like to take charge, that's fine with me. If you would like to bring a date, that's fine with me, too. Be warned, however— the wine's cheap and the women are easy."

Before he could respond, I went into the kitchen. Lily's face was glistening with sweat, but she did not appear anymore homicidal than usual. "Everything under control?" I asked.

She stared at me as if I'd wandered in naked. "I heard you fell in the cistern and cracked your skull like that other woman."

"Sherry Lynne told you that?"

"I overheard her talking to somebody in the sunroom."

"I may have slipped in the cistern, but I cracked nothing more than my tailbone and my dignity. Are you prepared to serve wine and canapes in fifteen minutes, and the meal in about an hour?"

"What do you think I've been doing all day?"

"I just wanted to confirm," I said as I edged toward the door. "Do you need any help?"

"Do I appear to need help?"

I would have felt more at ease if she'd blinked, even once. "Of course not, Lily. You've done a splendid job thus far. I'm sure whatever you've chosen to serve will be delicious."

"I hope there'll be enough for leftovers tomorrow. I'm going to spend the afternoon in my bedroom watching basketball on TV. It's an intriguingly contemporary version of classical Russian ballet, although with nihilistic overtones. I can almost visualize Baryshnikov slam-dunking those prissy little swans."

"The authors will be gone by noon," I said, clutching the doorknob behind my back as she picked up a carving knife.

"No, they won't. Lieutenant Rosen has informed me that they will not be allowed to leave until he has satisfied himself that none of them are involved—and that might require several days. I agreed to a discount for the convention. My rates will double as of tomorrow, or, if the Knicks lose, triple."

"Is that fair to the Thurber Farber Foundation?"

"Was it mentioned anywhere in the contract I signed that a dead body would be found in the cistern? I'd hoped for two diamonds from the AAA. Now I'll be lucky to be listed in the Chamber of Commerce brochures. My only chance is that this woman from New York will take to haunting the Azalea Inn. Ghosts are popular drawing cards so long as they'll materialize often enough to establish notoriety."

"A ghost in designer clothes, carrying a laptop computer as she pirouettes among the azaleas?"

"It's a new millennium," Lily said with a shrug. "I need to put the stuffed mushroom caps in the oven and start uncorking the wine. Unless you're inclined to do either. . . ."

"I'm sure you'll handle it admirably." I went back out to the sunroom, where I saw Peter nodding sympathetically as Allegra complained about the rigors of her tour. Their faces were so close that they must have been befogging each other's eyeballs. Red alert, Leslie.

Caron was not in the parlor, but some books had been taken out of the boxes and stacked on a cardtable. Laureen and Dilys were murmuring to each other as they browsed.

"Do you know where my daughter is?" I asked.

Laureen spun around and came over to give me a hug. "I wish you'd told us what happened, Claire. I would have insisted that you report it to the police. That lieutenant seems very concerned about you."

"One might go so far as to say he's obsessed," added Dilys.

"You could do worse, you know. He's attractive enough to have come out of one of Laureen's books, although I suppose he would have slate gray eyes, be wearing something more dashing, and have a cruel scar across his cheek. Why do they always have cruel scars, Laureen? Are they all ex-pirates?"

Laureen disregarded what was clearly a barb. "Seriously, Claire, there were only six people inside the Azalea Inn when you climbed down the ladder into the cistern. As much as I rely on old-fashioned coincidences to disentangle my heroines from sticky situations, I find it impossible to believe that someone was hiding in the garden or happened to come in through the gate while you were . . . doing whatever it was you were doing."

Dilys gasped. "So you're saying it must have been one of us!" She gazed at the ceiling. "Unless, of course, Lily has locked away a deranged relative in the attic. A great-aunt, I should think, who only dares to come out on dark and stormy nights."

"It wasn't dark," I said, "and it wasn't stormy."

"Did the perpetrator of this heinous deed have a cruel scar? Perhaps Lily has an ex-pirate in the basement as well as a great-aunt in the attic. If there is a chest of gold doubloons buried beneath the stones at the bottom of the cistern—"

"We don't get a lot of pirates around here." I turned back to Laureen. "Do you have any idea why someone in the publicity department at Paradigm House would suggest to Sally that she include Walter in the convention?"

Laureen lowered her voice to exclude Dilys, who was gazing alternatively at the floor and ceiling, and mumbling to herself in a way I would have found distressingly abnormal only a day ago. "That's not likely to have been the case. I would be more inclined to think that Roxanne was told that the four of us would be here, and realized she had an excuse to show up without warning and further torment Walter, should he be present. She would have done the same thing if we'd been scheduled to do a signing in a hut at the South Pole."

"Do you know why was she so determined to make his life miserable?"

"I've heard rumors, but he must be the one to tell you, if he chooses. Mysterydom is a tight community; if need be, we circle the wagons and take out our flintlocks to protect our own, no matter how objectionable they may be. Authors are powerless in the overall scheme of the publishing industry. We do what we can."

"So you do know," I said, frowning.

"And I also know that Caron is in Lily's office, making a phone call. Walter was last seen in his room."

"Will you keep watch over the stock until Caron gets back?" I asked. When she nodded, I went upstairs to the Petunia Room.

Walter's door was open. He was stretched out on the bed, holding the flask of scotch in one hand. His eyes opened as I tapped. "Ms. Malloy, I hear you've been quite the giddy superheroine today. Will you next be donning a leotard and a cape in order to leap off the roof? Please give me notice so that I can be watching from the lawn."

"Don't get your binoculars just yet," I said as I sat down on a chair across from him. "Why was Roxanne so dedicated to destroying you that she arranged for you to be invited to the convention this weekend?"

"I wondered if that was the case," he said, sitting up. "A drink, Ms. Malloy?"

"No, thank you, I'd rather have answers."

"And you think I have them?"

I crossed my arms and glowered. "Yes, Mr. Dahl, I think you do. This vendetta could not have started when she read your manuscript. She must have skimmed hundreds every week. The fact that you were sent a galley and a gracious letter from Paradigm House implies that Roxanne was trolling for you. She was in the flatboat, and you were nibbling on the algae at the bottom of the river until the plastic worm drifted into sight."

"I am not a bass, Ms. Malloy," he said stiffly.

"But you rose to the bait, did you not?" I looked at my watch. "We don't have much time. Laureen has acknowledged that she knows what this is about. If you won't tell me, then I have no choice but to inform Lieutenant Rosen, who will force her to reveal the details."

"If you're planning a career in blackmail, the procedure is for you to demand a sum of money in exchange for your silence. That's the classic approach. There is one thing I should point out about blackmailers in mystery fiction, however, and that is they rarely survive beyond the third chapter."

"If you're threatening me, Mr. Dahl, I am not impressed. You, on the other hand, are likely to spend the night in the Farberville jail. Watch out for the four-hundred-pound biker. He always insists on the only decent mattress. When you're released, you'll need to buy something to deal with lice."

He set the flask on the bedside table. "I wasn't threatening you, Claire. I knew Roxanne when her last name was Pickett, so I never thought twice about approaching someone at Paradigm House named R. P. Small. Had I known who she was, I would have flung myself off the edge of a very deep canyon. Make that a bottomless canyon."

"Does this go back to when you were teaching at Harvard and Roxanne was enrolled at Radcliffe?"

"How astute of you to make that connection. She took one of my classes. I saw nothing but a sea of shiny faces, but she began to drop by my office during hours, and eventually we lapsed into a relationship. Intimacy between teacher and student was forbidden, but she seemed old enough to know what she wanted." He paused as he looked down at the petunias on the bedspread. "God knows I wanted her. We spent two years together, staying in quaint inns on Cape Cod, skiing in Vermont, camping in Maine, and even just sitting in coffee shops, sharing the newspaper and a bagel. One summer we were lucky enough to be offered a tiny house on Nantucket. Every time I think of our picnics beside the cranberry bogs, I—" He broke off and wiped his eyes.

"I gather this relationship did not end well."

"She dumped me for a professor with tenure. I nearly went out of my mind with jealousy. I begged her to come back, sent flowers for weeks, and called her apartment until her roommates refused to take my messages. No one as beautiful as she had ever so much as smiled at me when I held open a door. I followed her when she went out at night, and lurked in the stacks when she studied at the library. When she went home for Thanksgiving, I spent four days and nights in my car at the end of her block. I was on the verge of losing my assistantship when I finally sought help at the campus infirmary. I received no counseling, but the medication helped."

"Was she aware of this?" I asked softly.

"I suspect it amused her."

"So why did she turn on you?"

He went to the window and pushed aside the drapes in order to stare at the house beyond the wall. "I did one thing for which I am still truly repentant. The grad assistants at Radcliffe and Harvard mingled in the bars we could afford. I dropped a few remarks hinting that her papers in my class were plagiarized, although I acknowledged that I could never find the original sources. The rumors spread. Unsubstantiated gossip is the grist that keeps the wheels of academia grinding ever so relentlessly."

"And they ground to the point that she was obliged to withdraw her senior thesis?"

"Nothing went on her transcript." He allowed the drapes to fall back. "She was tainted, though, and unable to get into any of the prestigious upper level seminars. She was in contention for editor of the school paper, but was passed over. Phi Beta Kappa did not invite her to the prom, so to speak."

"You are one twisted son of a bitch," I said. "It's no wonder she went after you like a Rottweiler. What's more, you deserved it. If there weren't a police officer on the patio, I'd invite you to take a stroll to view the cistern in the moonlight."

"I had no idea my idle remarks would do so much harm," he protested. "The male ego is fragile. Women like you think we're buffeted by testosterone, but inside—"

"Save it, Walter." I stood up, unwilling to allow him to look down at me. "Roxanne was playing hardball with you, and your response must have escalated to blind rage. Did you grit your teeth until you were able to ask her to join you in the garden to resolve the issue?"

"I most certainly did not! I'd intended to take a walk after the morning panel, but then I came up with an idea for my next novel. I returned here and began to jot down notes while they were fresh in my mind. I did not set foot out of this room until I heard all the shrieking downstairs. There is something about shrieking that stirs an author's soul."

"You didn't knock on the door of the Hibiscus Room?"

"If I had, Claire, I would hardly admit it. I am cognizant of the rules of evidence."

"But you will agree that someone inside the Azalea Inn was responsible for Roxanne's death? If not you, then who?"

He refilled his glass. "What about this other person found in the cistern?"

"He didn't do it," I said flatly. "He thought Sherry Lynne's cat was in there."

"Ah, thus accounting for 'Ding, dong, bell, pussy's in the well.' I myself might have tossed one in had the opportunity arose, were I not highly allergic to them. Whenever one has even been in proximity, my eyes begin to water and my sinuses to lock up. My allergist seems to think some of my symptoms are psychosomatic. I will admit to being raked across the face by a neighbor's cat when I was a small child, but I am not the sort to be manipulated by the unconscious impulses of my id. 'Id' is the first syllable in 'idiot.' I may be a pompous bastard, but I can assure you that I am not an idiot." His eyes gleamed in a way I found most alarming, in that I could provide neither a tissue nor a heartfelt avowal of camaraderie. His voice broke as he added,

"I hope, Claire, you will believe me when I say that I am not a murderer. Committing murder requires determination and spiritual fortitude. I am sadly lacking in both qualities."

I wasn't sure if he expected me to throw my arms around him and assure him that either I believed he was capable of murder or had never for a moment suspected him of it. The one thing I didn't want to do was breach the intangible gap between us and tacitly give him permission to stalk me in the same manner he'd stalked Roxanne ten years ago.

Which is exactly what he'd done, and I doubted it had ever amused her. When she'd learned of the rumors circulating in Cambridge bars, she must have been incensed. When they'd come home to roost, or in this case, to foul the nest, she must have vowed revenge. It had taken her ten long years, but she'd come close to presenting Walter's head on a platter to the Author's Guild only a few months ago.

"Then you never went near the cistern?" I asked.

"Until all this happened, I had no idea what a cistern might be. I'm still struggling to understand the concept of grits."

I left the room. What Walter Dahl thought was of minimal interest. Those who had paid over a hundred dollars to attend the convention were beginning to clog the hallway. Selling books was more important than solving mysteries, I thought as I went down the hallway. I could almost hear my accountant gurgling his agreement.

My intentions were pure, but Allegra popped out of the Magnolia Room and caught my arm.

"Do you have any idea how long we'll be forced to stay here?" she asked. "I don't know what to do about New York. My agent's out of the country, and my publicist is most likely double-dating with Ken and Barbie. She swears she's in her twenties, but I can never catch her at her desk before four o'clock. I don't even know the last name of Roxanne's current assistant; she went through them in the way the rest of us go through a box of chocolates. The nougats never lasted a day."

I was not inclined to wallow in the analogy. "You know more than I do, Allegra. Didn't Lieutenant Rosen say anything about when you would be permitted to leave?"

"Not really," she said, toying with the tip of the silk scarf around her neck. "He seems more upset about what happened to you today than he is about Roxanne's death. She could have fallen, I suppose."

"And Ammie Threety?"

"An unfortunate accident. She dozed off."

"The preliminary lab results suggested she had taken some sort of barbiturate." I recalled something Allegra had said at the airport. "You travelled with a prescription for antibiotics. Did you also have an array of prescription sleeping pills?"

Allegra stiffened. "I have a few precautionary medications in my purse, but I most certainly did not offer anything to Ammie. I barely spoke to her, and went upstairs shortly after supper. What's more, if I had given her a tablet of any kind, I most certainly would have said so. I had absolutely no reason to harm her."

I contemplated this for a moment. "You conceivably could have had a reason, Allegra," I said slowly. "What if you were worried that Ammie's manuscript might turn out to be the next best-seller? Roxanne might have abandoned you as she did Laureen, Sherry Lynne, and Dilys."

"My second book will be out in time for Christmas, and it's

already been bought by Hollywood for several million dollars. Foreign rights have been auctioned. Paradigm House is planning a major publicity blitz. The network talk shows are scrambling to schedule me. Because of my success, Roxanne's stature in the industry had never been higher. The only reason she would have abandoned me was if she was asked to be editor-in-chief, but she would never have let anyone forget who pulled my manuscript out of the slush pile."

"Will all this still happen without her?"

"I'm sure of it. I have a warm relationship with the publisher, who'll make sure I'm assigned to a senior editor. Laureen, Dilys, and Sherry Lynne are likely to experience more problems, though. None of them has been selling well. Laureen and Sherry Lynne will end up with entry-level editors with zero clout, and Dilys may spend the next ten years trying to get reversion rights to her backlist. Roxanne wasn't doing them any great favors, but at least she knew who they are. This is not good for them."

"So Walter Dahl was the only one of you who might have benefitted from Roxanne's . . . premature resignation?"

Allegra pulled me into the Magnolia Room and closed the door. "Do you think he did it?" she whispered, her heavily-shadowed eyes intent on me. "He lured her out to the garden and shoved her in the well? His room is next door. What if he decides he's jealous of my success? All he'd have to do is wait until everyone's gone to bed, and then . . ."

"Take his travel machete out of his suitcase and come after you?" I suggested. "A few days from now, Lily might open the refrigerator to take out a head of lettuce, and find that part of your anatomy gazing blankly from the depths of the vegetable bin?"

She sank down on the edge of the bed. "But if he killed Roxanne, who knows what else he's capable of? In his second or third book, his fictional psychologist is asked by the prosecuting attorney's office to evaluate a man accused of stabbing his ninety-year-old mother to death and shipping her corpse to Peoria via UPS. The psychologist found all of it highly symbolic, but I wanted to throw up."

"Your book was gruesome, was it not?"

"Only because the plot demanded it."

I smiled rather grimly. "The plot or the market?"

"Actually, Roxanne. My original draft was much tamer, but she knew what was selling. I nearly became addicted to Pepto-Bismol while writing the second book to her specifications. I have three scarves I cannot wear to this day. The advance did much to ease my symptoms, though, and I've always wanted a mocha brown Jaguar, something along the lines of Lieutenant Rosen's eyes."

"I'm sure the idea of leather upholstery helped settle your stomach," I said, struggling to keep any hint of hostility from my voice. "I'd better go downstairs and do what I can to help you make the payments. There's a deadbolt on the inside of your door. You should be safe when you go to bed."

She stopped in front of the mirror above the dresser and adjusted the scarf. "And I shall do my part, too. We won't have to do anything beyond this evening, will we?"

"Only what Lieutenant Rosen dictates."

"There's a man who's not the stereotypic small-town cop. It's not hard to envision him as the lead in my next movie. I certainly wouldn't object to doing rewrites on the script with him, preferably at my condo."

Peter was primed to be drawn and quartered. Leslie, Allegra, and I would collect our portions; his mother might want something to tuck into the family vault.

"Let's go, Allegra," I said.

We went downstairs and forced a path through the attendees in the parlor. Earlene was visibly agitated as she snatched proffered credit cards and jammed them through the machine.

"Where's Caron?" I asked as I sat down next to her.

"How should I know? I poked my head inside this room to see if everything was ready, and Laureen Parks told me to sell books until Caron returned to take over. I have no idea about sales tax! There's no cash box, so I've been stuffing checks and bills under a cushion, which is slipshod and not sanitary. It's very warm in here, you know. I am doing my best, but I'm feeling dizzy. Kimmie offered to spell me so I could step outside, but she cheerfully admits to forgetting to pick up her daughter at kindergarten more often than not. I didn't want to let you down, Claire, but—"

I patted her knee. "You've done a great job, Earlene. Why don't you go out on the porch until you've cooled off, then look around for Caron? Try Lily's office."

"Remind everyone that the authors are signing in the sunroom." Earlene lowered her head and charged through the bodies forcing their way into the room. I'd seen stampeding cattle with more decorum. In the movies, anyway. The cows in the bucolic environs surrounding Farberville might have been cut out of plywood and positioned in the pasture each morning before dawn and collected after dusk.

Eventually, the crowd diminished, and many of those who came into the parlor were carrying wineglasses, which indicated

Lily was adhering to the timetable. Caron did not appear, however, and I was increasingly annoyed with her. I'd made it clear that I needed her help. She may have been lacking in many of the character attributes necessary for participation in a scouting program, but she also knew enough about our financial situation to realize we were only a stone's throw away from consignment clothing stores.

There was only a scattering of customers in the parlor when Inez came through the doorway. She seemed startled to see me, but many aspects of life had the same effect on her. I would not have wanted to be within a mile when her mother first broached the topic of birds and bees. Inez must have required sedation.

"Where's Caron, Ms. Malloy?" she asked. "She told me she had to sell books."

"I wish I knew where she was."

"But she called not more than an hour ago. She thought maybe you'd let her leave in time for us to meet everybody at Streetcar Pizza. I came by to see if I could help."

"She didn't imply she would sneak off and meet you outside?"

"Oh, no," Inez said earnestly as she cleaned her glasses on her shirttail, resettled them on her nose and shot me a disapproving look. "We didn't care about the movie all that much. She figured you'd let her leave by ten o'clock."

"And now I can't let her do anything because I don't where she is. Will you please take over here while I look for her?"

Accommodating creature that she was, Inez would have donated a pint of blood or a stray kidney if I'd requested it of her. Once she was settled on the sofa and prepared to handle various transactions, I went to the foyer and leaned against the wall, savoring the relative coolness. Books sales had been better than I anticipated; I would be able to keep what books remained and sell them at the Book Depot on the strength of the publicity, albeit negative, generated by the convention.

It was a pity Farberville lacked a local tabloid, but there was always a chance some reporter might hear about the "Ding, dong, bell" message left on Roxanne's laptop. I was not above an anonymous phone call.

I pulled myself together and went to the sunroom. Authors and attendees were all busy eating off paper plates ladened with whatever Lily had provided; the color green predominated, but the scope was far from monochromatic and all seemed well-received. Wine bottles were back in full force. I scanned the room for Caron, although I doubted she had the nerve to flagrantly disregard my request for assistance in the makeshift bookroom.

To my dismay, Peter came out of the kitchen and joined me before I could flee through the hallway, scramble down the embankment, and leap onto the caboose of a train headed for Anchorage. It was a pleasant fantasy, although the next freight train was more likely to be destined for Topeka.

"I need your statement," he said.

"Here's one: I am looking for Caron. Is she in the kitchen, by any chance?"

"Not unless she's in the freezer."

"That's not as ludicrous as it sounds. She's disappeared. She made a phone call from Lily's office earlier, but no one has seen her since then. I'm beginning to get worried."

Peter's demeanor softened. "She's not in Lily's office. I was in there, making some calls. Could she be upstairs?"

"I don't know why she would be, but I guess I'd better make sure."

"You're awfully pale, Claire. Let's go out to the front porch for a minute, and then I'll go upstairs with you."

Struggling to keep my imagination from running amok, I followed him to the porch. Jorgeson was seated on a wicker settee, smoking a thin cigar and idly watching the college students heading toward Thurber Street for live music and beer.

"Have you seen Caron?" I asked him.

"I saw her earlier, when she and some woman unloaded a bunch of boxes and brought them inside on a cart. She's still in there, far as I know. If she's not, she had to have climbed out a window. The officer out back has orders not to let anyone go into the garden. He's a rookie, but I used words of one syllable and he seemed to understand."

I looked up at Peter, who had the maddening habit of being taller than I. "Then she has to be inside. Why would she pull stunt like this? She knew I needed her help—and she was getting paid. That, if nothing else, would have captured her attention."

Peter told Jorgeson to go the sunroom and get something to eat, then gestured at me to sit down on the settee. I was relieved when he sat down on a chair. Settees can be overly cozy.

"Is there anything you're not telling me?" he said bluntly.

I opted to stall. "Is there anything you're not telling *me*?"

"You're a civilian and I'm a detective. I'm not supposed to share all my information, especially with someone involved in the investigation."

I opened my mouth to claim I was most definitely not involved, then conceded his point. "I suppose you want to know what I've been doing since I left the hospital," I said, feigning meekness. I ran through my descent into the cistern, discussion with Laureen and Dilys, foray to Old Main, bubble bath, and subsequent conversations. I did not mention that I'd scrutinized the graduate assistantship files, since I didn't want to cause grief for the secretary, and may have edited my conversation with Arnie in my backyard as well. Other than those two lapses, I was forthcoming.

"Walter Dahl is the only one with much of a motive," I concluded. "Allegra believes her career will continue to thrive, but thinks Roxanne's death will cause more headaches for the others. I don't know enough about that end of the book business to have an opinion."

"You know more than I do. All I know is that these authors should all be locked away in padded cells, and the keys fed to crocodiles on a sandbank. I ask about their whereabouts, and I get long-winded theories about ghosts and antiquated relatives in the attic. There's no attic. Another is convinced that everything that's happened is due to ill-disguised animosity going back to toilet training. The next attempts to convince me to rely on animal instincts. The next tries to convince me that child molestation is a factor, even though there's not a child within blocks of this case. An then there's Lily."

"She does have an attitude," I said sympathetically. "She's only recently relinquished the cleaver."

Peter gripped his hair. "Not one of these people can remain focused for five seconds. They speculate rather than respond. Every question I pose becomes a potential plot—and what fun they have with it. There were moments when I was glad I wasn't carrying a weapon."

"I can't get a straight answer out of any of them, either," I said. "Can I get a couple out of you?"

"Such as?"

"Were there any fingerprints on Roxanne's laptop?"

"Her fingerprints were all over the case, but the keyboard had been wiped clean."

"And the ladder?"

"Nothing useful." Peter turned on the full intensity of his soulful eyes. "When this is over, will you talk to me?"

I stood up. "No, Lieutenant Rosen, I shall be thinking how best to end this relationship with grace and style. Should we throw an empty champagne bottle off one of the railroad bridges, or burn whatever diary entries have been made? I saved the mock-murder weekend brochure from the Mimosa Inn; we could watch as I feed it down the disposal. I think we need candles. The wicks flicker, sputter, and eventually go out once and for all."

Peter did not follow me into the Azalea Inn.

CHAPTER
15

Just in case Peter changed his mind, I locked the door and hurried up the staircase. He was a big boy, capable of creating enough havoc so that someone would eventually let him in.

I began opening bedroom doors and whispering Caron's name. The rooms were uniformly dark, and not so much as a whimper was offered in response. She had been kidnapped, bound, and gagged on one occasion; even then, she had not been an acquiescent victim, and the perpetrator had been eager to hand her over to me. And there was no reason why any of the authors would have detained her in such a crass manner. She was a teenager, granted, but her interactions with them had been minimal, and no one had complained about her. She knew almost nothing about what had happened, and she most definitely had not been present when Roxanne had been pushed into the cistern.

But she had not been in the sunroom, the kitchen, the parlor, or Lily's office. The rookie officer in the garden and Jorgeson on the front porch had barred the exits, although I suppose they would have allowed us out in an emergency. The Farberville Police Department deplores bad publicity in the same way the rest of us deplore the odd relative with stale jokes and the tendency to pass gas at the dinner table.

Sherry Lynne's room was as dark as the others, but I did pause in the doorway. The good news was that Wimple was not protesting his most recent incarceration. It was also the bad news, since he should have been. I switched on the light and gazed glumly at the bathroom door, which was open. The garbage bag that Caron had taken from the apartment was on the floor. Lily would have no doubts regarding the presence of a banned lodger when she spotted the kitty litter strewn across the floor like gravel in an alley.

Wimple was not crouched in the bathtub, or spitting at me from behind the commode. There was clear evidence of his presence; patches of wallpaper had been shredded and a bottle of shampoo still oozed on the floor.

It seemed obvious what had occurred. Caron had helped Earlene with the boxes of books, made the call to Inez, and then taken the bag up to Sherry Lynne's room and opened the bathroom door. Wimple had bolted; Caron had gone after him.

But where were they? They had not left through either the front or back door, and it did not seem probably that Wimple could have leaped out a window on the ground floor without attracting attention, much less a red-haired adolescent who was likely to have been loosing a stream of antifeline statements. Jorgeson could not have failed to notice a cat racing across the porch with Caron in pursuit. Even a rookie officer would have reported the incident once he'd recovered from momentary paralysis.

I returned to each of the bedrooms on the second floor, this time turning on the lights, peering under beds, opening closet doors, and making sure the bathtubs contained no hostages. The sheets and towels in the linen closet had not been disturbed. A door to the nonexistent attic had not materialized with a crescendo of lugubrious organ music.

That left downstairs, which was trickier, since Jorgeson would be returning to his post at any moment. Peter would not be pleased with my little ploy, and might, in all reality, have me hauled to a cell. I would not encounter Arnie's biker buddy, but I might spend the rest of the night being regaled with professional tips from prostitutes. And, of course, there was the lice thing.

I paused at the top of the stairs. The front door was still closed, and there was no way of knowing if Peter was pacing on the porch or Jorgeson was blithely eating pesto pasta.

My lips pursed, I hurried down the stairs and into the parlor, where Inez was packing away the remaining books.

"Have you seen Caron yet?"

"You scared me, Ms. Malloy. Are you okay?"

"I'm fine," I said brusquely. "I'd just like to know where Caron is."

"Is she still missing?"

I sat down and forced myself to take a deep breath. "Would I have said that if she weren't, Inez? I searched upstairs. If she's on the first floor, someone must have seen her."

Inez's eyes widened. "All I know is that she told me on the phone that she was supposed to sell books until you arrived to take over."

"Did she say anything else?"

"She wasn't very happy about having to deal with the cat again. My grandmother has a cat, but it doesn't do much more than eat, sleep, and demand to be stroked. If it typed a message, my grandmother would pack it off to the animal shelter and call her preacher to have the house cleansed of demonic forces. After she found a bat in the broom closet, she moved in with us for three months. She wore this necklace made out of garlic the entire time, and the house positively reeked."

"So Caron hadn't yet taken the provisions to the cat when she called you?"

Inez looked as if she wanted to slither under the coffee table. "She was going to do it right after she hung up. The cat tried to bite her last night, and she was afraid she might end up having to take rabies shots. Last fall Emily told us how her cousin was attacked by a stray dog and had to take all these really painful injections in his stomach. They used a great big needle, and—"

"Wimple may not have manners," I said, "but I can assure you he does not have rabies. He's undoubtedly had more vaccinations than you've ever had. Sherry Lynne is devoted to her assets."

"So what do you want me to do, Ms. Malloy?" asked Inez.

"I think everybody is pretty much done buying books. The cash, checks and credit card slips are in the bottom of this box of left-over books. Should I take it out to your car?"

"My car's in the garage, and Caron has the key. Leave the box behind the sofa and go undercover. Ask the woman in the kitchen if you might be allowed to make a quick call to your parents, then make sure Caron's not hiding under the desk. I think there's a bedroom adjoining it. Take a look around there, and if you get caught, say you were searching for a bathroom."

"What if the woman won't let me use the telephone? Some people don't trust teenagers, you know. I went into a shop on Thurber Street last week, and the clerk practically perched on my shoulder."

"Lily allowed Caron to use the telephone," I said. "Concoct some story about your ailing grandmother if need be."

"But she's on a Caribbean cruise."

"Inez, you may pretend to be an ingenue, but I know from past experience that you can be quite as devious as my daughter. Now finish packing the box and then go worm your way into Lily's private sanctum. If Caron's not there, mingle in the sunroom and take surreptitious peeks under the furniture."

She peered at me with the solemnity of an owl awakened by the sound of scurrying rodents. "What are you going to do, Ms. Malloy?"

The one thing I wasn't going to do was run into Peter, but I was not inclined to explain. "Please see if you can find Caron. For all I know, the people attending the convention have found her so adorable that they're keeping her glass filled with wine."

"They wouldn't do that, would they?"

"Go, Inez. Paste on an ingratiating smile and tell everyone how honored you feel to be in the presence of real writers. Simper if you must, but find Caron."

As soon as she left, I went to the window and cautiously squinted through the sheers at the porch. Jorgeson was back, but rather than eating or even smoking a cigar, he was in conversation with someone concealed by the azaleas. I made sure Peter was not lurking near the parlor, then went out the front door.

Jorgeson gave me what might be described as a baleful look. "Fancy that, the senator has joined us. Do remind me to vote for you in the next election."

"It's not Arnie, is it?" I whispered.

"I reckon not," said the black woman with the multilayered clothing who'd been on the balcony outside the skyboxes. "I don't know where he is, but he told me to find you if there was an emergency at . . . the apartment complex. Well, we got us one."

"What sort of emergency?" I said. "I can find you a phone if you need to call 911, or Sergeant Jorgeson can send a squad car."

"Think it through, honey," she said impatiently. "If you ain't gonna help, just say so."

Jorgeson looked at me. "What's this about, Ms. Malloy? Has she got information concerning Arnie Riggles? The lieutenant would like very much to hear it if she does."

The woman put her hands on her hips. "I barely got the shoes on my feet, and I don't keep track of trash like Arnie Riggles."

"She's not going to say anything in front of you," I said to Jorgeson. "Let me have a minute or two with her in private."

"I'm not supposed to let you leave."

"I am not leaving, Jorgeson; I am merely asking the woman to go out to the sidewalk and explain what she meant when she said there was an emergency."

He scratched the tip of his nose. "That's all?"

"We'll stay where you can see us." I went down the porch steps and beckoned to the woman to accompany me to the end of the walk. "What's this about?" I asked her in a low voice.

"It's about this skinny little girl going by the name of Wal-Mart who's having a baby."

"Arnie said she was due any day."

"Not any day—now. She says she can't make it down the steps so I can drive her to the hospital. If we call an ambulance, she, the baby, and all the rest of us will be sleeping in cardboard boxes. It can be mighty cold when the wind howls long about January. Most years I get myself arrested and do three months in jail. Better'n frostbite, if you ask me."

"What about the father of this girl's child?"

"She won't say nothing about him, but she was bruised and limping bad when Arnie found her slumped between two garbage cans behind a restaurant a couple of weeks ago. He's been looking after her since then, making sure she has milk to drink and something to eat every day. I think he has some kind of deal with the cafeteria workers to save the leftovers. I figured I'd hit bottom when I tasted the chicken divan."

I glanced back at Jorgeson, who was watching us. "What do you want me to do? I'm not an obstetrician."

"You had a baby, which is more than the rest of us can say. Arnie says it's like riding a bicycle."

"More like riding a bicycle into a brick wall. I wasn't paying attention to the details at the time. Is this girl local? Does she have family?"

"They kicked her out of the house when they found out she was pregnant. White folks might should go to church more often and learn about taking care of each other. Maybe that's why their skin's so pale. Nothing but ice underneath."

"How old is this girl?"

"She looks to be sixteen or seventeen, but she's getting older every second we stand here. Are you coming or not?"

I made sure Jorgeson was still on the porch. "What will you do if I refuse?"

"Arnie, that scuzzy crackhead that lives at the end of the row, and I are gonna birth a baby. You run along and have champagne and caviar with all your fancy friends inside."

I took a few steps toward a rusty behemoth of a car parked at the curb. "That yours?"

"It's a loaner. My Mercedes is in the shop."

Caron and Inez were sixteen. Had they found themselves in a dire situation, I would not have wanted them dismissed as unworthy of help. I'd seen a lot of deliveries, albeit fictionalized ones on TV and in movies. The vast majority of women in the world gave birth without sterile rooms, stethoscopes, and camcorders.

"Okay," I said, glancing back at Jorgeson once again. "I'll go with you and determine if there's anything I can do. Get in the car and start the engine. As soon as I jump in, drive like the wind. By the time the policeman on the porch realizes what happened, he won't have a chance to get a good look at the car or the license plate."

"What makes you think I got a license plate?"

The woman, who'd grudgingly allowed that her name was Bettina, parked on the sidewalk next to the stadium. "So they tow it," she muttered as she cut off the engine. "It'll cost 'em more than it cost me in the first place."

I felt as though I should be carrying a medical bag as we ascended to the tier of skyboxes. I also felt as though I needed to rededicate myself to aerobic exercise. "Do we have towels and blankets?" I said between gasps. "Is Arnie boiling water? Is there a phone if we have no choice but to call for an ambulance? Do you know the girl's name or how to get in touch with her family?"

Bettina stopped so abruptly that I bumped into her broad hips. "All I know, honey, is that the Lord is intent on bringing a new person into the world. It's gonna have a little-bitty heart, but a soul as big as yours and mine. We could stand here and talk about it, or we could get our butts upstairs and try to help this girl."

"Sorry," I said, then fell back into step behind her. We arrived on the balcony, passed several doors, and went into a skybox. The girl had fixed a makeshift bed of blankets and a stained sleeping bag. She was sitting on it, her arms resting on her bloated belly, but her face was ashen and her eyes dull above dark circles.

"Lemme have some water," she said to Arnie, who was kneeling beside her.

He looked at us. "Yo, Senator, am I glad to see you! Wal-Mart here's experiencing considerable pain, which may or may not be natural."

I sank down next to the girl. "What's your real name?"

"Ginger. This here's Gilligan, and the woman by the door is Mary Anne. The skipper when out to score some crack. Who are you?"

"Claire Malloy," I said, then stopped as the girl flopped back and began to moan. Whenever she could catch her breath, she cursed quite adeptly for someone her age. I looked at Arnie. "How far apart are the contractions?"

"My stopwatch is currently on the blink, but I'd estimate less than a minute."

There was no reason to think paramedics could arrive in time to take charge. Arnie was nearly as pale as the girl, and Bettina, although not pale, looked perilously close to fainting.

The girl gripped my hand so tightly I had to bite my lip. "I'm sorry about this, you know," she rasped. "Not about having my baby, but making you come here. I know it's not any of your concern." Her face contorted as another contraction began.

The time between contractions had been less than a quarter of a minute. "We need towels and blankets," I said as calmly as I could, although I doubted I'd be nominated for any awards in that area. "Some string and a pair of scissors, or at least a pocket-knife. Alcohol to sterilize the blade." I waited until Arnie left, then gestured to the woman. "Help me get her out of her socks and pants. This baby is on its way."

Less than five minutes later, the baby boy was wrapped in a towel and cradled between the girl's breasts. I was sitting on the end of the sleeping bag, unmindful of the bodily fluids that accompanied the birth. No matter how tiny his heart, as well as his fingers, nose, and dimpled knees, his soul had swelled to fill the room with a sense of awe. For the moment, his emergence into the world had quieted the tides of cynicism and hatred. Like every baby, he was the prophet who could bring us hope.

Bettina handed me a tissue. "Now we got to figure out what to do. She can't stay here."

"I'll take care of them," Arnie said, puffing out his chest but stopping short of passing out cigars.

I shook my head, gently so as not to disturb the baby. "No, Arnie, the baby needs to be checked by a doctor. If she was beaten, the battered women's shelter might take her in and help her get free medical care and a safer place to stay."

Arnie gave me an offended look. "What could be safer than the Wal-Mart box?"

"Almost any place without a crackhead living five doors away. Perhaps a reconciliation can be arranged with her parents. This is our baby, too; we have to do what's best for him."

"Little Arnie," he said.

The girl's eyes opened. "I changed my mind. I think I'm going to name him Skyler on account of where he was born."

"May I hold him?" I asked the girl whose name I'd never know.

"Yeah, sure."

I eased the baby into my arms, made sure all but his face was covered by the towel, and looked down at his smooth brow and curled eyelashes. Caron had looked much the same sixteen years ago: both innocent and wise.

Bettina said, "Arnie, you pack up Wal-Mart's things. Soon

as I get back, we'll ease her and the baby down the steps to my car. I don't suppose I'll have any problem finding the shelter."

I should have asked where she was going, but I was mesmerized by the life I'd helped bring into the world. My hands had supported him as he took his first breath. While Arnie had washed the girl's face, Bettina and I had tied off the umbilical cord and severed the lifeline to the womb. Skyler had fussed, but he hadn't cried. I dearly hoped he wasn't resigned to a future of homelessness, transient shelters, and abusive men who preyed on young women and children.

"You'll allow someone to contact your parents, won't you?" I asked the girl, now a mother.

She nodded, but held her arms out to reclaim her child. I stood up as Bettina returned with several items of clothing.

"I think you'd better change before you go back to the party," she said, thrusting them at me. "Arnie, find a clean blanket to wrap these two in while we drive to the shelter."

For the first time, I became aware that I was drenched with blood. "Unless I'm planning to haunt the garden, I guess I'd better." I took off my blouse and pulled on a man's dress shirt that could have contained two or three of me. The cardigan sweater was shapeless, missing all but one of its buttons, and smelled as thought it had provided a bed for a wet dog.

"No point in bringing you pants," Bettina said wrly. "We don't wear the same size."

Arnie returned and helped get Wal-Mart to her feet, allowing me one last chance to hold the baby. We cautiously went downstairs, keeping an eye out for campus security, and made it into the car without being pinned down by blinking blue lights and loud speakers.

"You can find the shelter?" I asked as Bettina drove toward the campus.

"In my sleep. Maybe I ought let you off at the corner by the mansion. I'm not willing to spend the night in a cell without my toothbrush."

Arnie was trying to persuade the girl to rethink her decision regarding the baby's name. I shushed him, leaned over the seat to take a last look, and forced myself to get out of the car. I stood beneath the streetlight until the taillights disappeared on the far side of the railroad bridge.

I was wondering how long I'd been gone as I started walking toward the Azalea Inn. Surely not more than half an hour, I decided, although that was quite long enough for Peter to have called in the APB. I could think of no plausible explanation for my absence that would not result in a raid on the skyboxes. I would be charged with jeopardizing the welfare of a minor by failing to act in a responsible manner. Guilty, your honor.

I had resigned myself to doing hard time when I reached the walk leading to the Azalea Inn, then froze as I saw a figure scuffling through the weeds at the top of the embankment. Although there was minimal light, the figure bore an eerie resemblance to my daughter.

"Caron?" I said as I went across the street. "Where have you been? What are you doing?"

"Looking for the cat. I feel as though I've spent my entire life looking for the cat. If I were to fall over dead, I'd spend all eternity looking for the cat."

I gave her a tight hug, then held her back. "You're caked with mud. What on earth happened?"

"I don't want to talk about it, but I can assure you none of

this was My Fault. How was I supposed to know the cat was in
the bathroom, poised to snarl at me and then dart between my
legs? You're lucky you won't have to pay a plastic surgeon to re-
construct my face." She stopped and took in my clothes." I may
have mud on me, Mother, but you look like you've been scav-
enging along the highway. That sweater is beyond description."

"Let's get you inside and cleaned up."

"What about the cat? Sherry Lynne Blackstone's just as
scary as the cat, and a lot bigger."

I put my arm around her and nudged her toward the inn. "I
was really worried about you, dear."

"Which is why you chose this designer outfit? I'm not sure
I see the connection."

I said nothing as we crossed the street. The red dot on the
porch warned me that Jorgeson was there, smoking his cigar
and waiting for us. Despite an urge to shriek at Caron to take
cover before we were slaughtered in our tracks, we continued to
the bottom of the porch steps.

"So the prodigal mother and daughter have returned," said
a voice that belonged not to Jorgeson, but to his insufferable superior.

"I wouldn't mind a fatted calf sandwich," I said. "This is
the second day in a row that I've subsisted on crumbs of cheese."

He stubbed out the cigar. "Would either of you care to explain?"

"I wouldn't," Caron said as she pulled free of my arm. "I
am sick and tired of being blamed for everything!" She ran past
him and into the house. The door slammed as a less than subtle
warning not to follow her.

"Goodness," I said under my breath, thinking of the days

when she would have cried on my shoulder and told me every-thing. She might have been wearing diapers at the time, but her candor had been heartwarming.

"How did she leave and where has she been?" asked Peter.

"She hasn't told me," I admitted. "Can I please ask Lily to fix me a cup of tea and something to eat? I don't know when I last had something. Thursday, probably, or maybe yesterday morning."

"Go ahead," he said with a sigh. "The convention people have gone to their homes and hotels. The authors are in the par-lor, drinking tea and arguing who had better sales this evening."

"Even Sherry Lynne?"

"I don't know. Jorgeson spotted her cat in the yard and managed somehow to grab it. She took it upstairs."

"And Jorgeson?"

"I told him to go on home and tend to his scratches. He looked as if he'd flung himself face-first into a thicket of partic-ularly nasty thorns." His eyes widened as I moved under the porch light. "You've changed your clothes since I last saw you."

"I'll explain later after I've spoken to Lily. I'm so hollow that my stomach isn't rumbling—it's echoing."

I left him on the porch and hurried by the doorway that opened into the parlor. I heard voices from within, but my name was not called. Lily was in the kitchen, washing wineglasses at the sink. She was not pleased with my request, but agreed to fix me a sandwich.

"Your daughter's taking a shower in my bathroom," she added. "She and her friend are supposed to meet some girls shortly. I offered to let her borrow a shirt and jeans from me. The key word is 'borrow.' I expect the clothes to be returned no later than tomorrow night." She winced at my current fashion statement, which seemed to be screaming at everyone. "Very interesting. You look like one of those white-haired ladies who paint watercolors in the central plaza in Santa Fe. They are almost always accompanied by neurotic little dogs that snap at ankles and soil the sidewalks."

I decided to make one more effort to coerce Caron into explaining what had happened. "I'll collect her dirty clothes and take them with me."

As I reached the open door, Lily said, "The door to my office and bedroom is on the other side of the refrigerator. That's the door to the basement."

"What's down there?"

"The washer and dryer, the furnace, canned peaches and tomatoes from last summer, a few boxes of junk, an old bicycle. Look for yourself if that sort of thing amuses you. There's a light switch just inside the door. I usually take a flashlight with me in case the mice have nibbled through the wires, but I couldn't find it earlier."

I turned on the light, which was dim at best, and descended the wobbly wooden steps. My garage and storage area were piled high with boxes overflowing with old magazines, clothing destined to be donated to a thrift shop when I got around to it, empty jars and coffee cans, and piles of newspapers. Lily's basement was tidier than my living room. The boxes purportedly containing junk held tools and jars of nails. The peaches and tomatoes were labelled with neat, hand-printed dates. The washing machine was churning serenely. The dryer was the only possible place to hide Ammie's notebooks and manuscript. I opened it with the tiniest tingle of adrenalin and found a jumble of warm towels.

I turned off the light as I came back into the kitchen. "Is Caron still in the shower?"

"I think I hear her blow-drying her hair. Don't bother with her clothes. They can go in with the next load of tablecloths. Your teacup and sandwich are on a tray in the parlor. If you don't mind, I'd like to take off my shoes and lie down. I'll tell Caron and Inez where you are."

The kitchen darkened behind me as I went into the sunroom. The conversation from the parlor was not as acrimonious as I'd feared; the debate over book sales had subsided and the topic seemed to be which of them was being most inconvenienced by remaining another night at the Azalea Inn.

"So I left a message with the publicist telling her to call Larry King's people," Allegra was saying to an indifferent audience, "but I'm screwed."

"And I'll miss the state dinner at the White House," Laureen murmured.

They all stared at me as I came into the room. "It's a long story," I said as I sat down next to Dilys and stuffed half the sandwich in my mouth. I'd never had testier sprouts (if I'd ever had sprouts; I wasn't sure).

"Are you all right?" asked Sherry Lynne.

"Yes. How about your friend upstairs?"

Walter stood up and pointed his finger at her. "Is your cat up there? I should have known when I started wheezing in the hall. Lily assured me that—"

"More importantly," Dilys interrupted smoothly, "is Caron

all right? I was coming downstairs when she came in from the porch, as muddy as a soldier in the trenches. I'm quite sure there were cobwebs in her hair. This is very mysterious, you know. Earlier, Earlene was skulking about and watching us as though she was convinced one of us would drag her out to the cistern. An hour later, Inez began asking if anyone had seen Caron. Laureen and I had, of course, but before the attendees arrived."

Allegra picked up a teacup. "Lieutenant Rose told me that there were police officers at both doors."

"A fascinating twist on the locked room mystery," Walter said as he sat back down. "Rather than a lone corpse lying on an Oriental carpet in the library, we have over a hundred people locked inside the allegorical room. How did Caron manage to leave without anyone seeing her? She could hardly have flung open a window, knocked off the screen, and toppled into the shrubbery. Some of us are more astute than others"—he gave Dilys a pointed look—"but surely someone would have noticed her curious behavior and commented on it."

"Shouldn't you be more concerned with why?" said Allegra. "I'd expect at least one theory about repressed memories or hysteria brought on by 'female problems.'"

Laureen put down her teacup and yawned. "I'll carry a few of these to the kitchen, and then retire."

"But it's so Gothic," said Dilys, clearly disappointed by Laureen's unwillingness to participate in idle plotting. "I think we should ask Lily for candles, turn off the lights, and explore the house. If anyone should lag behind, however, all that will be left of him"—her pointed look at Walter was a good deal sharper than his had been—"would be a muffled cry of pain, and then silence."

"Agatha Christie's already written that one," Sherry Lynne said. "But I suppose we all steal plots from wherever we can."

Laureen began to stack saucers and teacups. "Sometimes unwittingly."

"Plots may linger in the subconscious," Walter said in a voice that must have put many an undergraduate to sleep on a hot afternoon. "We are unable to differentiate that which we have experienced, even vicariously, from what we believe are spontaneous creations."

"Does anyone know if Lieutenant Rosen is still here?" I asked.

"I believe all of the police officers have left," said Dilys. "Lieutenant Rosen may be hoping we murder each other in our beds, thus saving himself from further investigation. One would think that anyone whose duty is to investigate crime would enjoy possible scenarios, but he became very grouchy when I brought up the likelihood of a pirate in the basement."

I finished the last bite of sandwich. "I looked, Dilys. No pirate, no bottle of rum."

"Have you considered a full frontal lobotomy?" Walter asked her.

"Why, no. Was yours successful?"

"Children," Laureen said wearily, "I think I'd better send you to your rooms. There will be no creeping around once the lights are off. Put on your pajamas, brush your teeth, and go to bed."

"Let me help you," I said to her. "Caron's still here, and I want to talk to her before she heads for the pizza place."

"No, dear, you've had a hard day." She refilled her teacup. "You stay right where you are. As for the rest of you, don't force me to behave like a stern nanny from one of Dilys's books."

Everybody trooped out of the room. I sank back, noticing for the first time my knees were stained with blood. None of the authors had commented, but perhaps they'd described too many bloodstains to find them of interest.

I could hear footsteps upstairs and a low buzz of voices. However, the Azalea Inn seemed to sigh in relief at the prospect of a quiet night. I was musing about Skyler's perfectly sculpted features when I heard Caron scream.

CHAPTER

16

I scrambled down the hall, looked wildly around the sunroom, then barged into the kitchen just as the overhead light came on. Caron and Inez were hanging onto each other, their faces immobilized with shock. Lily skittered into view behind them.

"What's wrong?" she demanded.

Caron held up a wobbly hand and gestured at the basement door. "There's something in there."

Inez nodded so vehemently that she had to grab her glasses before they flew off her nose. "That's right, Ms. Malloy."

"What makes you think there's something in there?" I

asked, trying to introduce an element of sensibility to what felt like the set of a bad movie.

Caron let go of Inez's arm, but stayed where she was. "We were on our way to go to the pizza place. All of a sudden, the door started creaking open. I am normally not this immature, but after all that's happened today, I lost it. I mean everybody knows there's a murderer loose in the house!"

I eyed the door, reminding myself I could not have overlooked a laboratory in the basement, replete with an array of coils, bunsen burners, and vats of pickled body parts.

Lily joined the girls. "Aren't you going to open the door?" she asked me.

"I don't live here," I said. "You open it."

She sneered. "What do you think you'll find—a modern-day version of Frankenstein's monster?"

"Don't be absurd."

We were at a standstill, literally as well as figuratively, when we heard a series of squeaks, followed immediately by a distinct thump.

"Let's get out of here," Caron said to Inez. "We're already late. I'll be home by midnight, Mother."

I held up my palm. "Nobody goes anywhere." Nobody went, but nobody seemed inclined to join me as I crept across the kitchen and slowly opened the door, recreating the creaks that had frightened the girls. The room was inky, but I caught a glimpse of an expanse of white, as if the basement had experienced a blizzard.

I flipped on the light and looked down at Laureen Parks, who was sprawled on the floor amidst hundreds of sheets of paper. "Are you hurt?"

"No, but I could use a hand to get up and navigate the steps. I gave up my aspirations of joining the U.S. Olympic Gymnastics team on my sixteenth birthday. I was informed that trifocals were not allowed on the balance beam."

Caron, Inez, and Lily followed me downstairs. Lily and I pulled Laureen up and held onto her as we started back to the kitchen. I considered asking the girls to gather up what I knew were the pages of Ammie's manuscript, then decided to leave it to the police.

"Run along," I told them. "Caron you need not concern yourself about our houseguest, who has found other lodgings. I'll expect you home by midnight. Lily, will you please make a pot of tea and bring it to the parlor?"

Laureen tried to smile. "And a side order of aspirin, please. Any flavor will suit me."

"What were you doing down there?" asked Lily.

I wasn't sure how much she knew of what had happened, but Laureen was trembling and I wanted to get her to a comfortable seat. "I'll explain later," I said, then helped Laureen to the parlor and deposited her on the sofa with various cushions propped around her.

"Can you explain it?" she asked me.

"I think so, but I doubt I can outline it easily enough so that it can be used for a plot for one of your novels."

"Why my novels instead of, say, Allegra's or Dilys's, or even Walter's?"

"You didn't mention Sherry Lynne's, but of course the cat was a player. She's the one most likely to have a book out next year titled, *The Murder at the Azalea Inn.*"

"I'd tackle it myself," she said with a shaky laugh, "but I

won't be writing another novel. I'm exiting the stage with a bang, or at least a whoosh."

"You might have gotten away with it had it not been for Wimple. He's caused you problems since you saw him sniffing around the cistern after you pushed Roxanne into it. Were you unable to pull the lid back into place?"

"I have a weakness in my hands and wrists. Pushing it open was difficult, but pulling it all the way back proved impossible. I really wasn't too concerned until I saw the cat. I was afraid he might decide to leap in, then be unable to claw his way up the stone sides. I would never harm an innocent creature."

"Unlike Roxanne Small, who had no reservations about harming Ammie, who was as innocent as they come. Allegra left her purse on the sofa when she went looking for wine. Did you see Roxanne take out a few sleeping pills?"

"Not at all. I simply deduced it when we were told of Ammie's otherwise inexplicable accident. Roxanne was the only one among us with a motive."

I nodded. "Because of Ammie's manuscript. You heard enough about it in the garden to realize there were some elements of it in Allegra's book."

"Quite a few, actually. What Roxanne didn't feed Allegra for the first book will show up in her next, which has been bought by a production company and is likely to splash down at the top of the *New York Times* list in November."

We both stopped as Lily came into the room with a tray. She clearly looked as if she intended to stay, but I shook my head and said, "I promise to have a cup of tea with you in the garden tomorrow."

"I am entitled to know what goes on in my own establishment," she said coldly.

Laureen sighed. "No matter how hard you glower, you are no contemporary Medusa and no one's turning to stone to gratify your delusions. Now run along and watch sitcoms, or better yet, read one of my books."

Once she was gone, I said, "I suppose Roxanne had never given Ammie a second thought until last evening. To her, Ammie was just some drab little thing who had dropped out of school to bury herself in a backwoods town. Then, out of nowhere, there she is, goggling at the famous authors. Roxanne must have realized Ammie was likely to buy one of each author's books to have it signed."

"So she had to be prevented from returning to the convention today." Laureen's hand shook almost uncontrollably as she tried to pour tea. "Could you do this, Claire? I'm awfully tired and my back is beginning to stiffen. There are some things a woman of a significant age should not do. Falling down stairs is one of them."

"Lemon or milk?" I asked.

"Milk, please. Dilys has converted me. One of these days I may find the courage to eat a fishpaste sandwich."

"Were you sitting here late this morning when Roxanne came into the inn with an armload of papers?"

"I knew what they were, naturally, but I pretended otherwise and insisted she accompany me to the garden. I took the papers from her and set them on a bench, then suggested we sit on the wall of the cistern so no one could see us from the back door. I assumed the role of a snoopy old biddy, asked Roxanne what she thought might be in the cistern, and even convinced her to help me slide back the lid. She was smirking as she indulged my whim. What a shame that was the last expression on her face, except for a brief flash of terror. I really don't like to dwell on things of that nature, however. Do you think I might have another lump of sugar?"

"Certainly," I said, empathizing with Alice as she faced the Mad Hatter across a tea table. "But you had to decide what to do with Ammie's manuscript and notebooks. Why not dispose of them?"

"Her life's work? Unthinkable. I simply found a place to hide them until the police—and you, my dear—were finished searching the inn. I suspected the presence of a tunnel as soon as I read the brochure with the history of the house. I've had more experience with old houses and tunnels than most. I knew where to look."

"Weren't you worried Dilys might insist on an expedition to explore the basement?"

"Dilys, like her Miss Palmer, prefers to spin her fanciful ideas from the relative comfort of a cozy parlor such as this one. If she'd persevered, I would merely have warned her of the potential for mice and scorpions."

I hoped Dilys was not eavesdropping from the staircase, but the sound of footsteps suggested as much. Dilys came to the door of the parlor, dressed in a flannel nightgown that sagged unevenly below her knees, her face slathered with a pink cream that may well have contributed to her husband's heart attack.

"I am not afraid of crawly things," she said indignantly. "It's not to say that I should clutch them to my bosom, but I do not fling my hands in the air and shriek."

Laureen smiled. "Go to bed, Dilys."

Dilys stared at me for a moment, and then at Laureen. "Are you quite sure about this?" she demanded with more intensity than I'd heard previously from her.

"Quite sure."

"You've been my best friend in the business," she said. "I love you."

"I know you do," Laureen said. "Now trot upstairs like a good girl."

I waited until she left, then said, "I went down to the basement, but I didn't see an entrance to any tunnel."

"It's in the shadows behind the furnace, and barely wide enough to slip through. A weathered piece of plywood was propped against it. Only someone with expertise would have spotted it."

"How did you slip by Lily?"

Laureen gave me a modest look. "It was not difficult. I waited outside until I saw her go down the hallway to the parlor, then dashed through the kitchen and into the basement. I will say I had to wait at the top of the stairs for a tiresome time until I heard the telephone ringing in her office and knew, to utilize a cliché, that the coast was clear. I really did think everything was under control until I looked out my bedroom window and saw Wimple. I must have misread his intentions."

"And this afternoon," I said with a cold stare, "did you see me from your window?"

"I feel bad about that, Claire, but I wanted to discourage you. I did wait until you were almost at the bottom. I did not wish you to break any bones."

"So very thoughtful of you. It must have been difficult for you to pull up the ladder."

"It wasn't nearly as heavy as I'd anticipated."

I was not amused. "And would you have replaced the lid if it weren't so heavy?"

Laureen held out her tea cup. "Just half a cup, please. I don't want to be up and down all night."

That was a question I chose not to pursue, especially since we had yet another visitor in the doorway. "Sherry Lynne," I said.

She stared at Laureen. "I cannot allow you to take the blame for this. You are a revered luminary in the genre."

"Come now," Laureen said, "I've already confessed. Besides, we all know you would never have done anything that might endanger one of your cats. Let him feast tonight on a can of particularly succulent salmon or whatever you feed him."

"Don't you think—"

"I think you should tend to your cat."

"But, Laureen—"

"Wimple needs you," said Laureen. She glared until Sherry Lynne scurried back upstairs. "Please continue with your conjectures, Claire."

I wasn't sure how crowded it might be on the landing, but I swallowed and said, "So you assumed you had everything under control until Caron came in through the front door. You knew the only way to leave the Azalea Inn without being seen was through the tunnel. Wimple was looking for an escape route, and Caron was chasing him."

"I did not actually enter the tunnel, and I had no idea it wasn't blocked after a hundred and fifty years of neglect. It wasn't so much the mud on her clothes as the cobwebs in her hair. I had a very good idea where she'd been."

"She didn't spot the manuscript and notebooks, probably because you carried away the flashlight." I paused to think. "In the morning she would have told me about the tunnel, however, and I would have insisted on seeing it, as would Lily and the police. With the aid of adequate illumination . . ."

"That's what occurred to me. I felt as though the papers were less likely to be discovered in my room, since it had already been searched. Do tell Caron and Inez how sorry I am that I scared them, although if they were more familiar with my novels, they would have realized that creaking doors are *de rigueur* in houses of this period."

I placed my teacup on the tray. "I hope Ammie, or at least her parents, will appreciate what you did."

"I know Walter will, as will Sherry Lynne and Dilys when they acknowledge that Roxanne would have squashed them as surely as if they were ants on the sidewalk. Allegra may grow as a writer once she's forced to rely on her own imagination. They're all good eggs."

"I'm feeling a bit hard-boiled, myself," said Allegra from the doorway, clad in a negligee as gossamer as her scarves. She might have been the cause of a heart attack or two, but for entirely different reasons. "Once I realized—"

"Stop right there," said Laureen. "Go to your condo, take lots of showers, then sit in your hot tub and concoct plots. You're not a bad writer. You can come up with something fresh, even if it's in a different subgenre. You didn't have a chance with Roxanne's fangs so firmly embedded in your neck, but now you do."

Allegra shook her head. "Once I realized—"

"You're repeating yourself, child. The denouement has concluded. Claire knows that I shoved Roxanne into the cistern. If you attend a memorial service, please shed a few tears on my behalf. There is nothing else to discuss."

"Laureen—" Allegra began.

"There is nothing else to discuss," she said emphatically.

"What about Ammie's manuscript?"

"It will be returned to her parents, who will never so much as glance at it. Someday, perhaps a cousin will find it in a drawer and read it, but you have nothing to worry about. Fame is ephemeral; take the money and invest wisely. Keep a lawyer under the deck, just for luck."

Allegra came into the parlor and clutched Laureen's hands. "Why are you doing this? You barely know me."

"Consider it a legacy from the senior class."

"A very observant member of the senior class, watching from her bedroom window?"

Laureen shrugged. "I would never have left the manuscript on the bench. Focus on the details, my child. A tightly-plotted novel has no gaping holes, unless, of course, they lead to tunnels. Tunnels are so helpful."

"I'll keep that in mind," said Allegra as she kissed Laureen's cheek.

Laureen and I remained silent until she had gone upstairs. "You'll have to talk to Lieutenant Rosen," I said as I picked up the tray. "Are you confident you can hide the truth?"

"Claire, my dear, I have murdered people in my fiction over the last fifty years, and not once has even the most astute reader anticipated the truth until the final chapter. What I tell Lieutenant Rosen shall be the shining culmination of my life's work. The only thing missing is the final love scene. What a pity." She grimaced as she rose unsteadily to her feet. She leaned over me to pat my cheek. "It's time for me to retire. Although I do not have another novel in me, I think I shall write one last literary masterpiece before I sleep."

She took a step, then nearly lost her balance. I caught her arm before she could fall.

"Are you okay?" I asked.

"Yes, thank you. I have a degenerative muscular disease, as you must have noticed. It can be neither reversed nor halted. What I did today was my parting gift to the genre. Now, if you'll excuse me. I shall make my own way upstairs. I've grown rather fond of the Rose Room; it reminds me of my garden at home. So restful."

She went around me and took each step slowly, her hand clutching the bannister.

I put the tray back down and let myself out of the Azalea Inn. I would have to return in the morning to supervise the other authors' departures. Laureen's departure might not require an airline ticket.

Peter was sitting on the settee. "Finished for the night?"

"Have you been here all the time? Didn't you hear Caron scream?"

"I decided to let you handle it."

I sat down on the top step. "That doesn't sound like the Supercop of olden days. I would have expected you to come charging inside like a blinded bull, waving your gun and warning everybody not to interfere with the crime scene."

"I thought you might enjoy hearing Laureen's confession so you could claim you solved the case."

I swung around and stared at him. "You heard?"

His teeth glinted in the muted glow from the streetlight. "No, I watched you two through the window. I had a gut feeling—a cop thing, I guess—that she wasn't advising you on how to get an agent."

I gave him a synopsis of what Laureen had claimed was her final plot, then added, "She went to bed, and she's not the sort to pack her bag and flee to avoid taking responsibility. She's . . . well, a good egg herself."

He joined me on the step. "I know you're exhausted, but I want to say one thing about this situation with Leslie."

I put my finger on his mouth. "You don't have to. Bringing a child into the world, especially one who'll have all the advantages, is a noble cause. I know you won't believe me, but I'd like to hold this child someday."

He rocked back. "That's not what I expected to hear from you. What caused you to change your mind?"

"I don't know, Peter. I guess I've been mulling it over in the back of my mind since you told me. I can't explain why I initially found it so threatening. It's not about me."

"All this time I've been waiting for you to tell me not to do it. If you had just once said that, I would have told Leslie to find someone else."

"Just like that?"

"Just like that," he said resting his hand on my shoulder. "Instead, I felt backed into a corner, with Leslie and my mother cutting off one avenue of escape and you the other."

"What did I do?" I protested.

"Your pigheaded refusal to so much as talk to me made me all the more defensive."

I moistened my lips. "Okay, don't do it, unless you're willing to take full responsibility and become a constant part of this child's life. Our society doesn't need any more absentee fathers."

"It's irrelevant, anyway," he said. "Leslie spent a week with her sister's children and has decided to buy another pair of wolfhounds." He tugged me to my feet. "Walk you home?"

"You gonna carry my books?"

"You don't have any books."

"Wow, Sherlock," I said as I gave him a kiss, "I can't fool you."

"If only that were true, Ms. Marple."